Prais 7/2|

THE
SECOND
HISTORY

"Silver Slayter's examination of how humans carry on through apocalyptic hardship is complicated, contradictory, urgent with warning—but the turn at the end, a small readjustment that changes every understanding, gives a prickling, green-shoot feeling of that thing in short supply these days, hope." —Marina Endicott

"*The Second History* brings the lovers Eban and Judy to life with such deep wisdom and exacting detail that they will last forever. This novel is about risks in desperate times, the paralyzing power of fear, and the struggle for freedom. But mostly it's about love, one of the most honest renderings of romantic love I've ever read. It's about how we pull each other through. Here is a truly mesmeric story, tender, unflinching, quakingly good." —Lisa Moore

"*The Second History* takes place in a post-post-apocalyptic world where cities, and even communities, are fabled things of the distant past. It follows a young couple wandering through the frozen wilderness in search of a colony of humans, a haven they think is called Heaven. On the way, they survive unimaginable human and natural predations only to arrive in a place no rumour could ever have conjured. In this harrowing novel of human resilience, Rebecca Silver Slayter creates a world of dread and beauty so convincing it feels like it might be about tomorrow. Gorgeously written and packed with unforgettable scenes, *The Second History* is a towering achievement." —Michael Redhill

"Told in luminous, propulsive prose, *The Second History* is a unique love story that looks ahead to find its way home. A balancing act of grace and suspense." —Iain Reid

THE SECOND HISTORY

- A NOVEL -

REBECCA SILVER SLAYTER

DOUBLEDAY CANADA

Doubleday Canada and colophon are registered trademarks of Penguin Random House Canada Limited

Excerpt from "No Long Way Round" in *Sea Change* by Jorie Graham. Copyright © 2008 by Jorie Graham. Used by permission of HarperCollins Publishers.

Library and Archives Canada Cataloguing in Publication

Title: The second history / Rebecca Silver Slayter.
Names: Silver Slayter, Rebecca, author.
Identifiers: Canadiana (print) 20200364103 | Canadiana (ebook) 20200364219 | ISBN 9780385694445 (softcover) | ISBN 9780385694452 (EPUB)
Classification: LCC PS8637.I36 S43 2021 | DDC C813/.6—dc23

Cover design: Emma Dolan
Cover image: Malorny/Getty Images

Printed in Canada

Published in Canada by Doubleday Canada, a division of Penguin Random House Canada Limited

www.penguinrandomhouse.ca

10 9 8 7 6 5 4 3 2 1

Penguin
Random House
DOUBLEDAY CANADA

For my mother and my father

You have your imagination, says the evening. It is all you have
                    left, but its neck is open, the throat is
cut, you have not forgotten how to sing, or to want
                    to sing.
                              — Jorie Graham, *Sea Change*

I

IT IS THE END of their last day. The sun is drawing up from the wood all around him, the tree shadows leaning in, long and black, and still she hasn't returned. He goes looking for her along the usual paths.

He finds her in the forest, bent to the ground beside a sack of bones. She's nearly a mile from where they sleep.

He calls her name again, but she doesn't answer.

Judy once told him that this was the way things happened. He doesn't remember now what she was talking about—the progress of some chore; the melting of the ice at spring. She said, "Things happen little by little, and then all at once."

Watching her now, he is slowly realizing something that, he suspects, it will soon seem he always knew.

She appears to be studying the ground, hunched on all fours, her head hung over the snow. He hesitates, wondering what she's searching for there, when her body claps to the ground.

He waits until she finishes retching. Something they ate. The water.

She wipes her mouth and stands, unsteady. It's near dark now, and she is mostly silhouette, her face unreadable, her black, tight curls feathering into the darkness as if she's dissolving into the night sky.

He turns his eyes away from her, toward the pit where few trees grow. Down at the centre, old machines rust under a thin carpet of grass and debris, erased now by a thicker cover of snow. The hills are full of the old dumps, and when they first arrived here, they dug up every one they could find within a day's walk. Judy knew of someone who'd contracted tetanus and died, his body arched like a bow, after stumbling into an old cache of steel netting, so she insisted they rebury anything they couldn't use. But there was so much they could. At this dump, he remembers, he found an axe head, the handle rotted away years before. He sharpened it and polished it until it shone, and traded it to a peddler for a bag of dried beans that fed them for a month.

For a long time, they stand like that, not looking at each other, and then he says, "You're pregnant again."

It isn't a question, and she doesn't answer. Instead, she empties her sack into the pit and begins trudging back toward the path.

He looks down to the bottom of the pit, at the smudge of pink she made with the waste of all the animals they skinned and smoked to take with them. At the tiny skeletons, broken in the snow. "Judy . . ."

Finally, he follows her, and only when they reach the camp does she turn back to him. "Please don't, Eban."

"Judy."

"It won't make any difference. Okay?"

He feels frustrated the way he is always frustrated by her. "You can't stop things from being the way they are just by pretending, just because you want them some other way—"

And then she looks at him. "Can you be very honest with me now?"

"Yes. Yes."

"How long do you believe this will be a problem?"

He twists under the conviction of her gaze. "I just want us to do what's safe. I didn't say it was a problem. I would never say that."

"No, you wouldn't. But I hear you think it." She shakes her head. "Why not go, when it never helped anything to stay?"

"No. No. We're not leaving, not when you're—"

She tells him she will go in the morning. That he can stay, but she will go. It's what she has told him again and again and again.

Anger and worry and something else he can't name fill his head, stoppering his mouth. But he knows at dawn they'll leave together.

They go to bed in silence, and she is soon asleep. Beside her, he lies awake, trying to recall the day she began to drift from him, first by inches, then by miles.

Things happen little by little, and then all at once.

He watches but doesn't touch her, though he feels the desire in his hand, to feel her hair, the hard muscles of her back, turned toward him. He watches her the way he wishes he'd been watching when it happened. Maybe only for a minute he turned his eyes from her, and that lit-up bit of her, star-bright and searing, went out. Something he loved is gone now from her face. And he understands that, without knowing it or meaning to, he is the one who took it away. In the end, that's why he agreed to leave. To evacuate the place that has been their home together.

Because somehow, he did what happened to her.

This is what he dreams.

His mother is waiting for him outside, where he discovers that the fire has burned through the plug of sod he always smothers it with before bed. She looks reproachfully at him and then up at the smoke, weaving into the sky. "They'll find you," she says.

He wants to explain that he didn't mean to be so careless, that he always checks the fire before bed. When she was alive, she never let them light a fire, but, he wants to tell her, it was different then. It had last snowed when his mother was eight years old, the year they closed the border and talks on rebuilding the cities collapsed. She rarely spoke to him about her childhood, but she loved to tell him about the last time it snowed. How she'd woken in the middle of the night and not known why. How she put her face to the window of the outland house her family had moved to one year earlier—the house that felt, still, like it belonged to the people who had abandoned it after the second tsunami, leaving their pictures on the walls and their books on the shelves. How slow and white and strange the snowfall was. One day, months later when, a hundred miles away, the fires began to burn, she glimpsed ash in the sky and thought that by some miracle in that scorched summer another snow had come. But she never saw snow again.

It was two winters after her death that he woke one morning to a white forest, and the winter after that he lost a toe to the cold and was in bed for weeks with a fever. It was, he and Judy decided, safer to light the fire. This year, the trees had scarcely dropped their leaves before the snow came, and so he dug a pit in the ground where the flames would be hidden from view, and on the upwind side he dug a tunnel to ventilate the fire, oxygen feeding the flames and raising the temperature, so the buried fire would release only a thin stream of smoke that vanished inches from the ground.

The firepit allowed them to cure and stockpile meat so they could better endure times of hardship, when illness or foul weather or bad luck would otherwise have left them hungry. Each afternoon he gathered green switches to bridge the hole, and suspended a pot overtop filled with whatever they'd managed to kill or preserve. They'd lit a fire every night for months, and no one, not even a peddler, had passed their hide. Don't worry, he wants to say to his mother. I've thought of everything.

But he finds himself unable to speak. The words stick to his tongue, and he feels only a deep sadness at seeing his mother again. He wants to appease her fears for him. He wants to take her into the shelter to see Judy. He wants to tell her he might be a father.

But he can tell she knows what he and Judy have planned. Somehow she knows that at dawn they'll leave the place where they were safe.

She beckons to him to follow her and then leads him along the ridge he climbs every day down to the brook. She wades through the water, looking back at him to ensure he is behind her. Silently, he follows. Though he has spent the last four years among these trees, these hills, the land soon becomes unrecognizable. She is, he realizes, taking him to the valley.

He tries to catch her, to stop her from going farther, but she is moving faster and faster and he can only chase her vanishing figure in the trees.

At last the woods thin and the mountains resolve into foothills, and she stops at a crest, pointing to the unending view before them, at the things he's known only from rumour, the houses, the cities, the people, the sea. "Look," she says.

And he does.

In the morning, Eban wakes to the noise of Judy gathering together their things outside. He can hear her hurry and impatience. She would have packed days sooner if he had let her. Now she'll be looking to fight with him, with a ready answer if he questions anything. In this mood, he knows, she'll leave important things behind, and he'll say nothing when, later, elsewhere, they find what they need missing.

It's still dark. Their shelter is the best he has ever built. Overhead, where the branches weave together in an artful bit of joinery he takes particular pride in, he can see light pierce through on certain mornings.

No light today.

He peels back the roll of woollen blankets, the synthetic sleeping bag with its dizzying design of colours he has never seen elsewhere. He lets the cold sink into him. Feels the nerve endings shrill to attention, a shiver of awakening all over his body.

When he stands and lights a stub of candle, he sees Beau has waited for him, huddled by the door in a ball of chestnut-coloured fur. Eban reaches out his hand and lets Beau push his black nose against it, though he knows the dog only stayed near because Judy shut him in. He follows her everywhere she goes, while his affection for Eban seems only dutiful. To Judy, he is devoted, adoring, a disciple of her fleeting attentions.

"Judy," Eban calls as he pushes open the door. During the night it must have snowed again; he has to push hard to scrape the door through the accumulated snow, though it has already been opened that morning. "Tell me what needs doing."

He sees their packs laid out by the firepit, already full. They've discussed for weeks what will be left behind. Nearly everything.

Judy appears from behind the shelter. He can hardly see her; the branches overhead make lace of a faint blue light, illuminating only the edge of her cheek, the end of her nose, a coil of hair. Her arms are full. He reaches to take what they hold, but she pushes past him. For a moment he wonders if she didn't see him, or didn't hear him call her name.

She kneels before the packs and slides more things—the axe, two of their smaller pots, the fishing kit—inside. There is something else. It's from the protective way she holds them, as she slips them into an outer pocket, that he knows what they are. Her books.

He recognizes at a glance the ones she has chosen. One translated from Russian, split into four volumes of tiny, scarcely legible writing. One about an island that he watched Judy copy from an edition of her father's, the first summer he knew her. A book of fairy tales, each page illustrated in fading paint. The pages of poetry they cut from a rotting binding, now tied together with string. He's surprised to see she has left out the stories about gods, the strange play that made her cry when she read it out loud to him, and the French books she sometimes would translate for him. He is not surprised to see she left his mother's compendium of medicinal plants and herbs, or the book about a robber and a nun he bought from a peddler, thinking to please her, which she at last, when he asked, explained was not serious.

And if she's brought the books, he knows she'll have brought her things. She keeps her things, wrapped in cloth, in a dirty yellow box, made of some ancient polymer. Its rusted hinges gave out years earlier, when she was a child, but still she keeps it. She ties the box shut with a braid of string, and rarely opens it in front of him. In the last year, she has found more and more objects to add to it, and opens it only to slip each new object inside.

He has come to understand the things she keeps. Beautiful objects from before that have no use. Things of metal mostly, or glass. Things that have endured since the time when they had purposes. A string of jewels with a pin that she calls an earring and says was her mother's, though he knows that's not true. A glove that isn't warm. A piece of a machine for counting time, and he forgets what else. A green shoe with a pointed heel, so it raises her inches from the ground when she crams her foot into it and stands, teetering, on one leg. She loves that shoe.

Even in their arguments, she never mentioned bringing her things, or the books, but he knows not to say anything now.

Only when she stands does she address him. "Can you manage the bedding?" she asks.

He nods, though she still isn't looking at him. Beau, at her heels as ever, barks. "*Ssh*," she says. "Beau, sit. *Stay*." She leaves the dog by the shelter, adoration fixing him to the ground, tail beating with gladness. Eban returns to the shelter and lights a second candle by the door.

The sleeping pad will have to stay behind. It won't compress enough to fit into his pack. He chooses the warmest, most tightly woven blankets and rolls them into as small a bundle as he can. He finds a tattered sack in the corner crate among the things they seldom use. He pounds the bedding into the sack with his fists, and then, in the remaining space, he fits the sleeping bag as best he can, though it bursts from the top of the bullet-shaped sack like a neon aneurysm.

He looks at the things they'll leave behind. The other blankets, the extra traps, the pouch filled with his mother's belongings, the chair he made for Judy, the dishes, the jars of dried and preserved summer forage, his drawings, Judy's dress. The shelter itself. It took him an entire summer to build, too much time. It had meant a hungry winter. But they'd be there longer than he had stayed anywhere before, maybe forever. It was, he thought, their home, his and hers, and should look like something that would last.

The structure is just a simple box, but has a feeling of permanence. Sometimes he pauses outside it in the last hours of the day and admires the wood and stone painted in auburn evening light. He'd carried loads of stone up from the river and laid them out, three-wide, in rows. With a pack of mud and clay he'd filled in the cracks between, where wind smuggled in the cold. Ribbons of grass and reed wove together a roof of weathered branches. When it rained, he hung a synthetic cover they'd purchased from a peddler over top. It was more than a shelter. It was a home. He'd imagined one day he might build a hearth. He'd built it right, so it would keep them warm and dry, and last. "No window," he'd explained patiently again and again to Judy, even after he didn't feel patient any longer. "Cold looks for weakness. Everything I did there with the leaves and mud and stone would be for nothing if I left a hole for wind to rush in."

Taking a final look around the shelter he made for them, he remembers how he and Judy first arrived here.

His mother had died three days after Judy's father, and neither of them wanted to remain in the place where they had buried the last of their families. They agreed to search out a new place, a place just for them. They travelled for weeks to find it, through the rain that had finally come and now fell without seeming like it would ever stop.

Eban had in mind a place higher in the hills, farther from the route the peddlers took. But, stopped one day for a drink at a brook that rilled between the trees, Judy suddenly looked up at him, her face alight.

"Look, Eban."

He looked with confusion into her eyes, where he saw happiness for the first time since her father's death.

"Can you see it?"

He couldn't, and shook his head.

"There's water here. Flat ground. These big trees that can't have been cut in a century, for shelter and shade. We passed an old dump not long ago. But we're a good distance from the route."

He turned his face up at the trees blotting out the sky above them. It was October and the last leaves of a fled season rattled on the branch. "You think here?"

"Just the night. Let's stay the night. Maybe a few days. See what you think."

"But you like it?" he persisted. "You think we could live here?" He tasted the word in his mouth before he spoke it. "Together?"

She turned her head so she could see him only from the corner of her eye, teasing him with her silence.

They decided not to eat. They decided not to even build the tent. The night was unusually warm and they sat with their feet in the brook till the moon came out. And then it was so yellow and bright that they rejoiced in its light and decided to follow the brook, climbing higher and higher, until they found a mountain pool. The water was cold and the air was warm, and they swam like dreamers slipping between worlds.

She called his name and he came to her, paddling furiously to stay afloat while she bobbed lightly and easily in the water. He was still shy then with Judy, but believed they would grow to be at ease with each other. That they would talk and touch freely, like family.

His teeth shook in his head. Maybe it was colder than he thought. But he was giddy, wild, and felt truth spilling over him, things he wanted to tell her and ask.

Moonlight made the water luminous, but where the stones that edged the brook cast their shadows, the water was dark and deep. It frightened him, but he dove into it, searching for the bottom, and then for her. He felt the water ripple around her kicking legs, felt eddies of water run over him like the stroke of a hand. Impulsively, he grasped one of her feet and felt her kick suddenly away from him. But he wouldn't release her. He pulled her under the water, and she wrapped her arms and legs around him, pressed her lips to his, and he opened his mouth and choked. Buoyed like bubbles, they burst to the surface, and she laughed so hard the night rang with the sound of their joy.

He was deeply relieved to find a breach in her grief, and in his own, and terrified of undoing it. And so he spoke without thinking, as he never did, his words clumsy and hurried.

"I never thought this," he told her. "I never imagined anything like this. Like you."

"What do you mean?"

"I didn't think a lot about the future. But I didn't think we'd ever leave where we were. I thought it would always be just me and my brother. I never thought I'd know anyone else this way."

Judy paddled a few inches closer, and he felt the heat of her nearness, the weight of her gaze. In the night there was only the sound of water parting and dashing against itself, stirred by their hands. "Eban, what happened to your brother? I don't even know his name or how he died. Will you tell me about him?"

He waited a long time for the words to arrive to answer her, and when they didn't, he shook his head, like they were both dreaming and needed to be roused. "Maybe we should get out of here," he said, and meant with the softness of his voice to tell her he was sorry. "It's so cold."

She looked so sadly at him then that he knew he must say something more.

"I'm sorry," he said at last. "I just can't. I can't talk about that."

She pulled herself up onto the rocks, huddling with her knees held to her chest. "I guess I don't know what that's like. I never had a brother. Or a sister. I only had my fathers."

He knew enough not to reach for her or touch her then. "We should make camp," he whispered.

"Can we sleep like this?"

"Here, you mean?"

"By this pool, just as we are. The water was cold but the air is warm and we'll soon dry. Can we sleep right here, under the moon?"

"All right," he said, glad for this small way to please her.

"And maybe we'll stay a few nights, like we said, and see if we could live here."

"I'll get the blankets," he said, already on his feet, heading to the place where they had left their packs.

She said they'd stay the night. They'd stay the night and then they'd see. They stayed four years.

Now a pale daylight spills into the room as Judy yanks open the door. "Done in here?"

He nods, heaving the sack of bedding over his shoulder and extinguishing the candles. "I guess there's nothing else we can fit now."

"Nothing else we need." Judy stalks back out, leaving the door open behind her.

After a moment's thought, he peels one of his drawings from the wall and rolls it up, tucks it into his fist. Most of the drawings are of her, but this is the only one she posed for. The others catch her accidentally in stillness, reading or writing or with her chin between her fists, thinking something out. But in this one, she sat in the afternoon light for as long as she could stand it, holding his gaze every time he looked at her, and then, for a moment, she grinned at him, so suddenly and briefly— he erased the mouth and eyes he'd drawn, to try to catch that expression. He missed it—the curve of her lips is more of a sneer than a smile, but her eyes are full of him. Just that, he will take.

After he fits the sleeping things into his pack, slipping the drawing into the side pocket where he normally keeps his eel jig, he stands awkwardly before her. "What else?"

She shakes her head. And all of a sudden she smiles. Her crooked teeth he loves. The gap between the ones at the front. "We're ready."

"The tent?"

"In my pack."

"The medicine bag."

"In yours."

"Matches," he murmurs, even as he slides his hand into his pocket and feels a box there.

"We've got enough. We can get more. There will be people out there. Peddlers. Someone."

Under the weight of the pack, she looks delicate. Her strong shoulders and back catch its burden as she stoops forward slightly, giving her upturned face the inquiring, timorous look of a bird. Her black hair is twisted into a knot at her neck, and her brown, freckled cheeks are flushed. It occurs to him that she looks happy. Over her shoulder, the barrel of the shotgun rises from the top of the pack, where she's strapped it.

He never wanted to leave this place, and never would have, not for any reason except her insistence. This dirt, these trees, the paths they know, the brook that has never yet run dry . . . it was a world, and it was theirs. In the years they lived here they never starved or thirsted or were visited by anyone who wished them harm.

And now they leave it to chase a mirage, a lie that he put in her head to slow her departure from him. But it has only carried her away, and all he can do now is stumble after.

The sun is rising, casting watery yellow light through the trees. The snow that fell during the night has settled in white beards over the firs. Between them, the snow bristles with the bare, mauve branches of dead scrub. But the path from the camp will be easy to travel, brush and snow worn thin. He doesn't know how far they'll get today. Maybe to the second river. Maybe farther.

"The map," he says softly, but she's already pulling it out of her coat. She made it the same summer he built their shelter. It traces all their usual routes from the camp, sites where they buried any kill they couldn't eat, locations of edible vegetation or medicinal herbs. It's badly drawn and so inexact as to be useless, but they know everything it attempts to depict anyway. And in two days, they'll be beyond its reach.

"We'll do what we said. Follow the lower path till we get past the boneyard, and then travel along the ridge from there."

He waits, not wanting to be the one to start. The map still in her hand, she begins walking, quickly, so that Beau has to trot to keep at her heels. She doesn't look back. But he does.

He thinks of having a child, as he once believed they would. Back then, he wondered if it would change the way Judy looked at him, to have made something of themselves together. He guessed, like Beau, the child would love her better, prefer her moods and warmth to his steady hand and efforts. He thinks now of how it would cry, and want to be fed, and need countless things, difficult to give or determine; how he would guess at its wants and never be sure—not even when the child was at last able to talk and demand or beg or make faces, to say one thing in a tone that meant another—what it was that he should give it. What to do.

He has never held a baby. When his brother was born, he was only three, and though he remembers begging to hold him, his mother forbade it. "You'll drop him," she said. "You don't realize how heavy even something so small can be. If you don't hold his head just so, you might break his neck."

She told him babies were born with softness in their heads, the bones not yet fused, so that if you weren't careful, if you were insufficiently gentle or did something else wrong, you might damage that thin tissue, bruise the tiny, growing brain it contained. He would stare in awe, then, at his brother, sleeping in his crib. He'd look at the soft bald flesh, its fur of golden hair. At his own hands, too rough, too strong, not to be trusted.

They didn't know then what was wrong with his brother. After they knew, they left that house. Came away, into the hills. Somewhere the house was still there, perhaps. The cradle, packed away in a closet. His brother, damaged, though Eban had kept his hands to himself.

As they trudge on through the drifts of snow, he can see the trees closing behind him, hiding the small clearing where they lived. For a moment, looking back over his shoulder, he thinks again that he chose the site well. They might never have been found.

Then he continues, walking in the half-buried tracks of other trips he has taken down this path, following Judy, her disappearing shape, the blazing colour of her red coat against the white forest.

And when he gets to the place where his tracks turn away, following another, more familiar path, he steps out of them and continues, walking side by side with the prints of her boots in the snow, shuffling on, trudging through the untouched field of snow.

II

LIGHT SINKS ACROSS THE HILLS as the moon lifts into the sky. For the last several miles, they have walked beside each other. Beau kept at their heels until he tired, and since then Eban has carried the dog in his arms. After the second river, the path widened and rose steeply, ascending higher and higher before them, and after that, the path was gone. They haven't eaten since they left.

The white wood is luminous and alien under the moon; he can see everything, but imperfectly. The altered, spectral trees and their long blue shadows. An altered, spectral Judy. There is no sound but their boots crushing the snow.

Back at the river, Judy refused to let him stop to melt a slab of ice in the sun or over a fire, so he scooped snow into his canteen and tucked it under his coat. He drinks it a few drops at a time as it slowly turns to water, and every few miles he sets the dog on the ground and pours him a little. Each time he offers the canteen to Judy, she shakes her head, though he has seen her snatch handfuls of snow from the ground in her mitten and lift them to her mouth when she thinks he isn't looking. He watches her for any sign the end has already begun, another pregnancy extinguished. A loss of colour from her cheeks. Her mouth pinched in that terrible way he remembers. But stealing glances at her, as they walk, he sees only expectation in her face. Expectation and something more. A private, almost insolent gladness.

He is a student of Judy's moods—he studies her every tone and gesture like a diviner casting the ground for what might lie beneath. The way he watched his brother in the first months of his infancy, with the sense of peering at someone who didn't belong to the world in the same way he does. A visitor.

He remembers back then studying his brother, restive as he always was in their mother's arms, filled with an urgent physical determination but no discernible objective—all darting eyes and thrust limbs and crying that never stopped.

Their mother dwelt at the outer edge of her patience for those endless months, and Eban feared her. And feared his brother even as he feared for him.

One night, the baby had cried so long and late that his mother at last threw open the door to Eban's own room, carrying the baby in a drawer. She shoved it onto the floor, where he lay bawling, and left the room without a word, her face white and frightening. Eban crept to the end of his bed to stare at the wild creature abruptly put into his care. He understood it was his brother's fault that his mother had become a threat to them both.

"Stop it," he told his brother's howling, shuddering body. "Stop, stop, stop, stop." He repeated the word until it became senseless and the howls slowly dissolved into gulps and gasps. At last, when light began to show through the shutters, the baby slept and Eban watched him still.

Judy, at times, seems as unknowable now as his brother did to him then.

———

They reach the edge of a frozen lake, and Judy steps out onto the ice without hesitating. Snow squeaks under her boots as she circles the centre of the lake, peering down. And then, with a whoop of triumph, she points to the ground. "Look, Eban! I can see those little sinkholes they make."

He frowns. "Eels, you mean."

She nods. "Maybe they got trapped by the freeze and just burrowed into the mud like another winter had come. We can smoke them to carry with us."

He lowers one boot onto the ice. Feeling the lake take his weight, he steps out with the other foot and makes his way to her. Is it so late in winter already? Have the eel already begun their run upriver from the sea?

She sets Beau down and pulls her spear from her bag. Without thinking, Eban's hand goes to the side pocket of his pack, before he remembers the drawing he took from the wall. "I don't have the eel jig," he tells her. "I left it."

She stares at him. "Well," she says at last. "Get the axe."

Obediently he finds the axe and begins to cut away at the ice. He makes three holes and then she slides the spear through the first, digging at the lakebed. It is blind, uncertain work.

Eban has never enjoyed eating eel, but Judy loves the meat, or pretends to. Each time they fish for eel, she tells him again that some of the yellowy adolescents they've glimpsed in their passage upstream will live to be centenarians. Judy claims they travel a thousand miles from a distant, southern ocean to arrive at these hills, and will return there again. Because she loves to, he lets her tell this story over and over, and the one about the time her father Daniel was taking specimens from the river and caught sight of an elver slinking along the mud. It had been decades since he'd seen an eel, and he'd believed them to be extinct. Without them, there were disturbances in the aquatic insect populations, too many of the wrong things, and other details Eban didn't understand and Judy only partly remembered. Dan was overjoyed at the discovery, and Judy seems to recover that moment of shared happiness with her father each time they fish the eel, which are now consistent summer traffic in the rivers and pools of the hills.

But as she jams the spear through the ice, again and again, rooting through the mud, the eagerness slips from Judy's face. At her feet, Beau turns in circles, restless. Eban begins to worry for her again.

After an hour, Judy throws the spear to the ground. "I'll do the fire," she says, as he bends to pick it up.

He prods at the mud, the spear handle slipping in his gloved hand, and at last he removes the glove so he can push the spear deeper. He thinks she must have been mistaken. It usually takes only a short while to pull an eel or two from a lake where they've nested in the silt.

And then, just as Judy emerges from the trees, a load of wood in her arms, he feels the spear pierce what feels like a bundle of wet blankets. In wonder, he withdraws it into the icy night air, producing an enormous, shining eel. "Judy," he whispers, turning toward her, the eel waving like a flag from the stick in his hands. But she already sees. She is watching as she drops the wood to the ground, smiles, and turns her back.

He pulls eight more eels from the lake in less than an hour. When all nine are wriggling on the ice, and he can see the fire blazing behind the snow wall Judy has built, he throws down the spear and lashes each eel in turn against the ice. Dead, they continue to twist and coil in the snow. Hooking his fingers under the gills of each one, he makes a circle cut around the head, peels back the skin and removes it in a single piece, as if he is stripping the eel of its clothes.

"Okay," Judy calls, and he makes a final cut down each eel, from end to end, and removes the organs and bones. By the time he reaches Judy, the nine skinned eels slung over his arm have finally ceased to move. Judy takes them from him wordlessly. Slipping a noose of twine under the gills of each head, she strings them up on a rack of green sticks over the fire, blanketing the rack with a tarp. Beside her, the dog, exhausted, sleeps on top of her pack, his body drawn into a tight little circle.

"What did you find to burn, for smoke?" Eban asks.

She takes a branch from the pile and hands it to him. "Crabapple," she says.

He runs his hand over the branch. "Delicious."

"Yeah."

He pulls his hands out of his gloves and rubs them together. He can see a mood settling in her, an ease, and he is afraid of wasting it. What can he tell her to make her smile, to keep her here beside him for this meal? "A good day's travel," he says.

"Eban?"

He waits.

"You want to build us someplace to sleep for the night?"

He stands up, brushing the snow from his pants. Her attention's gone back to the eels. She scoops up one that has begun to slip from its noose.

He finds a place, not too far from the fire, where the snow has drifted up against a line of trees. The trees will block the gathering northwest wind, and in the drift, there'll be room to tunnel down like worms. He takes a step towards their packs, and then he stops.

"What is it?" Judy calls. He turns to see her watching him.

"The shovel," he says softly. She cups her hand to her ear. "The shovel," he says more loudly.

Judy stares back at him for a moment and then shrugs. "So use your hands."

He hates that they don't have the shovel.

Shattering the crust of ice along the bank, he starts to dig. By the end, his gloves will be soaked and his hands frozen.

He begins to understand what his mother felt. After they left their home in the outland, she carried the burden of her tribulation without setting it down until the day she died. She wasn't interested in pity, and grew impatient with Eban if he was sentimental about the time before they came to the foothills. But at night, she would sometimes lie in the dark, cataloguing their one-time house, piece by piece. "Your father found that door. Steel it was. Rusted down an inch, would have went to dust in the dump he took it from, but he sanded it till it wasn't bad to look at. Kept the wind out, didn't it. Got a bucket of paint from a peddler, didn't we. I didn't like that colour. Used that same bit of paint on all the windows, so they wouldn't rot. Remember them little bugs that got in, round the corners, where the paint wore off? *Lyctus planicollus*. You remember any of your Latin, or would I have done better to spend the breath on whistling?"

His mother was a kind of genius, wasted. *Waste* was her word. She had her own names for everything, and in a certain mood she'd call the territory where they lived "the wasteland." She had brains and knew it. Eban always figured her brains would have come up talent and purpose in the right soil, something that would make her and those around her happy, but in the outland, they sowed only suspicion and fury.

As he works, and thinks of what he and Judy have left behind them, Eban feels something like his mother's anger planted in the core of him, its roots coiling. Judy has led them far away from a safety she didn't know to cling to, because she doesn't know to be afraid.

All Eban's life he has heard rumours of what happens in the cities, and what is done to those found in hiding by the wrong people. Fear of that kind grows thick in these hills, blooming in the shade like moss beneath a tree. He himself has glimpsed the cut tongues of peddlers, but can only guess what happened and why. They belong to the unillumined world beyond the outland that his mother warned him of when she taught him how fear was something you could live within, like gravity or time.

The lessons in fear began when he was still a child, as soon as he had passed the tests his mother set for him. As soon as she knew she could trust him, she taught him to trust no one else. He still remembers the lessons, and the tests. The first happened in the garden.

The house they lived in then had been built long ago by someone else, years before Eban was born. It had three rooms, each with a window that had wooden shutters they could pull closed when the winds came. In the biggest room was a fireplace built of clay brick, which he found beautiful though in all his life he never saw it lit.

On a shelf above the fireplace was a photograph in a tin frame of Eban's grandparents, outland poultry farmers whom he had never met. Their clothes belonged to another time—a shining yellow cross hung from a chain at her throat and her hair was almost the same bright colour, which his mother said she used to buy from a store. He was thin and bent-shouldered. Eban's mother told him the picture was taken three years before the drought closed her school and her parents wrung the necks of the last of their hens. In the picture they are poor but not starving, and their faces are lifted up to smile at the person who took their picture. Their teeth are as white and perfect as a child's.

Once there had been a second photograph, a yellowed picture of Eban's father, cut from a newspaper. He wore blue jeans and a thin cotton shirt, sitting in the grass, late sun slanting from the sky somewhere behind him. He looked worried. The sentence under the photograph was torn off at the end. It said his name, and that he taught at a university. He had designed something for the computers they used at hospitals. Eban's mother spoke only once about the university, where she had met his father. She showed Eban the picture, which had been taken from the wall years earlier, and she explained computers and hospitals. Her face and voice softened as she told him how, the year she turned seventeen, the university had been part of the first district to open in the newly consolidated cities. The voluntary relocation program had just concluded, halting all services to outlying communities. Eban's mother was eligible to attend the university, but her parents and their church had joined the revolt in the outland, and they told her if she went to the cities not to come back. "What did you do?" Eban asked her, and she said, "I went."

Later, briefly, there was a third photograph.

The first test came without a warning. Soon he'd learn to expect them. And always knew from his mother's eyes that he had passed them.

He was five years old. His mother led him outside by the hand and showed him something she had found. It was the frail shoot of a pear tree she had planted in their yard. She showed him the shining threads of a web strung between the branches, throbbing with the fly it held fast. Then she pointed to the spider waiting on one of the threads, and showed him what the spider did to make the fly stop throbbing, and what it did next.

"Why," she asked him, "wouldn't the spider eat the fly?"

He wouldn't answer her. He was upset and wanted to go back inside the house.

"The spider is hungry," she told him. "That fly can feed its hunger."

He tried to shake her hands from his shoulders.

"What reason could stop the spider, who is hungry, from eating the fly, who is food?"

"Because," he cried at last, angry with her, "the fly is hungry too."

"Good," she said, and let go of his shoulders, going back inside and leaving him alone with the pear tree. And the spider, who was not hungry anymore.

The other tests were more difficult, but he passed them as well. When the lessons came, about whom to fear and how to hide and what to say and when to be silent, he understood they were a reward for having answered all his mother's questions correctly.

He never saw her take his brother into the yard or what answer he gave.

Eban digs out a snow cave wide enough for him and Judy to sleep inside, puncturing the ceiling so they aren't smothered in the night. Then he digs a tunnel on a downward incline, so their body heat will rise and be trapped inside the snow walls, instead of escaping out the entrance. It takes a long time to finish, and by the time he returns to the fire to fetch the axe from Judy, she is unstringing the eels.

"Ready to eat?" she asks.

He nods. "I'll go get some branches for us to sleep on, while you finish that."

After he has laid several inches of boughs across the floor of the snow cave, he joins Judy by the fire. She has already cut one of the eels into pieces and she offers it to him on a tin plate.

"It's still hot," she says. "It's perfect."

They can't find the forks, and so they eat with their hands, oil trickling down their fingers. The sweet crabapple smoke has sharpened the tang of the eel meat. His tongue is burned by the hot, greasy meat, but he ignores the pain. He has to restrain himself from eating more than he can swallow. Beguiled by hunger, his belly is convinced he has eaten nothing better.

When they have finished eating, they look up, in surprise, at each other. He thinks the juices of the meat must be all over his face and hands. He feels embarrassed to have lost himself to his appetite like that. But Judy only laughs. "I think I forgot you were there," she says.

He can't remember when he last heard the deep bark of her laughter, unsoured by grief or grudge. "Who would have thought we'd eat so well, so far from home," he says.

She's still smiling. "My father said that in the cities they used to eat foods we couldn't dream of. Every kind of meat and fish, whenever they wanted it. Cherries in winter."

He stands up abruptly, holding his plate and reaching for hers, but she doesn't release it or even lower her gaze to his hands.

"How far do you think it is, Eban?"

"I don't know."

"But from the stories you heard."

"Everyone says something different. All I know is what I told you. Follow the setting sun below the barrens to pass between the two-horned mountains."

It has been weeks since the idea came to him, to tell her about Heaven colony. Though she knew about Heaven, of course. Everyone did. The rumours were the favourite gossip of every traveller who passed through the hills. She'd heard occasional things down in the allotment, but her fathers had been dismissive, and she hadn't been interested then in what was back in these hills. So he told her everything he'd heard, even the most doubtful reports from the least reliable of tellers. And he made up what he didn't know.

"I wonder if it might be closer than we imagine," Judy says. "The hills seem so vast, we've always assumed they go on for a thousand miles. But maybe they don't."

A city in the wood, he told her. A people like them, who had come into the hills not to hide from the world, but to build a new one. Safely concealed from those who could harm them, but findable to those who sought them. "We just don't know," he says now.

"But I'm saying we really have no idea. Everything might be closer than we think. If no one ever said how far Heaven is, only the direction to travel, it's possible, isn't it, that it's not nearly as far as we thought?"

"I think we should prepare ourselves," he says slowly.

"What do you mean?"

"It might be farther." He hesitates. "Or . . . different than you want it to be."

She looks a long time at the fire and then says, something hardened in her voice, "It might not be far at all."

Together they pack up the remaining eel meat; between that and the smoked meat they brought from the hide, it will be days until they have to worry about food again. He washes the plates in a pot of boiled water and then stamps out the fire. Judy puts out some scraps for Beau and hangs the remaining eel guts from the trees.

Finally they face each other, and Eban gestures toward the entrance to the snow cave. "You first."

She crawls inside and he hands her the sleeping bag to spread out. When she's finished, he passes her the dog and follows after.

He realizes he built the cave too small. There isn't room for him to stretch out all the way, and they will be pressed to each other like two clasped hands.

He slides himself into the sleeping bag and then lies down, his back to hers and the dog at her feet. After a moment, she turns and wraps her arm around him, tucking her chin over his shoulder.

He feels something that makes his eyes sting. He tells himself to choke whatever it is or it will become awkward and difficult and she'll turn away again.

Her breath on his cheek is hot and damp. It stinks of eel. He wonders if he takes her hand, if she will let him. Through their gloves, he
would feel none of her heat, the knots of her knuckles, the calluses of
her fingertips.

When he met her she had soft hands. She had lived at the outer
perimeter of the resource allotment, in a house with two floors and glass
windows. So much grander than the rotting, three-room cabin his
mother would index in the dark. Judy has described it to him a thousand
times, first proudly, when they met, and then with longing. And then she
stopped speaking of it at all.

Her father Daniel was the son of a famous entomologist. His mother
had taught him to read insects like tea leaves. He tracked them in the
woods and fields around their house, and noted changes in their habits
and populations. He made surmises and predictions, and wrote a quarterly report that sold well enough to support his family of three. She
never knew whom he sold it to, but four times a year a rider would arrive,
with pannier sacks slung across their horse, and a stack of hand-copied
reports would disappear into one of the sacks.

Eban never met Dan. It was nine days after his death that Eban
found Judy and her other father, Alphonse, camped out in a battered
tent in the foothills.

He approached them with caution, as he did all strangers in the
hills. He first watched them for several hours. It was spring and he had
been following the river, picking the heads of ostrich ferns. He saw their
tent first, a ragged, bright-coloured relic, made of some synthetic fibre.
From that, he knew they didn't belong here. They didn't know to hide.

And then he heard her voice. "Dad, it isn't here. Dad?"

She appeared in front of the tent, unzipping the door to speak to the
man who sat cross-legged inside. "I'm sorry," she said more softly. "We
must have left it behind."

Eban couldn't hear the man's answer.

"I know," she said. "I'm sorry. We have the others, the first three volumes. But the fourth must have been somewhere else. Maybe he had it in his—"

She sank to the ground and he thought she was about to cry. But she began to nod and he realized she was listening to her father. Her back to the tent, her knees to her chest, her body had a strange eloquence. She looked at first sorrowful, acquiescent, nodding steadily as she listened. And then the bobs of her head became impatient. And then she stopped nodding, her eyes darting around the wood.

"I can't," she said, her voice now dissipated almost to silence. "I've told you I don't want to . . . No. No, of course not. I would never fault you for . . . It's just, I can't, I can't keep . . ." She made her hands into fists and pressed them against her eyes. "Stop!"

Getting to her feet, she told the man inside the tent, "We have only twenty-two tablets left. Do you know what that means? And we have half that many jars of—"

Her father emerged from the tent. He was tall and lean, with long greying hair. He spoke with a trace of an accent—an extra, lingering attention to vowels—but his words were exact. "I know you are right. I know you are wise. I don't want to stop you from doing what we must. But I can't—I am useless to you. You are without help. You are without fathers . . ."

Then the man, who was older even than Eban's mother, without warning buckled to the ground and began to sob. Eban had not known it was possible to weep with such fervour. Without restraint of any degree.

He thought the daughter would embrace him and offer some comfort, but instead she backed away as if she, like Eban, were frightened by the man's grief. "We have to eat," she told him. "If we don't find our own food and water we'll soon have nothing left. I have to hunt for us."

Eban hesitated, wanting to follow the woman and make sure she was safe. He wanted, also, to watch her longer. To see her from closer. But the man and his grief transfixed Eban, and he stayed for some time, watching the man, who continued to cry long after the woman was gone, and then sat without moving, in terrible stillness, as the sun began to drop.

Eban knew he needed to leave then if he was to make it back to his mother before dark. It was clear that the man and his daughter posed no threat. If he left them, they would make their way or they would not, but they would harm no one but themselves. Maybe he could even visit them again. Leave things for them. Help. But for now he needed to return. And yet he waited.

It had just occurred to him that maybe he waited because he hoped to see her one more time, when he heard the whisper of her voice in his ear.

"I have a weapon," she said.

He swallowed. "I know."

"You know because you saw it. You saw me take it into the woods."

"Yes."

"You were watching us."

"Yes, but . . ."

She stepped before him. He noticed, with surprise, that her shotgun was lowered, almost forgotten, by her side. She had long, narrow black eyes and freckled brown skin. He liked her face.

"Yes but what?"

He didn't know what to say. "But I wasn't going to hurt anything. I was just watching to see if you were . . . dangerous."

A smile broke out over her face so suddenly that he flinched. And then she began to laugh. He stared and she lowered a hand over her eyes, shaking her head. "I'm sorry. I'm sorry. I don't know why I . . ." She dropped the hand. Though the laughter had seemed sincere, her expression now was as weary as if she'd wept. "I don't think we're dangerous. Do you?"

He shook his head.

"Will you leave us alone then?"

"Yes." He began to retreat into the woods, feeling ridiculous and angry and ashamed.

And then she called, "Can you help us?"

That first night, after Eban had brought them to the two canvas tents he and his mother shared, and Alphonse had taken his mother aside and said something in French that convinced her Eban was right to trust them, the four sat together, huddled over bowls of boiled fern heads and rabbit broth. He watched Judy, who gripped her spoon like a shovel and had hardly delivered one mouthful to her lips before sending the spoon diving for another.

She looked up then from her soup and caught him staring.

"What," she said.

"Nothing."

"What?"

"It's just the way you handle things. The way you move. It's like you're running out of time."

Eban's mother twisted her mouth wryly. "He's calling you clumsy, girl."

"Not clumsy." He hesitated. "I don't know. Maybe it's just strong."

He could tell Judy didn't like that, him trying to take the measure of her, but she said only, "You touch everything like it's going to run away."

And then she smiled. And he saw in that look how she took in all of him at once, devouring him in a single gulp. How he was stripped by her eyes. How she lost the defeated look from her face in an instant, shook it off with a lift of her chin.

She was nineteen years old. And he was seventeen.

Later, as he showed her how to wrap her tent in brush and skins for cover, they shared the brief stories of their lives. He went first, on her urging, and found he had little to tell. "I grew up near the foothills," he said, haltingly. "In the outland. With my mother." His brother's name stuck to his tongue for some reason and he waited for her to ask about him, but of course she didn't.

"What about your father?"

He couldn't think what to say. "He was there when I was very little. And then he left. I don't really remember him. We don't talk about him much."

She nodded. "Do you think he went to the cities?"

"I don't know," he said honestly.

She nodded again. "What about your mother? Did she always live in the outland?"

"She grew up here. But she was one of the first to attend university in the new cities, ten years after the original university closed. She was studying medicine there when she met my father. He taught in a different department."

He hesitated and then went on. "I used to ask my mother why they didn't stay in the cities, but it always put her in a terrible mood. I stopped asking eventually. But one time I found her holding this old picture of my father that I thought she'd burned years earlier. I knew enough not to ask about him. So I asked about the university. And it was like she couldn't stop herself from talking about that.

"She'd finished her first three years of coursework in two years," he told Judy, "which no one had done before. She began medical school the year the third and worst wave of the fourteen-year drought hit. The few other students she knew from the outland left and went home to their families, but she stayed. She said she sat in classrooms surrounded by people from the cities, who were perplexed by her and by everyone from the outland. She didn't make a single friend. And then she met my father. She said he liked her biting tongue and how serious she was. But he didn't understand the people she came from any more than her classmates did. He thought the government should use any means necessary to put a stop to the riots in the outland, where those who had refused to leave were now starving."

Eban told Judy about the day his mother had been working at the lab when a protestor broke into the university to set fire to the files of a researcher who had been publishing work on neurodivergent adaptation. His mother was one of the few who made it out in time, but she felt compassion for the protestor, who died with the others and then was reviled by people in the cities and hailed as a martyr by the resistance. She said the protestor had come from the outland and wouldn't have understood what fire would do in a medical laboratory filled with solvents and liquid oxygen.

The day classes resumed, she learned she was seven weeks pregnant, and Eban's father begged her not to return. But it was her only chance. She would keep her head low. She would finish her education.

The night the resistance tried for a coup in the new national assembly, they sent a line of demonstrators to stand around the university and prevent anyone from leaving. They didn't hurt anyone. But the police came and broke it up and word spread that there had been a massacre at the cities centre, and then, she said, it all was a dirty mess, with people fleeing and shouting, and no one sure who was attacking. A protestor was running toward her with her arm raised and suddenly fell forward on the grass. His mother recognized her from the cannery where her sisters had gone to work after their school closed. She was scarcely fifteen.

"She'd been shot. There was blood in her mouth and she just lay there pulling at her bloody shirt. My mother didn't know what to do but help her pull it off. A student pushed her aside. 'Get back,' he said, and he pinned the girl's arm to the ground under his boot. My mother screamed and he showed her the protestor's hand, closed around a tin-can grenade. The girl opened her mouth and no words came out, only a bright red bubble. The student stamped on her face and she didn't move again. 'Come on,' he said to my mother, but she just stayed there on her knees beside the girl.

"She had been studying physiology for three years but she had no supplies, no tools, no help, and she said she saw then that none of her education had made her any less helpless. So she just watched until the girl died. Another protestor appeared behind her and yanked her to her feet. My mother could only see the woman's tired eyes over her mask. She suddenly found herself shouting the name of her village, the names of her parents, and over and over again, 'I'm pregnant. Help me get out of here.'

"And the woman did. She helped her find my father so they could go home."

"Home?"

"She wanted to go back to the outland." His mother had described to him the ride out of the cities in the back seat of a tiny solar car that belonged to one of his father's colleagues. It had been three years since she was home, and all along the road she saw the difference. Houses plastered in dust. Cars deserted in the road, sometimes a door still open. A tiny cross in the ground in front of a line of empty cars, where someone had painted over the car windows, *Lily Mary Two Months Old Dead of Dust Pneumonia.*

"She said when they stopped the car in front of her family's house, two children from across the way came running over, holding out their hands. She remembered the babies they'd been but they'd hardly put on any weight in the three years since, even though now they were tall enough to crowd the doors of the car and reach inside. She said one didn't even speak, just pulled at her pockets. She said their eyes looked like holes."

"Did she give them anything?"

"She had brought a crate of canned meat and legumes, and she gave them one of the cans, and the older girl started pounding it with a rock, but her sister looked sullen and went back to gnawing at a bit of bone that had long been stripped of meat, and my mother said she looked at the bone, and she understood all at once that it was the bone of a . . ." Judy's eyes, watching him, were so round that he faltered. "She understood how bad things were then, worse than she'd even guessed."

"Did she go back to her family?"

"They wouldn't let her inside. She said she saw her father standing at the open door, looking twenty years older than he was. And he looked at her and shut the door.

"She found a friend from her school days who told her about a house that had been left. Lots of left houses, I guess. She said my father agreed to stay until the baby came, but she knew right then she'd never go back to the cities again."

Judy told him that Alphonse's mother was a professor too, like Eban's father. She had taught French literature in another country, and as climate migrants flooded the border, she managed to secure a visa to accept a new teaching job. She'd just immigrated when the second tsunami hit, four years after Eban's mother was born. And then everything was gone. The job, and the university. She and her young son travelled out to what would become the outer edge of the allotment, a decade later. She hired a local man and together they built the house where

Alphonse lived until the day he left it with Judy. And one day, when he was scarcely twenty, he met Daniel at the outer gate. Daniel, a decade older, who had grown up outside the old city and had moved with his family to the cities after consolidation, the previous year. Daniel who loved to walk into the allotment, creeping past the cameras to study the insects that fed on the remaining crops. Daniel who was handsome and kind, who had a gentle and faintly mournful way about him, became the first and only man Alphonse ever loved.

Some months later, Daniel arrived at Alphonse and his mother's house with a suitcase, and as far as Judy knew, he'd never returned or seen his family again. "Alphonse knows nothing about the cities. He was only six years old when his mother brought him to the outland. But Daniel spent an entire year there with his family. I used to beg him to tell me about the cities, and he would almost always change the subject."

"Maybe he was ashamed," Eban said, staring at the ground.

"Ashamed?"

"Of leaving them. His brothers and sisters. His parents."

"Yeah," she said slowly. "Yeah, maybe you're right. I remember once Daniel told me that in the cities all seven of them were living crowded together in two rooms, at the top of a building seven floors above the ground. That was all they could afford with the consolidation payout. He said he couldn't understand why his family seemed so happy there. He hated it. He said there was no outdoors in the cities, just concrete walls and floors and hardly any sky.

"He got a job as a field labourer so he could get out into the allotment, and then little by little, he learned the patrol schedule and where the cameras were, and he was able to slip into the outland and collect data. He shared it with his mother, who was working on the pollinator action plan, and she connected him with a group of scientists who disputed the government's species extinction doctrine and official climate projections. They paid him to share his research with them."

"What extinction doctrine?"

"He didn't know. He *said* he didn't know. Honestly, I don't think he really cared. He said he only ever cared about the research, not the politics. He wanted the stories the insects were telling to be heard. That was all." Judy smiled. "I think that part was true. But he did like that the work he did mattered. I know that was true too. Even after he came to the outland, he still sent research back to the cities, and he knew it was dangerous and he did it anyway."

"But what was dangerous about it?"

"I don't know. I must have asked him every day for years to tell me more, more about the cities, more about his work, more about everything else, and he always said he didn't know anything to tell me. All he knew was that the people who collected his research told him he needed to be very careful."

"Were the people . . ." Eban hesitated. "The people he gave his research to . . . were they the other ones?"

Judy looked puzzled. "What do you mean, 'other ones'?"

"Did they not . . . Did your fathers not tell you about the other ones?" She shook her head and he saw that he now held her attention completely. "Something happened to the people in the cities. They were altered somehow. My mother didn't like to talk about it. All she would say is that it made them dangerous.

"When I was little, I asked questions whenever I thought I could do it without making her angry. But it was like you said about your father."

"The more you asked, the less she would say."

The conversation was circling too closely around things Eban had never been able to talk about with anyone before, and he saw now how dangerous it could be to have someone to tell things to.

"What about your mother?" he asked, so she would talk instead.

So Judy told him how she'd come to have two fathers. How Daniel and Alphonse had found a woman willing to carry a child for them. How the mother had begged them to let her stay when the baby came, to keep her safe, and they agreed, but then, just minutes after giving birth, she died.

"How?" Eban asked, and Judy hesitated.

"Her heart . . ."

"Her heart?"

"Daniel said she had something wrong with her heart, something she'd been born with. But he said it's not something that would have been passed on to me. He said I don't have to worry."

Eban nodded. "That's good," he said. "That's good."

In the days and weeks that followed, Eban looked at Judy so much and so often he had to hide it. Alphonse caught him watching her once and said he used to find the English *beautiful* too ugly and lumbering a word, until he came to understand how complicated beauty was. He said it was a better word than the French one after all, because of the clumsiness of it. "Such a brutal word," he said. "So much weight and spoken with such force. And awkward, like a burden, something hard to carry. You see what I mean, or I think you will."

But he had misunderstood Eban, who didn't stare at Judy because she was beautiful, and wasn't sure she was, even in whatever complicated way Alphonse meant. He stared because she was written there, something true and essential marked on her face in text that was almost, almost legible. Even now he feels the weight of her head on his shoulder and wonders whether her eyes are closed or open, and what they see.

He wonders why his mother so disliked her. She prized deep feeling, and no one feels things more than Judy. He's seen how she borrows pain from anything that suffers. After she came to their hide, he taught her what he knew of fishing and hunting, and she learned the skills well. But he saw her, once, take a fish from the hook when she thought she was alone. He saw her bend her head over it, her hands fingering the wound left behind and whispering to it something he couldn't hear.

Their warmth has begun to moisten the cold air, their breath surrounding them, new oxygen leaking in only slowly. The warmth makes it less bearable to be in this tight space, but it also makes Judy feel closer. "Judy," he whispers, but she's sleeping. He takes off his glove. Takes her hand.

III

HE HAS LOST TRACK of the months.

His mother had told him to be very careful about the passage of time. She'd numbered the days and months on the wall in white paint, and marked their passage with a bit of chalk. She warned him that if he were to lose a day, it would be gone forever. Eventually, he would lose a week, and then a month, and then the seasons would become cryptic. Too much would be unknown—when to expect heavy rains or the migration of birds; when certain animals would be at rest for winter, or made savage by hunger or rut. Marking the time, his mother said, was a daily task, as important as gathering water and food.

He'd heeded her words; at least, he'd never intended not to. But after the cold weather came this year, not a single traveller passed their hide, not even a peddler. And somehow, in the many months since he and Judy last saw any face but their own, he occasionally forgot.

At first he'd remember in time and know a day or three had passed, and he'd mark those missing days. But then one day he couldn't recall how many days he'd lost, and a week later he forgot again, and then again.

Each time he forgot, the calendar he kept became more doubtful and therefore less and less important. Finally he stopped keeping time altogether. And now he feels this winter has stretched on far longer than it should have—somehow it has expanded beyond containment into a bloated, endless season, devouring all others. But he isn't certain, and now he will never know.

And so he counts the days of their walking. The new calendar in his head begins with their departure. It has taken five days to reach the bridge, longer than he'd hoped. The temperature has fallen further every day, and they walk with their faces lowered against the cold and struggle to keep warm at night. They smell the stench of eel on everything.

They cross the bridge in the middle of their fifth day. He guesses it's noon though the sun is smothered somewhere in the grey sky, impossible to locate. White shreds of sky slip from the clouds. Judy is the only mark of colour in the white and grey wood; he watches for her red coat and shining black pants as around her everything that isn't tree or snow is disappeared, a white, meticulous erasure.

At the end of the bridge, Judy stops short.

"What?" he asks. "What is it?"

"The dog." She's opening the zipper of her coat. "Beau, he . . ."

He steps toward her, and looks as she peels back the collar of her tattered coat to show him the dog inside, clutched to her chest. "What is it?"

She stares down at the bundle she holds. "Something's wrong."

"What do you mean?"

"He's shivering. I don't get it. His body isn't . . . It doesn't feel right."

He shakes his head even though he knows it's the wrong thing to do, but she doesn't seem to notice.

"The pads of his feet are cracked. I got ice out of the fur between his toes, but—"

"Judy, I told you . . ."

"It could be frostbite. Do you think?"

"I don't know."

"He whines when he walks now, like it hurts him. Could it be frostbite in one of the paws? From the ice?"

"Judy, I told you before we started. It's too far for him to walk. It's too cold."

She shifts from one foot to the other, her eyes sliding off to the trees. "No."

"No?"

"No, you said it. You don't know."

"Judy."

"It's a goddamn dog, Eban. It's a goddamn dog."

He doesn't know how to answer.

"Every other animal in this wood walks in the snow, sleeps in the cold. He's a dog. A wild animal."

"He's not a wild animal. He couldn't have been more than a month old when that peddler brought him to us. We're all he knows. He's never—"

"I'll keep him close by the fire tonight. I've just got to get him warm. It won't be too much longer."

"Judy, it could be weeks or months till we find them. All we know is a direction to walk. You have no idea how long it will take."

"What's the point of saying that, Eban?" She hisses the words like her mouth and tongue are shaping them around a knife edge. "What does it help *anything*?"

"I'm just saying. We shouldn't have brought him."

Sometimes when she looks at him, it's like she has removed him from the world with her eyes. Like he's gone. Like he was there and then he isn't anymore, because of how she can look at him like that.

"When I first wanted to go to the cities," she says slowly, "you told me it wasn't safe. And then when I said I would go anyway, we had Beau, and you said the cities were too far for him. And then you told me about

Heaven, and you said if we could find it, the people there could tell us if
it was safe now. If we could make it to the cities."

"I did."

"You said that it wasn't so far."

He shakes his head.

"You said that it would be safe. For us. For Beau."

"No, I . . . I said it was safer. Not safe. And I wanted to leave in
spring . . ."

"Yes. Then when I agreed to go to the colony first, you said it would
be safest to wait until spring. And that's when I understood. You
would never leave. There would always be another reason. Another
threat. Another delay. Another way to keep us trapped and call it safe."

A week after Judy miscarried for the first time, a peddler had turned
up at the camp, and they traded him some skins and dried meat for
a box of candles, a replacement for their rusted-out skillet, and tooth-
paste. Judy had been the one to notice the cage on the back of the
peddler's cart. It made no sense to Eban at all, a dog too small to guard,
no hunting blood in it, only one more mouth to be fed. But then there
was the look on Judy's face, and he'd found himself putting back the
candles and pointing a thumb at the pup already squirming in Judy's
hands. "We'll take the dog too," he'd muttered.

The same peddler had returned every season after that. He'd act
pleased at how big and healthy the dog had grown, his toothless grin
too wide as he stretched his hands apart to indicate the dog's size. Now
he had rabbits and wondered if they were interested. "PET?" he wrote
on the bit of slate strung around his neck. He was the only peddler
they'd ever come across who could write, or who would admit he could.
He was a fool to trust them with such a secret. When Eban shook his
head, the peddler put his hands to his mouth, as if to feed himself.
When Eban shook his head again, the peddler wrote "EAT?" as if he
thought Eban had only failed to understand him.

Judy thought it was nice he came around to check on the dog, but Eban said it was only that he'd found an easy mark in them, a buyer for the least of his wares. She gave him an unhappy look, and Eban wondered why he'd spoken.

It was around that time that the arguments began. At first Eban thought she was only being impulsive, as she always was. She wasn't serious, he thought. She wanted a reaction from him, or maybe just to have spoken brave words.

But the impulse, if that was what it was, took hold. For a long time it was all they could talk about, and if they weren't talking about it, they were silent. He came to welcome the silence, for the peace it brought.

"We can't stay here," she'd say. It was the staying that she got stuck on. That was the bit that seemed to catch her mind like a hook. She'd say, "Forever? Stay here forever? Live like this?"

It seemed cowardly at first, and there were moments when the woman he loved—who was flinty and stout-hearted, and could endure anything she had to, on the strength of her obstinacy—seemed to dissolve before his eyes. When he was left to wonder if she had ever been there at all.

He thought maybe it was the wilderness. The mud floor after her glass windows, the cold nights after her house's hearth. He had to put his mother from his mind, because he thought maybe this was what his mother had seen in her. A weakness.

But it was something else. She was as frightened of staying as he was of leaving. Something about their lives here appalled her. He saw it, as the months and arguments went on: the look of repulsion on her face. "We are living like rats in a HOLE," she once yelled, knocking a pot on the fire to the ground with her hand, and burning herself. "I can't live in fear, in hiding," she'd plead. "I can't spend the rest of my life wondering what will catch us here."

And even that wasn't it. It came out in pieces. "Something terrible has happened. It's happening now, right now. And we're just useless, just waiting till some bad meat kills us off, instead of trying to help, trying to fix . . ." She'd get hung up there, because nothing else she could say had any meaning at all; she knew nothing of the world or its fights.

At first he could stop her with the dog. Even if they waited till the melt, how many weeks or months would it take to reach the cities? Not even she knew. The dog took a dozen steps for every one of theirs. How could they drag him there with them, all that way, amidst hardship they couldn't even guess at?

With those questions, he would see surrender in her face. They might argue for hours more, but he'd have won. And then, after a while, she hardened her resolve against him. "If I have to, I'll carry him," she'd say. "I'll take him with me and do whatever he needs me to do."

He thought he'd lost her then. But one night, as she spoke of when they'd leave and what they'd bring, he said, "It would be wiser to visit the colony first. They could tell us."

He didn't know where the idea had come from, but he knew immediately it was the right one. He saw her listening, so he told her more. He told her every rumour he had ever heard of Heaven, and when she asked questions, he made up answers. He said when they found the colony, they would be among friends, who could tell them the truth about the cities. And then if they still wanted to travel on, they'd go prepared. And not in ignorance. He said this because he knew Judy despised her ignorance, and it might have been that single word that convinced her.

After it had been decided, he wondered what it was he'd meant to do by convincing her to seek the colony instead. To delay her? Distract her? Now they are headed deeper, higher into the hills, chasing no more than a whisper in the wood, a vapour.

He feels his whole life has been this, the evasion or pursuit of ghosts. If the colony is real, the truth can only be far darker and more troubling than Judy has considered. He knows what happens to people in the hills.

Is that what he hoped? That whatever they find will teach her fear at last? That it will end all talk of leaving?

And if the colony isn't real, what will he have gained? Will she, in exhaustion, at last consent to stay? Or will she only leave him then, there, a little later and a little farther from where she would have if he hadn't kept her close with a lie . . .

"Well," he says now. "Well, here we are. More than a hundred miles from home. Whatever you wanted, this is it. But we shouldn't have brought Beau along. It wasn't the right thing to do."

"Eban, I don't know if we were safe in our hide or not. I don't know how many months or years we could have scratched out enough dead squirrels and dirty water to keep blood moving in our veins. But I know staying there, whatever it was, wasn't 'the right thing to do.'"

She closes her coat back up and turns away, stepping off the bridge into the last mile of wood they've walked before.

Though he trudges behind Judy, he can hear the whine of the dog in her arms. From behind, he can see the stiff way she holds him. He sees every sound the dog makes in the clutch of her shoulders.

Late in the afternoon, they stop for the first meal they've had since dawn. They sit on their packs and eat cold eel. He remembers how they feasted on it, days ago. Now he has to chew slowly and swallow carefully, or his stomach will refuse the greasy, foul-smelling meat and the food will be wasted.

Judy keeps the dog inside her coat and coaxes him to eat from her hand, but he lies limp in her arms with his eyes closed.

"Here," she says. "Here."

Eban feels ill as he watches Judy slip the meat into the dog's mouth. The oils run over her fingers and the fur around the dog's black lips. "Judy."

He thinks the dog is dead, but after a few minutes, its wet eyes open.

He had known it was wrong to bring Beau with them. He knew the cold, long days would be hard on him. But he never guessed they would affect him so suddenly or severely. The dog is more than tired. Sick, and maybe dying. Maybe it was frostbite in his paws after all, maybe some infection. There's no way to know for certain.

"Judy," he says again. All he ever does is try to make her answer him. "He's suffering."

She looks at him, her face lowered so a shadow falls over her eyes. "What do you want from me." He hardly recognizes her voice.

"It's too far, Judy. It's too far to take him."

She buries her face in the dog and is silent.

"You know it."

When she speaks again, he has to lean close to hear the words. "Remember when we got him? Do you remember that, Eban? Remember how the peddler wrote on his slate that he was the strongest one in the litter?"

He offers her his canteen, and she pours water onto a plate and brings it to the dog's mouth, but he refuses that too. Then they lift their packs and continue on.

It's near dark when Eban catches sight of Judy again. She has hurried on ahead of him these last miles and he has let her. But now he sees her on her knees in the snow, and in a second he understands.

He drops to the ground beside her. It is always like this. Everything fine and then suddenly the pregnancy is over, a beginning and an ending with nothing in between.

"I'm here," he says. He puts his hands to her face, holds her face, as she stares at him.

"It's okay," he says. "It will be okay. I swear it." He looks around him, thinking about how he will make her warm, what he can build to keep her safe and dry. She'll pass the fetus sometime this day or the next, and then bleed for days after. If it goes longer than a week, they'll have to worry about infection. It might be some time till she has the strength to travel again, or to fight him as he tries to keep her resting.

She stares at him, confused, and then her face alters with understanding. She shoves Eban away and pulls the dog from her coat, setting him on the ground.

"Sit," she tells the dog, who slumps in the snow. "*Stay.*" Then she gets to her feet and continues forward, her face set and determined.

"I thought you—"

"I know what you thought."

He looks back at the dog, whose face is lowered, shaking. He's not so well trained that he'd let Judy disappear from sight. At least, he never would have before. Now he hardly seems to notice her departure. "Beau," he says softly. "Come here, boy."

"*No!*" Judy swings around, her face unreadable. "Don't call him. I want him to stay until we're out of sight."

"Until we're . . . ?"

"You were right. You were right, he can't travel with us. It's too far for him."

"But . . ."

"He won't stay in my arms. He fights me. You were right, okay? I know it. He'll do better on his own. It's wrong to drag him along with us. Here, he can rest as he needs to, and find shelter and—"

"Judy! This is . . ." She can't be in her right mind. Even her stubbornness can't be so great that she would harm this animal she loves. "He will die here."

"No." Judy turns her back and goes on walking away from them both.

"Judy, he will die on the spot you left him." As he speaks, the dog rises to his feet. As if to vindicate the owner he loves best, he takes a few leaps forward, and then pauses to sniff at something in the snow.

Eban shakes his head. Judy is nearly out of sight.

The dog is still on his feet, face buried in the snow, when Eban sees him last. Like Judy, the dog doesn't look back.

When Eban first knew Judy, she was weakened. It wasn't her nature to retreat, and they had left their home by the allotment and she worried they were wrong to leave it. At night, after his mother and her father had gone to bed, they would sit in the last light of evening, talking about her fears. She thought their departure was both rash and cowardly. She wanted to be a survivor, someone who could make it in these hills, but they'd come into them to hide, and in this world, Eban's world, she was helpless.

"I used to think I was practical. Level-headed. Brave." She looked at her hands. "Daniel told me I was. He asked me once if he should stop the work he did, because it might be dangerous for him, for us. I told him not to. I told him his work was too important."

She told Eban of the evening, only nine days before he met her, when she and Alphonse had left home for a walk after dinner. Daniel had stayed behind. She said they weren't gone long, maybe an hour. When they returned, they found Daniel sprawled over the steps of their house.

"I couldn't understand what I was looking at. I thought at first he was sleeping. But his eyes were open. I thought *drunk* before I thought *dead*. One of his arms, I remember, was stretched out behind him over the top stair, his thumb and finger pinched together like this." She showed him. "He kept a bowl of salt at the table and used to pinch salt into his meals like that. His hair was soaked in blood and his pistol was on the ground beside him.

"He wrote what he wanted to," she said, "and we let him. And they shot him. With his own pistol, they shot him."

"Who did?" Eban wondered, but she shook her head and didn't want to talk anymore.

Unlike Judy, Alphonse took to life in the hills with Eban and his mother, in his own awkward way, as if hardship and hunger were well

fitted to his grief. He was a romantic. He said he came from a country
where the wilderness was something you tempered yourself against.
Something that changed and improved you.

Alphonse made occasional efforts to help around the camp, but
soon accepted that he helped best by keeping out of the way of Eban
and his mother. He would sit in his tent and copy out books from the
tiny library he had carried in two leather suitcases from the allotment.
Judy said the eight-day walk might have taken only four if he hadn't
needed to stop so often to set down his suitcases, and Eban noticed
Alphonse had few other supplies of any kind, only the binding tools
and single change of clothes he had borne on his back. Everything else,
Judy had carried, and neither of them had enough to last a season in the
hills on their own. Still, Alphonse complained only of the shelves of
books, acquired over a lifetime from peddlers who knew his tastes, left
to stand unread in their deserted house.

Alphonse spent most of that first summer making a single book,
thinking to sell it to a peddler in the fall. He worked a pelt into leather
and then stitched it together. He had a sheaf of pages that he filled with
his tiny, beautiful writing. Judy explained to Eban that this skill had
bought Alphonse books and fine, strange things in the allotment. A particular peddler had acquired whatever he made every fall, and knew
the sorts of things he'd want in return—sometimes only the trade of
one book for another.

But the peddlers who came up to the hills didn't want or carry
such fanciful things. A month after Alphonse finished the book, a peddler passed through, and Alphonse brought the book to him, almost
shyly. As if prepared for admiration, Eban thought later. As if he didn't
know how dangerous he must have seemed to the man, then, or how
contemptuous. Eban couldn't tell from the way the peddler pushed the
book back into Alphonse's hands whether he'd taken it as a test or an
insult. But he seemed in a particular hurry to finish his business with

Eban, who traded cured meat and a clutch of pelts for a warm red coat for Judy, a box of birdshot and a spool of cotton wick. Nodding his goodbye, the peddler didn't look at Alphonse once, and they never saw the man again.

Alphonse didn't make any more books after that, but Judy did, and he helped her. In the last hours of autumn daylight, they would sit inside their tent. Alphonse would read, a few words at a time, as Judy filled a stack of pages, line by line. Sometimes Eban sat outside their tent door to listen to stories he'd never heard before unfolding, metered out in half-sentences as Alphonse waited for Judy to catch up, her pen scratching against the paper and sometimes tearing it in her hurry. In Eban's house there had been only his mother's medical texts and a single book of stories from her own childhood, where the children pictured on the pages mostly met bad ends.

Once, Alphonse offered to show Eban how to write, and then watched admiringly as Eban produced four pages of clear, precise print. "Did you like the story?" Alphonse asked, and Eban didn't know how to answer—he had copied the words one letter at a time and never thought to assemble in his head what sentences they made. After that, he paid closer attention when Alphonse read, trying to make sense even of the French, and studied the books in secrecy whenever he could. Alphonse loved poetry and stories where few of the characters survived, with great sad speeches, things written in the distant past. A play about a mad king and another called *Cyrano de Bergerac*. *The Tale of Genji*. A poem called "Le Dormeur du Val." Judy loved books of far-off battles and revolutions, stories with heroes and sacrifice. *Field of Honour*. *Quatrevingt-treize*. *Les Trois Mousquetaires*. The *Iliad*.

Impressed by Eban's steady, tidy handwriting, Alphonse asked him to copy a book of his own one day, but Eban declined, because he'd seen the hard look Judy gave his pages, and knew she was embarrassed by hers. Her nervy, clumsy handwriting swelled and shrank in size, slid down the page, turned to the left and then to the right, or became outright illegible as she grew tired. Alphonse would look on it without a word, and Judy and Eban both understood it was the outer limit of his patience to say nothing.

Eban was surprised by the way he took to book-making—he enjoyed the slow, exact labour of it. It gave him something to do in the evenings, when he used to study his mother's medical texts until he knew them almost by heart. When he was bone-tired from the day, there was satisfaction in sitting with Alphonse in silence and stitching pages to leather, while Judy wrote and his mother slept.

He spent weeks on a small book of unmarked paper, etching a design of leaves across the leather cover with a nail heated over a flame. Once his mother found him working on it and stood over him for several minutes, until he laid the nail by his side and waited for her to speak.

"For her," his mother said. "You're making that for her."

He nodded and raised his eyes to see her, thinking she might look pleased in her own way.

"I'd have hoped—" she began and then fell silent. At last, she returned to her tent, leaving him there.

When he finished the book, he left it where he knew Judy would find it. She came to him the next day with it in her hands, but didn't thank him. He was prepared to tell her it was nothing, but didn't know what to say when she only stood there, looking at him and running her thumb over the cover he had made so carefully for her.

"I thought you might like to write in it," he said at last. "Things of your own, I mean. Stories, or what you want."

Then she smiled and stuck the book in a pocket of the green sweater with too-long sleeves she always wore then, which he guessed she'd made herself. "Okay," she said. "I will."

They make camp in silence, when the sky is dark already. They fumble, dropping things in the snow.

They build a fire and warm what remains of the eel. He watches her face in shifting gold light and shadow. At first, she eats hurriedly, as always, and then suddenly her expression changes. She freezes, and drops the hand that holds her fork to her lap.

"We can go back," he says.

She doesn't answer or even move.

"Judy? We can go back. Tonight. Or first thing in the morning. He won't have gone far. We can find him."

She flings her fork to the ground as she stands. Watching her stumble to the tent, he calls after her, and she says over her shoulder, "Don't. Don't you follow me."

He lets her go, and then after he has cleared up the food and stamped out the fire, he pulls a tarp from his pack, spreads it over the snow and lies down. The night is clear, and for a moment, looking up, he could imagine the sky is a huge, dark blanket full of holes, thrown over something blindingly bright.

He loves the night sky in winter, turned away from the Milky Way's dust and clutter of light. In winter, staring into deeper space, where the stars are bright and clear, he can pick out the constellations he likes best, one by one.

When they were very young, one night he carried his brother outside to see the winter sky. His brother had been slow to learn to walk, and still stumbled when Eban set him on the ground. Had his mother known he'd woken his brother and brought him out of the crib he still slept in, she would have been furious. But he wanted to show his brother the stars so badly that he took the risk. It was Eban's mother who had taught him to map the stars, but somehow even then he suspected his brother would not receive the same lessons.

"Look," he said, pointing up, but his brother only stared back at him. "Look," he said again. "It's a surprise for you," he whispered helplessly as his brother began to cry and wouldn't stop. At last, Eban lugged him back to bed, and listened as his mother stirred at the sound of her baby's sobbing. As she rocked the baby into the early hours of daylight, he lay awake, shaking with anger at the brother who had refused the gift he'd offered him.

Now, reaching one hand up over his head, he traces with his finger the lines of Taurus, the bull protecting the red star Aldebaran, one of the stars his mother taught him to navigate by when they first travelled into the foothills. Among Judy's things is a tiny round instrument made of yellow metal. A compass. She insists on consulting it, but he's tried to make sense of it before, of the silver arrow that's meant to point north but is now rusted into place. She can't possibly believe it's of use, but once or twice every day she pulls it from the yellow box in her pack and studies it.

He would like to lie like this again with Judy, to touch her under the lit-up sky. She might ask him to name the stars for her, the way she used to when she was new to the hills. He would tell her every star he knows and even remember some of their stories, always her favourite part. He thinks to himself that he should remember to do this, the next bright winter evening that she isn't angry with him. Of course, she prefers the summer night sky; once she said it was like an ocean made of light, and he asked her how she knew what the ocean looked like, and she said, "Everyone knows what the ocean looks like. Like you know what a giraffe is." And he lowered his face, and after a moment, she said, "Let me get my paper and pencil, and I'll draw one for you."

He waits out there a long time before he goes to the tent. Inside, she is sitting, cross-legged, with a candle in her hands, burned down almost to her fingertips. With a start, as he makes out her face, he realizes she's staring at him.

"I don't know why," she says, her eyes reddened but dry. "I don't know why I did it. Every time I looked at him, I felt the cold the way he must feel it. I couldn't stand it. But I swear I thought I was doing something strong. I don't know how to make you believe me, but I didn't see it was cruel. I just wanted to know the right thing to do, the hard, right thing. But now he's out there, Eban, in the cold, because I am so wrong. Because I'm always wrong here."

"It's not so cold," he says.

"Why didn't you stop me?" she asks, almost as if she's testing whether it's a joke.

He answers seriously. "I tried."

"I know you did." She rubs her hands back and forth over her face. "I have this feeling, sometimes. I just want to scratch every thought out of my head and run down the hills like an animal chasing a smell. This life we have is so small. I don't know how to fit in it. But is that brave, to try to fit? Or to run away like an animal? I thought maybe it was brave to leave Beau, and now I think what if the only thing in the world that I had the chance to do was keep that dog safe."

He waits, unsure how to answer, and she looks at him as if she wants him to say something so particular that he feels there's no hope he could come up with it. Then she gasps as the flame at last burns her hands and she drops the candle to the ground. He dives for it, but it has already gone out.

The darkness now is total, and he hears her breathing and can almost hear the noise of her thoughts but can't possibly guess what they mean.

"Sometimes," she says, so softly he almost isn't sure she's said it, "I can't stand to look at you. When I do, all I see is what's wrong with me. How unhappy I am with this tiny life that somehow is enough for you. How patient you are with me. Sometimes it makes me want to do things I know are wrong. Just to have a choice."

"Judy," he says, lying down by her side, "we'll look for him in the morning." And this time she listens, or at least she says nothing, and puts herself into his arms.

"It's warm," Eban whispers, his face so close to hers that if their eyes were open they would only see each other.

Those are the last words he speaks before they both fall asleep, and so they still echo in his ears when, a few hours later, they wake to find the tent doubled up around them in a howling wind, as the trees outside bend and shriek.

How could he have been so stupid? It's been months since the foehn winds blew, but they always come in the last weeks of winter or summer, in the earliest days of season change. The eerie warm air that settles before the winds blow provides their only warning.

He hardly hears Judy, as the tent flaps around them. He grabs at the tent pole and pulls open the zipper. "Get out," he cries. "We've got to find shelter. Get out, get out!"

Outside, Eban throws himself onto the tent to keep from losing it. Already one of the tent poles has torn lose, shredding the fabric that contained it. The gusts of wind come sudden and fierce. For a moment, the air will seem to calm, and then a roar of wind will throw down everything before it, trees buckling as if shoved to the ground by an unseen hand.

Judy scrambles down the hill, bent almost to her hands and knees. Eban tries to follow with the tent clutched in his arms, but it's torn out of his grasp. He watches as it disappears into the black sky. He has no time to think about what it means to lose it. Instead he stumbles after Judy, and finds her huddled down the hill in a recess in the ridge wall. He squeezes in beside her. The winds still pull at them, but at least they are out of the way of the blowing snow and the debris being volleyed through the air.

"It's okay," Judy whispers. "It's okay. It's okay."

And then, for just a moment, he thinks he hears something. A thin voice in the distance, calling out, that could be the wind itself.

IV

"NO," EBAN SAYS, "no, no, no," the words dismantled by the wind, as Judy leans away from the ledge, staring into the wild darkness, searching for the source of the call.

The voice, if it is a voice, is the first they've heard since a crowd of travellers passed dangerously close to their hide the previous summer but continued on without spotting them.

Judy ignores Eban and pulls herself above the ledge, emerging from its shelter. For a moment the wind draws back, as if inhaling, gathering lung power, and then it surges again. Something caught up in the gust strikes Judy's shoulder and she falls back. Eban seizes her by the hips and pulls her to him.

"I think they're close by," Judy shouts. "The wind makes them seem farther. But I think we can get to them . . ."

Eban sees that whatever hit her shoulder caught the side of her face too. Bright blood runs along her jaw, a scarlet flag unravelling down her throat. "We can't help them now. We have to wait. Until it stops."

Judy lowers her head, and he knows if he weren't here she would heave herself, her life, into the wind for the sake of a stranger. But he knows he is right. And she must know it too, because she remains in his arms and doesn't resist his hold on her.

They wait.

Impossibly, Eban sleeps. Or must have. Because when he opens his eyes, he finds the winds have stilled. And Judy is gone.

He climbs out of the shelter, and hauls himself up onto the ledge. "Judy?" he calls.

He finds her crouched on her knees in the woods, not far from the remains of their fire the night before. Everything—circle of stones, charred logs, wire cook rack—all of it is gone and all that's left is a black smudge in the snow.

Judy is bent over, studying the ground.

"What is it?"

"I just can't tell. Is that a footprint?"

He looks at the mark in the snow and the way the edge of it has crushed the snow down to the softening mud below. "No," he says, almost sure.

"If it is, it's too large to be yours or mine."

"It isn't. Probably in the wind a branch or something fell and left that mark."

She looks around, shaking her head slowly. "I've walked all over. I can't find any sign. No footprints but ours. No sign of a camp or a fire. I did see what looked like some broken brush . . . and places where the snow looked swept, like maybe someone tried to clear away their footprints? But why would they do that?"

"It's just the wake of the wind. It always leaves its mark on the wood."

"I was sure, Eban. I was sure I heard someone. And you were too."

"It was just the wind," he says.

———

An hour later, Eban leaves Judy alone to hunt for the tent the wind tore away, knowing she will also continue searching for someone who doesn't exist, while he hikes into the wood to find a meal. The day is clear. A pale winter sun is melting the ice from the banks of a narrow river. Everywhere, he can hear water trickle and stream.

The day is warm. He ties his scarf to a tree to mark it and leaves his hat and gloves at the base, opening his coat.

He follows the river up the hill, where it meets with other feeder streams, leading him farther and farther, and higher and higher into the hills. At last he finds the springhead. There, he crouches down and fills his canteen with clean, cold water.

He drinks his canteen to the bottom. It's the first time in days that he has drunk his fill. The water tastes of the minerals and earth it sprang from. The hide he lived in with his mother was built around a seep spring, and he remembers still the taste of that water. Since those days, he and Judy have always had to boil whatever they drink or use the purification tablets the peddlers sell.

The summer his mother died, the spring ran dry. It had never happened before, but that summer, a blazing sun rose each day, scorching every cloud in the sky and every drop of water in the soil. He found fish dead and wilted over the parched bottom of what had once been a brook. He travelled farther and farther in search of water and found only enough to sustain them from one day to the next as they grew weak and dry-lipped, hollow-eyed.

They opened up the emergency barrels and drank the sick-smelling water there. They left out sheets of plastic to catch dew, and sealed plant leaves in airtight bags to release their moisture. They hardly spoke to one another. Alphonse, who'd once kept goats in the outland, kept saying that if he had brought just one with him they could have drunk its milk, till Judy silenced him. "I suppose," he remarked softly, "it would have wanted water too."

They grew foul-tempered. They spent their days in the shade, moving as little as possible for fear of shedding sweat. And that was how the girl found them, stretched out beneath the trees, under a network of tarps, complaining to one another.

The girl, whose name he can no longer recall, was maybe eleven years old. Though her thinness might have made her appear younger than she was. Eban had never seen anyone carry much weight on their body—sparse food and hard work made the people of the hills all lean—but the girl was different. Her wrists seemed to reach to her armpits, with nothing beneath her pale flesh but bone. He wondered how she had been able to carry the heavy pack on her back as far as she must have. But then, she never told them where she had come from.

It was for that reason that his mother wanted to send her on, away from their camp. No one was allowed near their site without a convincing account of themselves. She met new peddlers from the heel end of a rifle.

But the girl was sick, her skin damp and flushed with the fever she carried, and she shook her head violently when Judy offered the little food and water that was her portion. Eban and his mother discussed what to do. Neither felt comfortable allowing the girl to stay, but they also couldn't stomach leaving a sick child in the wilderness alone. And as the discussions continued, unresolved, Eban watched Judy and the girl. He saw the set of her mouth when she offered the girl what would not have been enough even for herself. He saw her anguish, and wanted to be the one who could help.

And so, in the days that followed, Eban told his mother of the girl and of her goodness. Though he had spoken scarcely a few words to the girl, he told his mother they had talked at length, and that she showed him kindness and strength, despite her illness. He said it was evident she was like them, not like the other ones, and not from the cities. He said he thought she was getting better, keeping down the food Judy gave her, and that she was quick with a bow and might well be a benefit to their camp. "She has a child's resilience," he told her. "Maybe she's stronger than us. Maybe she can walk to water when we can't."

He went on saying things like this to his mother for a week, while the girl stayed on, supine in a tent at the edge of the camp, rocking with chills despite the heat and wrapping herself in the blankets that Judy brought her, unable to keep down food or water.

And at last his mother agreed that the girl would stay, and Eban went to Judy with the news. He doesn't remember now what he hoped for. She rushed past him to the girl, to tell her. And they spent the night carrying the girl's things to the house he had built for Judy.

He is startled by the sudden sound of feet hammering against the ground, as if something is charging toward him, something heavy and closer with each step. He half leaps to his feet, drawing his rifle from his pack, when he spies the bird, perched on a stump in a nearby stand of apple trees. Grouse fool him every time with the accelerating drum roll of their beating wings, summoning a mate.

The apple trees reach out of the ground like gnarled hands. As he takes aim, he wonders briefly who tended them, who lived here and when, leaving no trace but these ancient-looking trees.

With just one shot he takes the grouse down. It flutters and is still and he wrings its neck for good measure. Several of the surrounding trees still cling to the last of their harvest of fruit. The hard-looking golden-brown apples are shaded by taller trees, and he thinks that if they froze before they rotted and have not yet thawed, there might be food here for them. He plucks one and opens it with his knife. The flesh inside is threaded with golden veins, but he sees no sign of infection or rot. He takes a bite. The cold has robbed the tart sweet flavour from the apple, but he knows one squeeze will release its honey. He plucks a half-dozen of the best-looking apples, wraps them in a handkerchief and slips them into his pockets. He will cook them with the grouse. What a meal they will have. And he thinks of Judy smiling, taking bird and apples from his hands.

As he stumbles down the hill, he tells himself he hurries because the warm sun is on the grouse he carries, and not because of what Judy's face might look like when she sees what he has brought her.

He is descending the hill so quickly that he almost misses it. His gaze slides over the dark shape at the river edge but then is caught by the trail of prints. Maybe only because he thought for a moment it might be an easy catch, he looks again at the wounded animal crouched to drink at the edge of the river.

He whispers the dog's name as he drops to his knees. "You found us," he says in wonder.

But Beau barely stirs at the sound of his name. Eban reaches for him. Can he be dreaming? Or could some other dog, a stranger's dog, have wandered into the wood and only happened to cross his path?

But as he lifts the dog's trembling body into his hands, he realizes Beau didn't respond because he couldn't. Black blood soaks the fur across the dog's hindquarters, and his belly is soft and distended. He is bleeding internally. Eban is sure of it. "Poor little creature," he murmurs. "I'm sorry. I'm sorry. I will let you be."

He lays the dog back into the dirty snow at the river edge. He must have come for one last drink, Eban thinks. "I'll let you be," he says again.

He tells himself that there is no way to bring Judy here in time. The dog may have only a few breaths yet to spend. Eban wonders if he was injured in the storm. He imagines the dog searching for them as the winds gathered, stumbling on as the sky heaved and flung out refuse from the wood, and knows he can never tell Judy what he saw here.

"I'll wait with you," he tells the dog, letting his fingertips travel gently over the depression between his eyes where he liked to be tickled. He worries his touch hurts the dog and yet it seems wrong to watch him die without extending even that kindness.

The dog lies for some time with his eyes closed, head nodding slightly, showing no sign of recognizing Eban's nearness. Long enough that Eban begins to wonder if he should have gone for Judy.

He turns his back, unable to watch. The dog's shallow, shuddering breaths slow, but do not end. He doesn't know what pain a dog feels, but he feels sure it is wrong for this to continue.

He fires a single shot into the dog. His nodding skull shatters and all is still.

Eban digs a hole with his hands in the snow and then in the thawing ground beneath. He cannot dig deep enough and it may be that the dog will be found by some larger animal when the spring comes, but there is nothing he can do about that.

He lays the dog's body in the hole, covers it over, and stands for a moment, looking down and thinking he should say something. Then he heads back the way he came.

After resting the grouse and apples in the snow where they made camp, he glimpses a trail of footprints ascending the steep ridge above. Judy. His feet sometimes losing purchase in the snow and mud, Eban clings to fir branches as he follows the prints.

After some time, he notices that it has become easier to fit himself between the trees, and without intending it, he has begun to follow a weaving route that levels the ascent. Pausing to study the brush around him, he realizes he is walking what must once have been a path. Here, the brush grows thick and low, with paper birch and eastern juniper springing up between the towering black spruce and balsam. As he travels, the sun slips in the sky, the temperature falls, and the bank of snow begins to rise.

Cresting the hilltop, he finds an alpine clearing—the lowest entrance to the barrens his mother told him never to travel into, where the tree line dwindles and snow lies like a sheet of paper over the hills and everything can be seen.

He sees Judy in the clearing and calls her name. Coming closer, he finds she has dug out a trough in the snow, and sits inside it, looking at her hand against the ground.

"It's a boat," she says.

Not understanding at first, he looks down and sees she has unburied the keel of a corroded vessel—he runs his hand along its curved edge, struck silent.

"They made it out of aluminum. I'd have thought they'd make a boat of wood. How long do you think that would last up here? Where would they get it from?"

He shakes his head, absently combing snow away from it with his hand. He finds beneath it the buried branches of the low-growing scrub that rings the barrens—the thing was hiked into the air by the growing forest, or by the winds, which might be wild enough at these heights to fling something so heavy so far.

"I guess you didn't find the tent," he says.

She doesn't answer.

"Please don't worry, Judy. We'll figure something out." Though he can't think what. "Judy?"

And then he guesses where she has been and what she has looked for. Her ungloved hands are reddened from the cold and they both look at them. She has short fingers for her height, the hands of a child almost. A child used to work. Right then, for all the strength he knows is in them, they seem fragile and he wishes he could take them in his own.

"Did you . . . did you find any sign of Beau out there?" he asks.

Her mouth is drawn as tight as a stitch. "Nothing."

He knows it is in this moment that he must say something if he is ever to.

There is a streak of blood, bright as a coin, on Judy's left hand. Judy never complains about pain. He has only seen hurt register on her face when others suffer. Her father. The sick girl. The animal kills that feed them.

He thinks maybe that is what his mother saw in Judy. That there was no wisdom or strength in her goodness. How little it means to feel things, if you don't do the right things.

"I should get back," he says at last.

"That voice we heard today, Eban . . ."

"It wasn't a voice. I know you looked. We saw no sign of anyone."

"But if there was someone."

"Even if there was—it could be just another traveller. Maybe a peddler keeping low."

"It's just a thought I keep having. I can't shake it. I had a dream last night that we found the person we heard. It was a man, and he was so surprised to see us. He kept asking what we were doing up here. He kept asking me to go down into the valley and didn't understand why I wouldn't. He kept saying, 'Why would you want to raise a baby here?'"

"Judy . . . it's just a dream."

"All my life I've been told to hide, but no one has ever really told me why. You worry every time we light a stick of wood, because you were taught to. But he didn't know what I was talking about. He didn't know about any sickness or the other ones or whatever it is that's wrong down there. He said everything was ready. He said everyone was waiting."

"What are you . . . What do you think—"

She looks at him for a moment longer, and then down into the trees. "What if it isn't true? What if none of it is true?"

Eban once asked Alphonse what it had been like. They were washing dishes together in the river; it was a sunny, perfect day, and the two had talked more easily than usual, though occasionally they could hear the moaning of the girl from her house and Judy's efforts to shush her. Maybe they spoke only to stop hearing it.

Eban told Alphonse his mother didn't like to talk about what had happened. He said although she spent three years in the cities, he wasn't sure how much she even knew.

Alphonse was quiet for a few minutes and then said it was Dan who had known the cities.

He looked afraid of something. He said again that he didn't know, that he had been scarcely six years old when he came into the outland, at the allotment border. "But," he said, "when we found Judy, we knew how bad things were."

Eban asked him what he meant.

"Judy thinks we went looking for her. Or for a child to adopt. That we sought her out."

"Didn't you?"

"Eban, Judy's mother was from there. From the cities."

"Do you mean—"

"Yes. But Judy isn't. Judy is like us."

"I know," Eban said. Because of the fierceness in the other man's expression, but he wasn't sure he understood.

"There are," Alphonse said slowly, "restrictions. Limits on women having children. And penalties. This is what we heard. I don't know if this mother had too many or wasn't permitted any at all. But she brought her baby to the outland to die."

He said it was Daniel who'd seen her lay the infant in the grass and cover its tiny mouth and nose with her hand. He'd been out hunting and, without thinking, had fired a shot near her. The mother ran away, and then stood in the distance, watching him from the road. She didn't protest as he lifted the baby into his arms, slipping the rifle under his shoulder. They looked at each other for some time before she turned away, walking back down the road, back to whatever place she'd come from.

Alphonse gathered up the clean dishes on the bank and stood. "Judy doesn't know," he said.

"But . . ." Eban searched for the right question.

"And you can't tell her."

"I won't. Of course I won't. But she . . . she showed me an earring that belonged to her mother. She said her mother died when she was only a few minutes old. She said that with her last words she asked if the baby was a girl, and when Daniel told her it was, she asked him to take the earring from her ear and to tell the girl it had belonged to the mother who loved her."

Alphonse smiled faintly. "Daniel told me not to, but she wanted the story of how she was born. Maybe I shouldn't have done it. But I had an earring left me by a great-aunt, something she'd thought would still have worth. So I told Judy a story, and it made her happy. And I gave her something that had no value to me."

"She loves it," whispered Eban. "I've seen her hold it to the light, close it in her fist. She puts it in that yellow box and takes it out again a dozen times a day."

"I know she does."

"Does it matter that it isn't true?"

Alphonse looked at the plates in his hand. "I don't know," he said.

And then he returned to the one-room house where his adopted daughter kept watch over a dying girl, which they all now knew her to be, though none of them would ever say the words aloud.

"Are you ready to go back to camp?" Eban asks Judy now gently. "I found us a grouse. And some apples..."

She stares out at the barrens. "There might be a lake down there."

"Or there was."

"Or there was." He realizes she is sitting on the hull of the over-turned craft. "You saw the path?"

He nods.

"You aren't thinking—what are you thinking?" she asks.

"Nothing. Nothing."

"But are you thinking about them?"

"*Them?*"

"The colony? Are you thinking this might have been it? And nothing is left?"

He draws a breath and looks more closely at her, and then turns his gaze back to the snowscape around them. "No."

"No?"

"This could be anyone's old camp or settlement. And aluminum corrodes but takes a long time to give out. This boat could be from a hundred years ago."

"Okay," she says after a while. He reaches out his hand to help her from the boat, but she just pushes herself to her feet, and they follow their own footprints down.

He thinks he understands why she hesitated there. He felt what she did, the wrong-footedness of it, the boat in the trees, the lake beneath the snow or whatever might remain of it after the drought years. It should have felt like they were among ghosts, whoever made or travelled in that boat, and knew what it was to see water spread out farther than you could cross, and to sail over its surface, like you owned the wind and water. But under the measureless grey sky and falling snow, they were the ghosts.

One night, in the last week before his mother died, Eban sat up with her till dawn.

It had been almost a month since first Alphonse and then Eban's mother had caught the girl's fever. She lay in blankets that had been changed daily until then, stained with sweat and bodily waste. She hadn't excreted anything since the day before, and it was no longer worth the suffering of moving her. Her skin was yellowed as blood left her face and extremities to serve her failing organs. On her arms and hands were spots like bruises, where blood pooled. He could scarcely look at her, at the caves around her still-open eyes as they withdrew into her skull, everything retreating inward, as if death were an exit not out of the body but deep into its interior.

He heard then what he was saying to her. "I'm sorry. I'm sorry. I'm so sorry."

He tried to explain. "She died four days ago. I didn't tell you. She died here, at our camp, and she wasn't any of the things I told you. She wasn't good, or if she was, I never saw it. She wasn't anything, only dying. She could have been one of the other ones. She could have meant us harm. And you were right to fear her, to guess what she was, might be. But you let her stay for me, and . . ." He took her hand in his, struggling, the words stuck on his dry tongue. "Because of your love for me, you did this, and now you are—"

Whatever else he'd intended to say fell from his mouth as she narrowed her eyes and snatched her hand from his. From her face, he saw he had got it wrong. And then he guessed. It wasn't for him she did it. Nothing he'd said to her had mattered. She'd never bent her will to anything but her own resolve.

It was for his brother.

As they descend the path, Judy surprises him, stopping so suddenly he stumbles to avoid colliding with her. "I wish it was like that," she says.

He understands she is talking about the boat, the lake.

"They had everything. They had the whole goddamn world. And all we do is pick their bones."

"Judy, we have—we have each other. We have enough."

"It *isn't* enough. Are you listening to me? That is exactly the thing I'm saying to you. I am saying it *isn't* enough. Not even close."

"We're the lucky ones," he says, stubbornly. "We have enough to eat. We can find food and water. We keep warm. We've always been sheltered."

"I might have been good at something." Her face and voice harden. "And you. Someone might have loved you."

He stares at her until she looks away. He drinks in her shame, her anger dropping from her like a shrug. He fills himself with it like he's starved. Like it will fill the hole she made in the middle of the squandered world.

"My father used to say we didn't earn a perfect world," she says softly. "I don't have a clue what that means."

He thinks she is impressed by her own outburst, the intensity of her feelings. For a moment, he despises her.

"Shouldn't we get to know what it is we don't have? Shouldn't it be easier or harder to imagine? What would it mean? No one would die? Cherry trees?"

This answer he knows. "We would be good. It would be a good world." He thinks of his mother. "It was."

V

THAT NIGHT, AS THEY SLEEP, the temperature plummets. The first time he wakes, he's shaking with cold. His eyes open for a moment. The sky is black, moonless, pricked with stars.

They lie in the fold of a crude tarp-tent, on a bed of fir branches. He buries his head under the sleeping bag and pushes himself against Judy. She makes a sound but doesn't move away. He sleeps again, in her warmth.

The second time he wakes, Judy is frowning at him.

"It's soaked," she says. "The sleeping bag is soaked. How could we sleep through that?"

"It's okay," he says instinctively. "It's okay."

She is quiet for a moment. "Eban?"

"What is it?"

"I shouldn't have said it. Up on the path yesterday."

He looks away. "Why did you say it?"

"I don't know. I don't know why I do the things I do anymore. I don't know why I'm angry with you when none of it's your fault."

"No, it isn't." He doesn't want to talk about it anymore. "We can't travel today, not with everything wet, in this kind of cold."

"I fooled myself that we could make it into summer like this, if we had to. Stupid. We're lucky it was snow and not rain or everything in our packs would be soaked too."

Eban hesitates. Then he says, "I could build us something. Here, or near here. Wherever you wanted. Something safe. Something lasting."

"We're not stopping."

"Just till a peddler comes along, until we can get a tent to—"

"No. Eban." She shakes her head, a little sadly. "We can't wait."

He draws a deep breath. "It will be okay," he tells her, not knowing what else to say. "We've got extra blankets in the pack. We'll use those for now. If there's sun tomorrow, we can dry out the sleeping bag."

They should have waited. In a month or three, it might be warm enough that food would be easier found, and the rivers would run, and there would be no risk of death by exposure. He feels a ravaging hunger in his stomach. "We need meat," he tells Judy.

After Judy has gone to check the rabbit traps again, rifle over her shoulder, Eban sets to splitting kindling to rebuild the fire. He has struck just one blow of the axe when something makes him turn. Afterward, he can't recall whether it was a sound that warned him or some precognitive sense of being watched.

He sees them at once. Just ahead, so close he could strike them with a well-aimed stone, they walk in a loose line. They walk slowly, as if in no particular hurry. He thinks at first, for one wild minute, that they will pass on by like that, if he says nothing, does nothing. But it is soon clear what they are up to. Slowly, without urgency, they are forming a circle around him, and with each step tightening it. There are five of them. Six.

Eban grips the axe, his eyes searching the ground for the other rifle, but he must have left it where they slept. He thinks desperately of Judy. Stay away, he thinks. Have the sense to stay away.

One of the figures steps out of the circle then, a false smile drawn across his face. "Now, I know what you're thinking. But don't you worry. We're no marauders." He crouches in the snow beside Eban and his grin widens. "We're a family."

Eban hesitates to speak. All he can think of is Judy. How long has it been? How far might she be? How soon will she be back?

The man is tall and brawny. Even stooped and idle, he intimates wasted strength with every gesture. He studies Eban as if pleasantly surprised by him. "Well then. Let's get the pleasantries out of the way. That one's my brother-in-law." He points to a thin man who has already taken a seat, leaning against a tree with his eyes turned away from the scene unfolding before him. He looks like a sulking adolescent, all lanky limbs and hooded eyes, but he has grey in his hair. "His name is Dean. And I'm Tristan."

Tristan holds out a hand as if to accept something Eban has offered him, but Eban's hands are empty. Gently, Tristan takes Eban's hand by the wrist and holds it in his own. "Like this," he says, wagging it.

When the other man has released his hand, Eban draws it back as if it doesn't belong to him anymore, cradling it in the other hand.

"No one does things like that now," the man says. "But I like to. It's not my habit to get moony about the old ways, but that one makes sense to me. Show a man you mean no harm. Harder to betray someone, like you're itching to do, after you've shaken hands. Yes, I see those eyes darting around. How many more you waiting on? Where are they—up the trees? You got a camp near here?"

Eban shakes his head.

"Sure. Just out for a stroll in the woods, I'm sure. Maybe you got lost on your way back from a picnic. That it? That your picnic basket you got there?"

Eban can only shake his head again.

"Well, anyway. You see my point. You're more likely to hesitate to cut the throat of a man whose hand you've held."

"You might spare him the profundity, Daddy. He thinks you're going to rob him, and I think he's looking forward to it shutting you up for a minute." The four women of the group have removed their packs and settled into seated positions on top of them, with a shared expression of weary patience. The eldest is clearly mother to the others—two of the younger women seem only to repeat her, a faint reverberation of her own slight form and thin fair hair. The third daughter, who looks to be the youngest, takes after her father, with a solid frame and dark, ravelled hair that falls to her waist. It's the third daughter who spoke.

"My daughter Inge," says the man, without looking at her. "She was born insolent. The other two have about as much to say as a couple of nails. Bethany and Doll."

"Dollia," says their mother.

"She goes by Doll."

Doll herself, identified by a nod from Tristan, does not appear to care what she's called. Head lowered, she lets a tail of near-white hair fall over her eyes, and escapes behind it.

"And their mother is Vi. What do they call you?"

"My name's Eban." He steadies his breathing. "I suppose I'd better get on my way."

"Sure. And you will." Tristan swings his pack to the ground and nods to Bethany, who opens it and begins setting up the tent she pulls out from it. "Eban, is it? Well, we're just travellers like yourself, Eban. Picnicker, wasn't it? I think you'll be glad for a little company. Gets lonesome in the hills. Don't worry. We'll settle in for the night. Keep the conversation going. And who knows—maybe we'll find some other folks join us after all. Show up in those trees."

Eban is careful to steer his eyes from the hills where they want to search out Judy. "There's no one."

"So you say. So you say." Vi and her daughters seem to have taken Tristan's words as instructions and have gone to work, unpacking their belongings, building a fire and setting up camp. Only Dean remains unmoving under his tree, looking incalculably bored. "Now, why don't you go ahead and put that axe down, Eban?"

He lowers it slowly to the ground, resting the handle against the stacked firewood.

"That's better. Friendlier. And while we're enjoying each other's company, we ought to have some entertainment. Long day left yet, and we can't fill it all with yapping."

Eban doesn't understand why Dean has begun scowling until Tristan barks, "You heard me," and the younger man rises reluctantly to his feet. He reaches into his pack and produces a misshapen black case. It opens to reveal a coiling machine of gold.

Looking at the shining object, its whorl of pipes that open into a wide bell, Eban feels strangely moved. He doesn't know why. Dean handles the machine so gently, fitting his hands around it so precisely— as it, in turn, seems fitted to those hands—that the value of the thing he holds is as evident as if it were named aloud.

"What is it?" Eban whispers.

"French horn." Tristan looks faintly awed himself, watching as Dean blows into his machine. "I would have rathered a guitar, but it beats the quiet anyway. The quiet out here can put you right out of your head."

"Horn," Dean says so quietly that Eban scarcely catches it. "They called it just the horn."

"It's for . . . it makes . . ." The word seems absurd and Eban stumbles on it before a voice he wanted desperately not to hear speaks it for him.

"Music," says Judy.

Tristan turns so slowly that Eban hopes she will be gone by the time his gaze reaches the place where she stands, between the very trees he gestured to, minutes ago. She doesn't seem to notice him, or Eban. She is watching Dean, transfixed, as he raises the horn to his lips.

"Strauss," he says, his voice without expression. "Nocturno. Opus seven."

Eban flinches at the sound Judy makes as the man begins to play. It is a cry of something so pure and so unhappy that it is a music of its own. He can't bear to look at her.

"Listen to him," murmurs Tristan. "Listen to that." And Eban does.

The sound that slides from the horn and winds like running water between the air, the trees, the molecules and material of all the world, is not like a human voice. It sings, rises and falls, like a voice might. But it is a machine. He plays only for a count of minutes. But when he has finished, even the light seems to have changed in the wood.

"Please," says Judy. "Will you play it again?"

Dean doesn't seem to hear. "Too cold," he mutters, giving the horn a shake. "Gone flat on—"

"I guess we've found some more company," says Tristan, drawing closer to Eban, who is trying not to look at Judy. "That the last of you? Or are there more out there?"

Eban wonders if it's better that the man thinks there might be more of them, at wait beyond the camp. Back in the outland, when he was still a boy, marauders would often pass through. He came to know from the sound of his mother's voice when she had spotted them. She'd send him and his brother to their room, and sometimes they'd have to wait for hours till she came for them. Once she was dragged out of the house before she had time to send them away. "Get out!" she screamed as three men hoisted her by her elbows, her heels leaving two furrows across the dirt floor. Eban thought she was talking to the men, but when he forced himself to lift his head and look at her, her eyes, staring back, were filled with fury. "You get out of here, you and your brother, or I'll beat you raw!" He felt curiously stubborn as he realized that there was no way she could enforce her words. "No," he said. He was searching the room for something to use against the men. He found nothing, and by then they were gone. "Don't listen," he told his brother, closing the door against the noises from outside. She came back several hours later, and he was feeding his brother at the table. They looked at her, looking for some sign of what had happened, but there was none.

"Well, we'll find them if there are. Or maybe they'll find themselves, like young miss here." Tristan raises his voice now. "Will you introduce yourself? I think this one's not too happy with you. But we'd be glad to make your acquaintance."

Inge, who is digging a firepit with a blackened trowel, says, "Quit the speeches, Daddy. You sound a fool."

Tristan gives no sign of having heard her. "Tristan," he says, stepping toward Judy with his hand outstretched. "I'm not one for the old ways, but this is a better custom than most. Hard to betray a man you've—"

Inge turns her head to watch Judy as she passes, her gaze dropping and lifting to take her in. "He thinks he's a pirate," she says, still eyeing Judy, who has accepted Tristan's offered hand. "He likes to think we're all very, very impressed. And frightened."

"I'm Judy."

"Well, we're very pleased to meet you, Judy," says Tristan. "You and this man, who I guess belongs to you."

"We're together. As you are." She looks at the other women. "Hello."

Tristan introduces them and Judy nods at each before turning back to Dean. "I'm Judy," she says again.

The man has pulled a u-shaped pipe from his horn and is shaking it over the snow. "Dean."

"Dean," Judy says. "It was so beautiful. That music. How did you learn it?"

Dean doesn't respond or look like he intends to.

Tristan answers for him. "His grandmother used to play in the orchestra."

"Grandfather," says Vi.

"He learned from her."

"Him."

"I like to hear him play. And you meet a lot of people in these hills that like to hear it too. Oh, we can get by with buckshot and fishing line, same as anyone, but it was my idea to do something different from the rest. Entertainers, that's what we are. And people don't mind paying a price to hear something you won't find anywhere else, living up here."

"Are you . . ." Judy looks at Eban for the first time since she emerged from the wood. "I mean, the orchestra . . . that horn. To have things like that . . . Are you from the cities?"

Dean looks like he will speak then, but Tristan says, quickly, "Why would we go back there, when we can find all we need in these hills? With company to be found—"

"The cold," says Bethany. Her voice is ghostly and startling and they all turn to hear her. "That cold never goes, it never gets out of you. Not up here, not in the . . ." She waves her thin hands, like she's trying to stir up the right words, but her mother hushes her and she falls silent again.

Tristan regards her for a few minutes and then says, "Well. The ones that haven't seen it have trouble understanding. They think it would be easier."

"Not easier," says Judy. "That's not it."

"No?"

"You've been there, haven't you? That's what you're saying? Not your mother or your grandmother—you know it yourself?"

It's not clear whether he is considering the question or Judy herself. At last he opens his mouth to speak, but Judy interrupts him.

"It's what we left our camp to look for. We want to know about the cities. We want to know why . . ."

He smiles, and there is a warmth in his eyes and in his voice as he asks, "What *why* is it that you want to know?"

"Why we . . . Why we can't go. Why it isn't safe. If it's safe."

"Here's what I'll tell you," says Tristan. "You take that rifle I see you've got cocked ready in your coat, and you go find us something good to eat. Not a bunch of scrawny rabbits. Something hearty, a good meal that'll leave us with full bellies and in the mood to talk. And then, we'll have a chat. We'll let you see the show—yes, there's a show, and I think you'll like it, if you liked that one tooting away."

Judy lets the gunstock slide from her coat, resting in the palm of her hand, but she doesn't move. "Will you really tell us? Do you really know?"

The smile is gone. "Get our dinner while I'm still in the mood to tell you. No more questions."

After Judy has hurried off into the trees, with one parting look at Eban that reveals nothing of what she might be thinking, Tristan pays no further attention to Eban. But Eban understands he is to stay within the man's sight.

Tristan vanishes into the tent Vi and his daughters assembled, and the women follow him inside. Then all is quiet. Eban guesses that they travel by dark and sleep what hours they can during the day. For a moment, he thinks of the cry they heard in the foehn winds, and wonders. Then he gets to work.

After building a fire, Eban strings up the sodden bedding. He doubts it will dry in this weather but hopes the heat of the fire will at least speed the job along. They will need to take the first chance they get to run.

As he knots a length of twine around a fir trunk, he thinks, and not for the first time, that there is something similar in Judy and his brother. Certainty, he supposes, or will. And something more than that. Something that is almost, but not quite, invincibility.

It is an intensely vulnerable feeling to live beside someone with that quality. Even as a child, his brother showed no sign of the worried mind that Eban had been born to. He never had nightmares. Never begged their mother to waste a candle burning in the dark at bedtime.

One night Eban whispered his brother's name, testing whether he slept. He always fell asleep easily and quickly, while Eban battled his own consciousness every night, sometimes for hours.

"What, Eban?" came the steady, familiar voice, from an arm's length away.

"Do you ever think about what will happen to us?"

"Tomorrow?"

"No. I mean, later. When we're grown up. When we're her age."

"No."

"I mean . . ." He hesitated, frightened even of the words, spoken aloud. "When she dies. When it's just us?"

"No."

"You never think about that?"

"No, Eban."

"Oh." He turned away, irritated and unsure why. "But . . . think about it now. Think what it will be like. Only the two of us."

"Yeah."

"What will we do?"

He was quiet so long that Eban thought he'd gone back to sleep, and felt angry enough to tear the blankets back and shake him till he woke. Then his brother said, "Maybe I'll learn to make things out of wood. I would like that. And you could get some seeds and make a garden. Maybe you could do that."

Eban shook his head. "You don't understand. We'd be alone, just the two of us, forever."

"Yeah," his brother answered. "Just the two of us. Just me and Eban."

"Never mind."

"Are you angry, Eban?"

"Just go to sleep."

"You're angry at me."

"I said just go to sleep."

He heard an obedient shifting of blankets and then the slowed breathing of sleep, and sometime after that, it was morning, and they never spoke again of what might happen in the years to come.

At twelve, Eban began his study of the human body. His mother gave him her old textbooks for his birthday that year. She opened one and leafed to a series of transparent pages, each illustrating an isolated system of the body.

On the top page, a stiffly posed male, palms turned out in supplication, presented the integumentary system—a corner cross-section revealing its weave of hair and glands and dermal fibres. With a turn of the page, that system flicked away, disrobing the skeletal system, and then lymphatic, respiratory, circulatory . . . At the muscular system, he paused, studying the pink web of tissue in the shape of a man. It was the only system beneath the skin that perfectly reproduced the body's form. It enabled a man to move and to work. It was, he thought, the central human system.

His mother slid open the next page, which depicted the sinuous roots of the nervous system, woven through the man's limbs and spine and blossoming at his skull. As if disputing the thought Eban was sure he hadn't spoken aloud, she said, "That is what you are." She flipped back through the earlier pages, and said, "Bones, cells, lungs, blood, these glands, those vessels, that's what you're made of. I'm going to teach you that. But *this*"—she returned to the nervous system—"this is what you think, what you feel, and what you are. I want you to understand that."

He didn't know what he'd previously imagined might lie within him—what bled or ached or breathed—but he was stunned by the simplicity of the revelation. Seeing the body divided into a handful of pages, he realized he had, however vaguely, guessed at something much more complicated. He found he liked to think of the body as it was on those pages, and he nodded at his mother.

She told him she would teach him the physiology of the body, so he would understand it, and then she would teach him to use that knowledge to treat illness and injury as she did. "Here," she said, "we have nothing. Those drugs the peddlers sell are spoiled or worse. I have no tools, no equipment. Just what I can scratch out of the wood—the balsam gum, yarrow, sweet flag, fireweed—but it's a handful of sand thrown against the wind. That's all we've got here, and that's what I'm going to teach you. When I'm dead someday, you can take care of yourself and your brother. That is something, at least. To understand somebody's pain, and know what's the cause of it and how to stop it . . ."

She paused as if taken by a new thought. "That," she said, "is what we are, that too. Hurting just because someone else is hurting, and wanting to fix it. The good of that. It's what makes us different from those other ones."

That evening, Eban's brother found him reading by lamplight and took the stool across the table.

"You have a new book, Eban?" he asked.

Eban nodded.

"Read it to me, Eban?"

Eban had felt sorry for his brother the day their mother threw down the tattered book of stories about children from before and declared him unable to learn, but his brother had seemed only happy to be released from his lessons. Though he had always shown an intense dislike for the effort of sounding out letters and words, he loved the stories themselves, more than Eban ever had, even though they were written for much younger children. He would beg Eban to read them until Eban gave in, so often that they both could have recited the brief tales from memory.

Tonight, Eban refused, enjoying too greatly the sense of importance of his new undertaking, eager to learn every word of the pages his mother had assigned to him. But as usual his brother's determination outlasted his own, and finally he began to read aloud, hurrying through the paragraphs on biochemistry in an affectless tone that he hoped would dull and exhaust even his brother's persistence.

But his brother listened, chin in his hands on the tabletop, until Eban had read every line up to his mother's pencil mark, and then read on, to the end of the chapter, and the beginning of the next, on organic chemistry. At last, his throat dry and eyes aching from reading by the low light, he stopped.

"That's enough," he told his brother, who nodded in acceptance and raised his head from the table.

"Why are you reading that, Eban?" he asked.

"Because I have to."

"But why?"

"Because she told me to. Because I'm supposed to learn it."

His brother thought about this. "Why do you want to learn it?"

"So I can help. If someone is injured or sick, I can help them get better." He hesitated. "Do you want to learn it too? I could help you. I could read the books with you, if you wanted. We could be physicians, like she was. We could do it together." The more he spoke, the more he liked the idea. They could study together in the evenings. His brother could be very quick to learn certain things. They might help each other. Somehow the bright light of knowledge his mother had described seemed more possible, more powerful, if the two of them might share and practise it together.

His brother shook his head. "No, Eban."

"Why?" he asked, hearing in the word an echo of his brother's own questions, and hating it.

His brother shuffled towards the bed, his back to Eban. "It isn't interesting."

It's near dark when Judy returns. She is bruised and filthy, bent under the weight she carries over her shoulders. His mouth falls open as he sees what she has brought them.

"Well done," says Tristan, pushing his way through his tent door. "Well *done!*" He strokes the muzzle of the deer Judy wears like a yoke almost fondly. "I haven't had venison in years. I hardly thought they came this high, or thought maybe they were all shot dead a decade ago." He turns to Eban. "Some hunter, your girl. A wonder you look half-starved if this is how you eat."

Judy's expression is dark as she swings her load to the ground and the women hurriedly crouch beside it and begin gutting the animal.

Judy remains standing over the bowed women and Eban touches her hand to try to call back her attention from wherever it has fled. What he took for a bruise running down her jaw and shoulder is a streak of purpling blood. When she doesn't move or even flinch, he finds a rag from a coat pocket and tries to wipe her clean.

"It's okay," she says softly, and when he hesitates, "Please, Eban. Don't."

No one bothers them as the women string the deer up from a branch and stoke the fire they've kept smouldering all day. Tristan lies at the root of a tree beside the one where the deer hangs, smiling faintly as he watches the women work. Eban doesn't know where Dean has gone.

While the family is preoccupied, Eban and Judy kneel on the ground and whisper to each other.

"Are we in danger?" Judy asks him.

He looks at Tristan. His eyes are half-closed. Is he really watching the women or watching him and Judy? "We could be."

Eban remembers that he's angry with Judy but feels too tired to chide or reproach her, so he only says, "I wish you'd stayed hidden. I might have been able to get away. At least you would be all right."

Judy doesn't dismiss the words as he expected. "But I couldn't," she says simply. "I could see them and you and knew I could have hidden for hours or maybe more, maybe waited till they slept and got you out. But then that man took out that horn and I thought how could anyone know how to use something like that and want to harm us? How could anyone able to do something so beautiful do anything terrible or wrong?"

Eban frowns. "Do you really believe that?"

She sighs. "I don't know. Maybe not. I just couldn't, Eban. I couldn't just hide and not listen to that sound, or listen and not want to come closer or talk to the people who knew how to do that. And I thought you could only learn something like that in the cities. I thought we could end our travel here if they could tell us what we're searching for Heaven to find out. We could go to the cities tonight."

"I don't know if I believe they've ever left these hills," Eban mutters. "People like them belong here like the dirt and the rats do. And Judy, where did you find that deer anyway? How did you do this?"

She looks away without answering.

"I've hunted since I was five years old and never seen one," he says. "I wouldn't even have recognized it except for a picture in my mother's old book on field dressing."

"I've seen one once before. In the outland."

"Were you able to get a clear shot then?"

She shakes her head. "No, no. It wasn't like that. My fathers . . . They never would have done that."

Eban doesn't understand, but he can see she has more to say. He waits.

"I walked for hours," Judy tells him. "I didn't see anything. Not one thing. Not a bird, not a rodent, not a single living thing I could have brought back. You heard what he told me. I had to bring him something good enough that he'd tell us what he knows, and I couldn't find even a squirrel."

"And then?"

"I'd told myself I wouldn't come back till I found something. I thought I'd walk until I starved before I came back empty-handed." She rubs her belly. "But I felt ill, and the sun was high and I was exhausted. I sat down, just to rest for a little while, but I fell asleep. I woke up and didn't know how much time had passed, and I was so ashamed. And then I saw it."

"The deer?"

"It came like it was looking for me. I swear I don't know how else to tell it. It wasn't even frightened. I thought at first it didn't see me, and I sat up so slowly, so carefully. But it was grazing maybe a stone's throw from me and all at once it looked right at me. Chewing, considering me, not afraid at all. It made it so much worse that it wasn't afraid."

"Judy . . ."

"Alphonse said there was a special dispensation for beautiful living things. My fathers wouldn't have eaten that deer no matter how hungry they were."

"It's different," Eban said. "Your fathers didn't live up here."

"It has nothing to do with the hills. It has nothing to do with how we live. I wasn't hungry, or no hungrier than I ever am. I just was desperate to know what he knows. Whatever that man can tell us." She drops her hands from her belly and they rest palm up in her lap like they don't belong to her. "I shot it before I could think about it. I knew it was the only way I could."

"It's okay, Judy. I swear it. It will be okay. It's how we always live, how everything does. One animal feeds another."

A dark look spreads like weather over her face. "It walked for an hour before it fell. I followed it. When I got there, it was still alive. I shot it again, standing over it, close enough I could have touched it. Her."

Eban is wondering whether it was the deer's bad luck or their own that led it to cross Judy's path, when Tristan rises to his feet.

"Mind if I interrupt?" He stands over them, his expression inscrutable—ironic or angry, Eban can't tell. "If you're done your chatting, Vi and the girls got the deer hanged, and we've got a few hours yet till we can eat. Time enough to put on the show."

"Can we talk first?" Judy asks. "I want to hear what you said you'd tell us."

The look on her face would have arrested Eban in any action, but Tristan barely glances at her. "Show first," he says, without animosity. "And then we eat. Then talk."

VI

THE SKY IS FADING overhead, and they sit in the shadow of the trees, seated on blankets the women spread over the snow. They face a rickety arch of steel rods and rails, hung with red cloth. The women have vanished and Dean stands in front of the arch, puffing soundlessly into his horn, while Tristan checks the deer.

"What is that?" Judy asks.

"What?" Dean looks up from his horn.

"The curtains, the poles. Is it another tent?"

He sneers. "It's a stage, cave dweller." He eyes the torn cloth and rusted bars as he blows air again into the horn, and then he drops the horn to his side in disgust. "I mean, isn't it elegant? Our proscenium arch? Aren't you *transported* by the artifice?"

Judy doesn't seem to hear his scorn. "A stage? Like a theatre? Your show—is it a play?"

"No. You'd need talent for that. Brains and a plan. That's not what this is."

"But what is it?"

"Tristan flexing." Dean glances at Tristan, his expression defiant, but Eban notices he has lowered his voice. "He insists on the stage. He likes to insist on things. He doesn't like the horn, but he insists I play."

"And the women?"

"The same. A game for him." He hooks a curtain with one finger, and peers through the gap between it and the other. When he lets it go, his expression has softened. Saddened, Eban thinks. "Not Vi though. Vi's the real thing. I mean, she could have been. Our mother was."

"Let's go," hollers Tristan. "What the hell is taking so long?"

There's silence and then a voice that sounds like Bethany's. "It's *cold*."

He claps his hands together. "No more dallying. We've got a hot meal waiting. Open that curtain or I'll do it for you."

Hands appear between the curtains and slowly pull them to either side. The second curtain snags partway, and after two or three tugs, a sigh is heard, and the hand disappears.

Revealed by the open curtains is Vi, standing on a flat slab of stone with her head bowed, her bare arms bent and elbows jagged above her shoulders, hands dangling like leaves from a tree. Her ankles are crossed, her bare legs, muscular, vein-knotted and thin. Her hair hides her face, and there is something terrible in the eyes that can't be seen.

"She'll freeze," whispers Judy, who has laid a hand on Eban's own, digging her fingers into his palm. More loudly, she repeats, "She'll freeze!"

Eban hadn't even noticed, transfixed by her shape against the dusking wood. But she wears only a strange black garment that fits her body tightly, leaving her arms and legs uncovered. The thin cloth shows the line of her hips and hangs to just below her knees, unravelling there into rags and threads. She looks like something else. A dark bird, the bone remains of an animal, weather.

"Not if she hurries up," Tristan retorts.

She looks like a streak of charcoal on a white page. And as still as that.

Then they hear the horn, and turn, startled, to remember Dean is there. He releases a long note that rises and falls, dissolving into a whisper. They look again at Vi as her left arm twists, snake-like, to the side, drawing her body with it, until she is bent at an impossible angle, head cocked like she is listening for something.

Judy's grip on Eban's hand tightens. "Oh Eban. Her feet."

She wears no shoes.

The music suddenly speeds and swells, note following note, higher and higher, and there is no rhythm or melody Eban can discern, and it's nothing like any music he has heard, which is almost none—the things his mother would hum to make his brother sleep, a peddler with a dented guitar.

How could anyone able to do something so beautiful do anything terrible or wrong? Eban thinks of Judy's words, and of his brother, who used to sing without seeming to notice it, at the table, chasing flies around the yard, always in a nasal, atonal voice Eban found intolerable.

Vi slowly lifts a clenched bare foot like it's something she has found in the snow. As her leg extends above her head, he stops breathing. And then she begins to dance.

The delicacy of Vi's first movements yields to a savage grace. She spins from foot to foot, vaulting into the air again and again, rising higher above the ground than Eban would have ever guessed possible. She dances with a kind of frenzied glee that reminds him of the way he and his brother used to chase each other through the dust, arms wheeling. And yet, there's something vicious to it that he can't quite identify, something brutal about the way, after each soaring leap, she is yanked back to the ground.

The daughters appear behind Vi. Though they wear boots, they aren't dressed for the season. Wrapped in loose rags dyed bright colours, they swing the tails of cloth as they turn and jump, but none of them has their mother's gift.

Then Inge, who has stood slightly behind the others, her performance listless, approaches the centre and bends forward. Vi arches her spine until she rests, splayed, across her daughter's back, helplessly paddling the air above her, and now they can see her bony, reddened feet, the shaking of her legs as she is flung to her feet on the stone. With a shudder that seems to pass through her whole body, she rises inches higher, standing on the very ends of her toes, teetering as she rotates in a circle before them. It is monstrous. And beautiful.

The horn music seems to circle around her. She is slowly lowering herself forward, her eyes staring straight out through and past all of them, when Judy stands up.

"Stop it," Judy says. "Stop it. Please, please stop." She bends over Vi, trying to help her to her feet, but the woman turns her face away.

Eban feels as though he has woken from a dream. He addresses Tristan. "If her toes freeze, she will lose them."

"You. Keep playing," Tristan orders Dean, who has lowered his horn and is studying Eban thoughtfully. "She's fine," he tells Eban. "The dancing warms her up."

Eban shakes his head. "Not the toes." He begins to unfasten his boot. "Have you ever seen someone lose a toe to frostbite?"

Tristan stares at Eban's foot as he withdraws it and tugs at the end of the sock. Tristan looks for a moment at the quarter inch of flesh and bone that remains of Eban's second toe, and then he looks away.

"Get your clothes on, girls," he growls. "It's time to eat."

It worries Eban that they have made Tristan angry, and he watches him as they take their seats around the fire, searching for any warning of what will happen when they finish the meal. But as plates of venison pass around their small circle, the mood seems lightened.

They eat quickly, the meat still steaming, tearing it from the bone with burning fingertips. Though Tristan eats the most, he finishes first and heaves the stripped, shining bones into the trees. He catches Eban looking after the flung bones, and says, "Go and fetch them if it bothers you. I won't stop you. Don't know what you imagine might creep out of the trees and come after them. Seen many bears around these hills of late?"

"Never saw a deer either." Inge continues eating, eyes on her food, showing no sign of having spoken, and Tristan seems, after looking at her for a moment, to doubt she did.

Eban doesn't move, and Tristan appears pleased. He leans back against an ironwood tree and pulls a clay jug from his pack. "Juneberry hooch," he explains, though the words mean nothing to Eban. "Did you like the show?"

"Yes," Eban answers. Judy is cleaning her hands and doesn't look up.

"I thought you would. You know, I gave Vi her name. Better for the stage than what they used to call her. It was my mother's name. Violetta the aerialist. She used to fly around the circus tent on a red sash. You know what that is, the circus?"

Eban shakes his head.

"People would come from miles around to sit in a big tent and see people who could do remarkable things. Dance on a wire as thin as your finger. Stick their head in the mouth of a lion. That's what my grandfather did." He pauses. "You know what a lion is? Well, about four hundred pounds of muscle and fur and just about as many teeth. You had to be born to that kind of fearlessness. You couldn't be taught it. My father never learned it. He added up numbers for a living. My mother left him when I was ten years old and tried to go back to kicking sawdust, that's what they called it. But by then nobody wanted to come to the circus anymore."

"You don't know anything about it," Vi says.

"Don't I?" Tristan turns back to Eban and Judy and doesn't appear troubled. "Vi's mother was a dancer, a proper one, from before. I saw Vi and her mother dance in one of those slummy outland shows they had back then, and I had the idea to tell them I was from a dance school in the cities. You could smell the stink on Vi, how bad she wanted that. I could have led her anywhere. So I led her here. To be a sideshow act in the back of beyond for retreaters like you and your girl." He laughs heartily.

"Judy." She has finished cleaning her hands and lays the greasy cloth she wiped them with beside her. "Judy."

"All you lot up here in these woods, trying to outrun your own shadows. I knew you'd pay for a thrill. And I knew it wouldn't take much. A second-rate circus in the hills." He gives a sour look to the other members of his family. None of them raise their eyes to meet his. "But Vi didn't want to be in the circus. She was at me every waking hour, and sobbing half the night to boot. I got one of those sashes for her and she was dead useless at it, or pretended to be. I couldn't make her. And I tried." He throws up his hands. "So we have this, this shabby little show and a one-horn band. But still, people pay to see it. Like you will." He points to what remains of the deer, still smoking over the fire. "We'll take the rest of that with us when we go."

Only Inge is still eating, digging with her teeth and fingers at a lump of meat. As she tears a piece away, Eban realizes it is the deer heart she is consuming, still raw and running with blood.

"She always does that," Tristan says. "Inge has some screwy ideas. She heard something about eating heartmeat. Doesn't even put it over the fire. Tell them why you do it, girl. She thinks it gives her power. Something like that. Just as easy to let her do what she wants. Doesn't bother me any."

He stares at Judy, who is perfectly still, watching him. She seems to sense it is better to wait for him to tell her what she wants to know than to ask. "It really is something that you found that deer. I wouldn't have believed it if I hadn't seen it myself. We'd come into these woods to hunt some when I was a boy, and back then you'd still hope to see one, maybe. But we never did. Didn't bother me any. Things always change. My grandfather told me there used to be caribou in the northernmost peaks of these hills."

"That's true," says Judy. "My father told me that too."

"But not for a hundred years or more. Two hundred."

"There was a parasite," Judy says slowly, as if she's reading the words from a dimly lit book. "Something in the hooves of the deer. There weren't always deer here, but people brought them, and the deer brought the parasite with them. It didn't hurt them any, but it made the caribou brainsick. They lost their fear of people or stumbled in circles until they died. They all died."

"And then there were deer," Tristan says, looking pleased. "And then there weren't. That's what they get wrong down in the cities, worrying about these things. Only someone with too much time or not enough in their heads worries about weather. The world turns, that's how it is. It rains, it snows, things change, deer die and some of us survive."

Judy is drawn tight and taut like a bow string, crouched in the snow, watching Tristan with wide eyes. "So you have been there, down in the cities."

Tristan has begun to sink lower on the ground, spreading like a puddle over the snow while his head still rests against the tree trunk. His eyes, under heavy lids, are vague, and Eban wonders if he's drunk. The clay jug is turned over beside him.

"Ask me that again," he says, the pleasant tone gone from his voice.

Judy rises to her knees. "Tell me about the cities. Tell me when you were down there and what you saw."

"Are you telling me what to do?"

"No. No." Judy lowers her voice and speaks as softly as if she were addressing a lover. "I wanted to ask you if you would tell me. I would like to hear what you know, if you will tell me. Please."

He lifts the jug to his mouth and upends it. A few drops spill to the ground. Without warning, he swings the arm that holds it and the jug shatters against the tree. Judy gasps and the women only cover their faces, without making a sound.

"We should be getting to bed," he says. "Early start in the morning."

"Please," Judy says again, her voice strained.

"You girls clean up this mess. And you." He stands and points a finger down at Judy. "You find a better question if you want me to answer."

"But you told me. You promised. You told me you would tell me about the cities."

He stands with one hand supporting himself against the tree, his back to Judy and Eban. "I've never been to the cities. I can't tell you a thing."

Eban begged Judy to sleep while he sat watch, but hours after the others have all disappeared into their tents, she lies with her back to him beneath the blankets, her eyes open, staring out at nothing.

"Please, Judy," he says once again to her back. "Please take this chance to sleep. He was never going to tell us anything. He has nothing to tell. We don't need him. All we need to do is wait until they leave and let him put some miles between us. He doesn't seem to want any trouble, but I don't trust him."

Some time later, Judy's eyes close at last, and Eban fights to keep his own open.

"You're right to set watch," says a woman's voice, which seems to come from only a few steps away in the dark. "And you are right not to trust him."

Without a sound, the woman moves closer, and a flash of moonlight illuminates her face just enough for him to recognize Inge's features.

"Most of everything he says is a lie," she continues, crouching in the snow beside him. "We do the same route through these hills, five times a year, and then we go back to the cities with whatever we managed to lay our hands on. There's no good reason why he lied about that except he'd finally gotten tired of talking."

Eban feels no more inclined to believe this woman than her father. "But how do you keep hidden from them . . . the other ones?"

"The other ones!" She strikes a match and draws deep on a pipe. "Haven't heard those words in a while. What do you know about that? About them?"

"The same as anyone knows. What do you mean?"

"I mean . . . well, who am I? One of them or one of you?"

"Well, you're . . ."

"Like you? What makes you sure? And for that matter, what makes you sure about yourself?"

"My mother gave me the tests."

Inge laughs. "The tests!"

"Are you saying," asks Eban slowly, "that people in the cities aren't . . . different?"

She shapes an *o* with her lips and releases a ribbon of smoke. "I'm saying that it isn't the way you imagine it. People didn't just change. Everything changed around them. That's what my mother told me. It happened slowly, but it took a long time for people to see and understand it. And then because they weren't ready, they thought it had happened suddenly."

"Little by little, and then all at once."

She nods. "Like that. More and more babies had it. And then the babies were grown. And then the weather changed. And the government changed. And the rules changed. And by the end you couldn't tell. Did the rules change because the government changed because the weather changed? Or because the people changed? Or was there no connection between any of it?"

"But *are* you like us, then?"

"Why does it matter? The only difference between you and the ones you call the other ones is some ancient reflex. Plenty of people think what those other ones did was right. It was the world that went wrong. And your people just didn't like that they didn't want to sit around weeping over it. But all that matters is what you do, and who cares what you feel doing it?"

"But they turned against people . . . like us. Didn't they? Drove us out . . ."

An image—a memory—takes form in Eban's mind as if it has always been there. His brother standing with his back to the front door, after pulling closed its heavy wooden bolt. He was five years old, and Eban was surprised he could lift something so heavy. "Safe," the little boy said. And Eban smiled at his brother, wondering who he imagined he was keeping out. And then Eban stopped smiling. He went to the window and stood there for some time, peering out into the dark through the open shutters. "Safe," his brother said again, firmly, and left the room.

Inge shrugs, and wears her father's expression as she dismisses the comment and, with it, the conversation. "There was less to eat, less to drink, less of everything. Some people got moved around. Why? Because the people in charge thought it would be better that way. Were they right? Maybe not, but they were in charge. And that's how it always is when someone else makes the rules, and that's why I live here and not there."

"But you're saying it's safe now? That we could—"

"I'm not saying anything. What you do is your own business. But here's what I came to tell you." She peers into the bowl of her pipe. "Lousy tinker tobacco. Don't burn right. Never did." She dumps the bowl's contents into the snow and looks intently at him. "My father told you he'd take the rest of the deer meat and let you go in the morning."

"Yes."

"I told you he's a liar."

"What do you mean? He won't let us go?"

"Won't let you go for that price." She shakes her head, and the gesture has a quality of theatre about it, like a movement from her mother's dance. "He would never let anyone go for a few paltry cuts of meat. Food we can get, easy. He wants something we can take back to the cities and sell." She leans closer, eyes bright. "You got anything like that?"

"We have nothing. Nothing of value."

"You sure of that?"

"Inge," says Eban, "he told us he'd take the deer as payment."

"It was a lie. He takes everything."

"But if we have nothing to take?"

"Find something. Find something worth more than the two of you."

"What do you mean—he would make us go with you?"

She nods. "It's why Dean is here. Don't you think he'd rather be anywhere else? My mother's different, though. She likes strong people. When he first came for her, I think she probably thought he'd keep her safe. She knows now she was never in more danger than she is with him. All of us are."

Her expression has turned soft, and Eban finds he is moved by her. How tough she has been made by years at the side of this tyrant. He knows Judy believes that she and Eban are prisoners of a kind, as if a thousand miles of hill and wood could be a jail. But he knows with certainty, watching this hard, clever girl lower her gaze from him, that they are free.

"I'm sorry," he says. "I truly am."

"Yes. Well." She makes a twist of her mouth. "So it is."

"Have you ever tried? To go? Alone?"

"Of course I have."

"But he found you?"

"He'd see me dead before he'd let me go. You don't know how he is.

Obsessive. A single idea will fix itself in his head and then he'll care for nothing else."

He hesitates. "Could we help you? If you could leave with us . . . maybe we could keep you safe. We've lived for years in these hills. We know how to hide."

"And yet we found you, didn't we?"

"But that was an accident."

"Do you really think that?"

He feels foolish suddenly. "I suppose . . ."

"We hunted you for four days. And watched you for one, to be sure of who you travelled with and what weapons you carried."

He shakes his head, and she rises to her feet.

"I'd tell you to get some sleep," she whispers, "but I don't really think it's a good idea. I should get to my tent. If you really have nothing to give him, I guess we'll have plenty of time to get to know each other."

He nods, distracted, trying to make up his mind. "Wait!" he cries. Judy stirs slightly at the sound and then her breathing slows once more. Lowering his voice, he calls again, "Inge, wait!"

He is surprised to hear her answer him from only a short distance away, and wonders if she waited for him, knowing he would ask her to return.

"Yes?"

"There is something." He shakes his head, not quite believing what he is about to do, and then he rises and retrieves Judy's pack. "It's in here." The yellow box is close to the top. She must have looked in it that day. He feels a tightness in his throat, which he ignores. It was the only way, he imagines telling her. They would never have let us go, he will say. "This."

She takes the box from him, weighing it in her hand as if to assess its worth by poundage.

"See if something in there will satisfy him. Please."

She smiles, keeping her eyes on him as she lifts the lid. He recognizes the sound of it cracking open. Sometimes it is the first thing Judy does in the morning, reaching her hand inside, touching one object and then another, or laying them out across the ground only to look at them. There was nothing else to give, he will tell her. Forgive me, he will say.

He cannot watch as Inge shoves her hand inside the box. There is a brutality in the way she roots through its contents.

"This," she says, withdrawing her hand, and something glints between her thumb and finger.

"Is it the earring?" Eban asks, not wanting to look any closer.

She studies it, a smile crossing her face. "Is that what you call it?"

"That's what Judy called it. She said it was her mother's."

"Did she?" Inge touches her finger to its sharp, hooked end. "They would put it in their ear, would they?"

"Through their ear. That's what she told me. They had holes there just for that purpose." He touches the lobes of his own ears. "I don't know if it was true. People say these things."

"Yes. Yes, they do. Well, in any case, that jewel is worth your passage, I'm sure of it. My father will be pleased."

Eban nods, unable to say anything more.

"In fact, you can get some sleep if you want it. I don't think he'll bother you after all. If he does, I'll show him this."

He knows he should protest, but he feels suddenly, terribly tired.

"That's it. Lie down beside your girl there. You've earned it."

He lets himself obey her, easing himself onto his back, pulling the sleeping bag over him. "Inge," he whispers, not sure if she is still there.

"Yes?"

"Don't tell Judy. "

"She'll notice it missing."

"Not that. I'll tell her that." He reaches one hand out to touch her sleeping form, as lightly as he can. "Don't tell her what you told me. Don't tell her you've been there."

"To the cities?"

"Please."

She shakes her head, smiles briefly and then nods at him. "Good night, Eban."

By the time she is gone, he is already asleep, but he dreams all night that he sits watch still, and that when they come for him, he's ready.

Judy's voice begins the day. "What did you do, Eban?" she asks.

He pushes aside the covers and tries to clear his head. He is guilty but can't remember why.

"You slept," Judy says, reproachfully. "You should have woken me for my turn to keep watch."

"I'm sorry," he murmurs. "I should have. I didn't mean to fall asleep. I'm sorry."

Judy has already begun packing up their things. The tents belonging to the others are as silent and inscrutable as two closed eyes.

"Should we leave before they wake?" Judy asks him as he listens for any sound that might indicate they are stirring.

"Better not," says Dean, stepping out of the trees behind them, his own tent collapsed and bundled in his arms. "They wouldn't like that." He crouches over the fire without looking at them and pours water and something from a sack into the empty pot.

"We want to make some distance today," Judy says carefully. "We shouldn't linger too long."

"Suit yourselves," calls Inge from the second tent as she opens its door. "Doesn't matter to any of us." Half-dressed, she emerges, her legs bare in defiance of the cold morning, her feet encased in enormous fur boots.

"Do you think," Judy asks her, "that there is any use in me asking him again? Do you think he might have more to tell me? Or is there anything you can say?" Her tone is soft, almost pleading, as if she believes Inge a friend.

Inge eyes Eban before answering, smiling slightly, and he notices something at her ear. A gleam. And then, with a quick intake of breath, he realizes what she has done, just as Judy, too, drops her hands and stares at the other woman.

"Is that—do you have my . . ."

Inge touches her ear, which is swollen and marked by a stain of dried blood. "Sure," she says. "Why don't you ask him?"

Judy takes her eyes from Inge and looks questioningly at him. "She has my mother's earring, Eban."

"It's all right," Inge tells her. "We worked it out. He'll explain it to you."

"I had to, Judy," he whispers. "She said they'd never let us go unless we—"

"Unless you what?" Tristan peels open the door of his tent and pulls his boots on. "How did she threaten you?"

Eban doesn't answer, watching instead as Judy turns away, the shape of her somehow sorrowful-looking.

"She's sly, that one," Tristan says indulgently. "What did she convince you to give away?"

Inge, sullen-eyed, ignores him, taking a seat beside Dean.

Tristan laughs, long and low. "Whatever it is, it's hers now. She can't let anybody get past us without relieving them of their belongings."

"She told me it was you. That you wouldn't let us leave."

He shakes his head. "We were even. I said as much. I wouldn't have bothered you. I don't hurt anybody unless they get in my way. But that one would slit your throat without blinking and only be sorry for bloodying her knife. I suppose she told you her sad story. We all have sad stories. You ought to remember that. You shouldn't sell your pity so cheap. Or your trust."

Eban turns his back on the man, his stomach sick. And then, through the tent door that Tristan left open behind him, he notices Vi and her daughters, sprawled naked together in the swell of bedding. The girls sleep with their heads resting on their mother's stomach, their bodies only partly covered. As Eban watches, Vi opens her eyes, regards him, and then pulls the covers higher, till her face is hidden from him. Eban glances at Judy and can tell from her face that she saw it too.

"Get us some water, girl," Tristan orders Inge.

"Get it yourself," she answers, and to Eban's surprise, Tristan chuckles and plucks a jug from the ground and heads off into the wood.

"Have a seat," says Dean. "Get your bowl and you can eat with us."

"I'm not hungry." Eban stares at the man and woman seated on the ground, spooning food into their mouths like they're starved. "I saw," he says. More loudly, he repeats, "We saw them there. In the tent. Your mother and your sisters."

Inge pauses, the spoon in her hand briefly arrested in its passage to her mouth. "Did you get a nice long look?"

Dean throws his bowl to the ground and glares at Eban. "Leave it," he growls. "Leave it alone."

"Dean, take down my tent," Inge orders.

Reluctantly, Dean rises and begins the work of packing up the second tent.

"He doesn't like it," Inge says simply.

"Does your mother? Your sisters—"

"I doubt they know what things they do because they like it and what they do because they're afraid. And I doubt it matters much. He tried that with me too and I woke him with a knife between his teeth and told him next time it would be between his ribs."

"Then why do you stay with him?" Judy asks.

Inge narrows her eyes. "You must not know anything about anything."

"Can't you fight? Can't Dean? If the two of you—"

"He tried. Twice." She leans closer, as if to make certain they understand her. "I don't think he will again."

"But you have weapons . . . You aren't helpless. You could—"

"Dean belongs to Tristan now, like I do and they do. Like my mother does." Inge looks toward the tent, where the three women sleep on. "But she'll kill him one day."

"You leaving or what?" demands Dean, jamming the tent fabric into a sack.

"Yes," says Judy. "We are."

They wait until it is almost dark before they continue. Eban wants to be sure the others are gone. If Inge didn't lie, if they were hunted for days without knowing it, he wants to believe that it is only because they weren't looking for signs of pursuit. He remembers the cry they heard in the wind, and decides not to think of it again. They never guessed they were followed, and, he tells himself, now that he is looking for such signs, he will see them if they're there. But he and Judy aren't of interest to that terrible family any longer. He is sure of it.

Of course it must have been a lie, what Inge said about going to the cities. She only wanted a bauble to amuse herself. He thinks there is no reason to tell Judy what Inge told him, because there is no reason to believe any of it was true.

A hard, icy rain falls, and the moon is lost in the sky. Judy and Eban talk little, instead driving their shoulders into the wind and setting their teeth against the cold.

At last they stop. There's no discussion, but they seem to understand each other perfectly, lowering their packs at once when they reach a small opening in the wood.

Once there is a fire, coaxed, smoking, out of the sodden wood, once Judy has found the driest clothing left in their packs and set it out for them to wear, once they have prepared a dinner of boiled beans,

Judy leans toward Eban and says, "I have to show you something."

As he follows her, Eban notices that something has altered ever so slightly in the carriage of her body, the way she walks. He stares at her back, her profile, and wonders if her shape has changed in some way she's now accommodating. And he remembers how he once had to tell her, this woman who knew about animals and countries he'd never heard named, why she had stopped menstruating, what she carried and how it would be born. The way she looked at him then, caught and ashamed. The way she needed him.

Judy leads him now to a place where the ridge veers sharply and the old stump of a tree, cleaved in two, still stands.

"Look," she says. "I saw it when I was gathering wood for the fire."

At first he thinks it's the tree Judy has just taken down to burn, but drawing closer, he sees the cut was made and the tree felled a dozen years or more ago.

"Look," she says again, and Eban does.

Carved into the severed trunk, where its heartwood is exposed, are four curved lines that nearly meet at the centre, a curling *x* with no apex.

"Do you know what that is?" Judy asks. He shakes his head. "I think it might stand for Heaven. Look at the other half."

From the other side, he can see eight letter *u*'s roughly hewn into the wood, and beneath, seven vertical lines, maybe capital *i*'s. "You think it means something?" he asks.

"They're numbers. Each unit is shown with a different symbol. Dan used this in his reports, to protect dates and locations. There was some danger that meant he had to keep those numbers safe. If you didn't know to look for them, you'd think they were just accidental markings, meaningless. I thought it was a code between him and whoever he sent his reports to. But maybe there are others who know the system."

"Then it can't be safe," Eban says quietly.

"This mark," Judy says, pointing to the *u*'s, "means units of ten. The other is ones. So the number is eighty-seven. I think we're only eighty-seven miles away now."

He wipes away the water dripping from his hair with his hand, which is no drier. "From the colony. But what reason is there to believe that's what it means? That *x* could stand for anything. Or nothing at all."

She takes his hand in hers and raises it to point at the mountain peaks rising from the forest before them. "One. Two. Three. Four. Four peaks. With a gully between them."

He frowns. "You think those are the two-horned mountains? You think if we pass between them we'll find . . ."

Her eyes won't release his. Her smile stretches all the way across. "Heaven," she whispers.

He bows his head slowly. "Okay."

If it is true, they are close enough they might be watched even now. But then there is no use in hiding. No use in putting out the fire or sitting watch through the night. They are caught, or they are welcome.

After they eat, they sit in silence. Tired but not yet ready to climb into their soaked bedding and attempt to sleep.

"How awful they must be," Eban says. "How awful the cities must be to drive people to lives like those."

"No," says Judy. "It's the other way around. How could they be any worse?"

They fall asleep beside one another, still cold, still hungry. Eban feels as though he doesn't sleep at all, but then there are flashes of dream, sharp and clear, singing like the sweep of a blade through the air, dreams where he shakes with cold. But he wakes dripping with sweat and certain something is wrong.

VII

DAWN IS ALREADY LIGHTING up the sky, so that the mountain and trees above look like they have been set on fire, though it will be another hour at least till the sun clears the hills and is revealed. The sky is lake-blue.

It rained in the night, and Eban's clothes are soaked through, his hair and skin damp. His wet face feels hot, though he is shivering.

"Judy," he whispers, but she turns in her sleep without answering.

He can't seem to free his mind from the half-dream of danger—its formless, shadowy innuendo—that woke him. Sitting up and rubbing his face with his hand, he tries to see the thing he only senses. Something troubling. Something missing. Something that should be there.

"Gone." The word falls from his mouth like a stone.

He takes it in, piece by piece, everything missing revealing itself, one and then another and another.

Gone is the shelter Eban stitched together out of tarp and twine.

Gone his pack.

Gone the axe Judy leaned against the stack of split firewood.

Gone the sack of fire nests Eban had forgotten to return to the cook kit, half-remembering as he slid into sleep and thinking no harm could come to it in the night.

Gone the water.

Gone the fuel tank.

Gone the food.

Slumping back onto the ground, Eban tries to clear his head. Anger crowds his mind, blotting out the sequence of concrete, explicit fears just past the outer reach of his thoughts. And something else, some sinewy gravity clings to him, slowing and delaying his thinking.

"Judy," he whispers again, but softly, almost wishing she won't wake.

It is impossible to know what she will think or say.

At last he rises to his feet. He is burning and frozen at the same time, and impulsively he strips off his clothes, hooking his coat over a branch with shaking hands, and letting the sodden rest fall to the ground. One less thing, and what does it matter now.

Slinking over his damp skin, the cold air wakes him up, nerve ending by nerve ending. He is something past awake, electric, quivering in readiness. He kicks off one boot and stares at his foot, white and shrivelled like something that has never seen light. He plants both feet on the wet, melting ground, feels myriad radicles spring from each phalanx and tunnel into the earth, a rhizomatic, anarchic root system, tethering him like a tree—

"Eban!"

He doesn't want to turn. To turn would be to stop the explosion of sensation, cold air broadcasting over his head and throat, his chest, his back, the rush of sky across his body.

"Eban, what are you doing?"

And that's it. That's what fear sounds like in her voice.

He turns and smiles at her. It comes to him in a flash what he looks like. White, and grimy with sweat. Yet somehow he feels only a proud certainty, standing naked before her. He tells her, "It's gone."

She is already looking around as he says the words, discovering what he already knows. The way she comes to understand it is systematic. He can see that she is counting things, unpacking what was put where, what they need and how badly, and where it was left and where it isn't and why it isn't and how far they have to travel and what they will find and what will be impossible now. He watches how each thought turns the next, its argument and answer.

"They left my pack," she says at last. "It must have been those marauders. They must have circled back for us."

"Yes."

She frowns. "Why?"

He shrugs. The gesture pleases him and he repeats it. It is the perfect expression of his state; he is perched somewhere that only overlooks what happens to her, to him, things blurred and trivialized by distance. He says, "Beau would have barked."

Judy looks into the woods for a long time, as he begins to feel the cold.

"He would have barked. He would have woken us up." He looks at the soaked clothing he stepped out of, piled at his feet, and realizes it is all he has to wear now. "If you'd kept him. If you'd kept him with us."

Then Judy snatches her pack up by the straps, turns it over and lets the contents fall out over the ground. She opens every pocket, pulls out what's inside and adds it to the pile. She empties the pockets of her coat and his. And then they stand and look at everything they have.

She tells him, "I'd put aside some things to wash whenever we reached water. There are pants of yours in there. Dirty but dry. Put them on."

He obeys her and then stands shirtless before her.

She looks him over and bites her lip. Then she pulls a long-sleeved shirt from her pack. And a sweater of hers that once belonged to

Alphonse, made of some light violet wool—who knows where he got it or who made it for him. Where would a sheep have been found to shear? He takes it from her hands.

As she watches, he pulls on the sweater. It is stretched taut across his shoulders, and the sleeves reach just below his elbows, but it fits. There is an unpleasant, animal smell to the damp wool.

Dressed, he looks at her again and waits to be told what to do next.

"What's wrong with you," she asks.

He isn't sure. "I feel strange," he says at last.

She nods. "You must have caught a chill in the rain last night. Do you feel feverish?"

"I feel hot. And cold."

"We still have the medicine kit, thank god. We need to know if it's hypothermia." She digs out the thermometer and hands it to him, and then kneels over what remains of the fire. "We're going to have to get this going again and dry out your coat. We can't leave here until you're warm and in your right mind."

It takes her nearly an hour to get the soaked wood to burn without the fire nests, and she comments tonelessly that only one box of matches remains. Even without his parka, in only her shirt and sweater, he begins to warm. His temperature reads 40.6 degrees—a moderate fever, not hypothermia. He slips in and out of sleep, lets dreams overlap with the figure of Judy before him, tending the fire, putting her hand to his brow to check his temperature and then letting it rest a moment against his cheek, or maybe that, too, is a dream.

He wakes and she feeds him their last tin of stewed beans. He worries that she has kept nothing for herself. She boils snow over the fire and makes him drink it, which he does, scalding his lips and tongue. A moment later the water spills back out of his mouth, and he sees fear in her face as she whispers that it's all right, and in her arms, he feels himself lowered to the ground.

He wakes again and it is late afternoon. "I slept all day," he says, sitting up. His clothes are dry, and he realizes he is in his coat again, which is smoke-soaked and fire-warmed, the steel buttons searing-hot. His hands shake, not working as they should, as he undoes the buttons. The air feels surprisingly warm, and the fire is high and bright. Judy is, he realizes, no longer worried about being found or caught.

"Five days," she says, smiling wanly.

He presses the heels of his hands to his eyes, clearing his head of strange dreams. He remembers his last moments of consciousness. The theft.

Judy seems to read his face. "I made a list of what we still have."

"Will we—" He can't think how to end the question without some histrionic word like *survive*. "Will it be enough?"

She begins reading from the list and then stops. "Till we get there."

"So you still want to go ahead."

"We never had much, really. And now we don't have any other choice. I've torn up every scrap of wood I could to keep the fire going. I had to feed it all night long. I don't want to waste the few matches we have left. We have no rifle now. Nothing to fish with. I foraged what I could. But we're both weak."

Eban pushes himself to his feet and tries to hide from her the way his legs wobble beneath him. "Then let's gather up and leave."

"I'm not sure you're ready . . ."

He leans his weight against the papery trunk of a birch that is weaving in the light wind. The snow is all but gone from the wood, melted away while he slept. "Maybe I can't do a full day's walking. But if we leave now, I can get my legs used to working again, put in a half day before dark, and then leave at dawn tomorrow. If we do long days, we might make it by the day after tomorrow, if you're right about the markings on that stump."

She is thinking. "The day after tomorrow," she murmurs. "Much longer and it will start to get harder. We'll be slower. Weaker."

"But we can get by till then. Even without food."

"Even without food."

The slanting sunlight overhead burns his eyes, and already he feels tired. But he helps her pack up what remains of their things. She insists on carrying her pack. He protests, but when she isn't looking, he tests himself. Suspending the pack in the air, his arm shakes, and he holds tight, letting the muscles grab and release, lengthening and shortening under the strain.

Once, Eban used to work his body until his muscles shivered. He enjoyed the shaking, and the next-day cramping, because he knew they were signs he was being remade. Bettered.

He began with push-ups; only thirty or fewer at first, but he soon had a regimen of one hundred, three times daily. And then chin-ups from the lowest branch of the nearest poplar, until one day, the branch broke at the trunk.

He watched his muscles swell with something different from pride. Relief, maybe. His frame was thin, but he got ropey, tight across the back and shoulders. Strength coursed through him, wasted and in wait even as he walked across the house or took a plate from a cupboard.

One birthday, his mother gave him a set of iron barbells and plates. He loved and was perplexed by them; objects with no use but their own weight. He wondered how she had convinced a peddler to find such an obscure thing and to carry the load so far. What it had cost her. Once he scrubbed his mother's steel baking platter till it gleamed, scratching out the blackened crust that ringed it, and then leaned it against the wall outside, receiving the sun and casting back his altered image as he studied his own face and body.

There is something in that memory. Some flicker around the edge. He struggles to recall it.

His brother. He had found his brother at the door, watching him bend his arm and bring the weights toward him, in first one hand and then the other. He didn't know what his brother saw. If he watched Eban himself or his reflection.

His brother had been a runner. He had been a runner the way a fish is a swimmer. His passion was slavish, almost devout. Each run, a devotion. It was in watching his brother—seeing him quit the house in the morning before the day's first meal and return hours later, pale and sweat-soaked— that Eban came to long for strength. His brother grew leaner daily, while Eban thickened. Broadened. Gained what his brother shed.

He didn't know where his brother ran. He tried once to follow him and tired after only a few miles. They had been warned never to take even a step in the direction that his brother sprinted, half-flying over the ground, wild-limbed. It would take a person weeks to reach the cities at any pace, but there was no way to know who might be on that road.

Some days, his brother would be gone till near dark. Eban wondered if his mother knew how far he ran. If she wondered about him, as he did. What did he think of when he ran? Where did he go? Why did he do it?

Their mother told his brother she couldn't afford to feed him enough to waste himself pounding the road at all hours of the night and day. She said he was melting away before her eyes, burning up every calorie she could put on the table for him. Running like a rat on a wheel. Going nowhere. Using himself up. One night, he refused to eat the plate of boiled squash and lentils she set in front of him, sitting at the table still shining with his own sweat, his chest still heaving, his shoulders and elbows poking out of his T-shirt like a wire hanger. With a howl she hurled the plate to the floor and then turned away, leaned her face into her hands, and cried, her shoulders shaking. Eban stared at her in fear, but his brother didn't seem surprised or troubled. He cleaned up the mess she'd made and left the table. If he was hungry, he didn't complain.

After that night, she began to openly berate his brother each time he left and returned from his runs, though she never stopped him, and maybe she couldn't have. Maybe she knew that.

And in between the things she said that made no sense, the angry, senseless slurs and reproaches, she would sometimes mutter something that helped Eban understand why she hated his brother's running. The loneliness of it, the fanatic solitude, was wrong. And that wrong told a truth about him.

It was during one of his runs that Eban's brother found the man and his child.

His brother had left only a short while before, so Eban and his mother looked up in surprise when he came loping back into the yard.

"Yes?" Eban's mother said, her voice faintly irritated as it always seemed to be now when she spoke to her younger son. "What's the matter?"

"I have to get a rope," the boy said.

"What do you need a rope for?"

"Can you get it for me? A good long one. Maybe that one." He pointed to the length of dogbane twine strung from the house to a post, where they hung their clothes to dry.

"Tell me why you need a rope."

He looked surprised. "To get the man."

Eban and his mother followed him all the way to the outer edge of the foothills, where a stand of spreading trees rimmed the valley. He led them to the trapping pit Eban and his mother had dug two years before, during a hungry summer when they'd had little luck hunting. "Maybe we'll catch something big," his mother had said. She'd heard rumours that there were still bears in the foothills. They'd checked the trap every day that first summer, but never caught anything except voles and pine lizards, and once a hare that had already begun to rot in the sun. It became Eban's job to check the trap, but it was always empty and he frequently forgot.

"Down there," the boy said.

Frowning, they stepped closer, and then they saw what was at the bottom of the pit.

"No," Eban's mother whispered.

Eban's brother held out the end of the thick hemp cable she had produced from a drawer. "Will you tie this to that tree?" he asked, not seeming to notice her expression of horror as she stared into the hole.

The man must have been carrying the child when he stepped onto the lattice of fir boughs that hid the hole below. The child, who looked to have been barely old enough to walk, had been dead for several days.

The man's body half covered the child, almost protectively. His face was turned down into the mud below.

"If you tie it, I can climb down there," Eban's brother said.

"Climb down?" Eban repeated stupidly as their mother staggered back from the hole that he had helped her dig.

"To check. To see if the man is okay."

Eban pressed his hands over his eyes and then his ears. He could remember when his brother was the child's size. He didn't want to look into the hole again.

After a while, he heard his brother shuffling around the tree, grunting as he pulled the rope tight. Eban began walking away, away from the pit and from his mother. When he looked back, his brother was lowering himself down into the hole, clinging to a series of knots he'd tied to the free end.

At first Eban thought the cry came from his mother. That her guilt for the part she had played in the child and his father's deaths had produced this incoherent string of sounds. But when he went to comfort her, he found her kneeling silently on the ground, covering her face with her hands.

The sound came from the hole. Eban had to look down inside it again to understand. The man lived. Eban's brother, not yet ten years old, had dragged him from his child and was struggling to help him to his feet.

"Pull us up, Eban," he called. "Pull us up."

His brother had tried to tie bowline knots around the man's legs, but the harness was slack and even if Eban could have lifted a grown man up the sheer wall of the hole, the man didn't want to be lifted. He tugged at the knots until they released. And then he mumbled something, and looked into the eyes of the boy trying to help him.

Something seemed to give way in him then, and he allowed Eban's brother to show him where to put his hands around the rope, and slowly dragged himself to the surface, where he lay limp on the ground. Then he rolled to his side, and for a moment, Eban thought he'd throw himself into the hole again. The man kept his eyes squeezed closed, his head turning slightly back and forth as he whispered in whatever language he spoke.

Eban's mother took her hands from her face and watched him. "Oh god," she said. "I am so sorry . . . I am . . ." Her voice broke, her mouth still open but empty of words.

"Water."

Eban stirred at his brother's voice but didn't answer.

"Eban, he needs water."

His brother's face was calm and his eyes steady. He darted off into the trees, and returned carrying a crock of water and a shovel.

"Here," he said to the man, who seemed to be committed to dying on the ground beside his child's grave. But to Eban's surprise, the man jerked up and seized the water from his brother, spilling it as he gulped it down. He drank till it was gone.

"I'm sorry," Eban's brother said. "I'm sorry about your son."

The man gave no sign he understood.

"Leave him be," Eban's mother said sharply. "Leave that man be."

But her son ignored her. "I brought a shovel," he said.

The man didn't budge, but sat in silence as Eban's brother dug a second, smaller hole beside the one where the child lay. And when the pile of freshly displaced dirt reached his waist, he offered the shovel to the man.

"No . . ." cried Eban's mother.

The man stared at Eban's brother for a long time, and then took the shovel in his own hands, looked at it, and filled the blade with dirt. He whispered some words to himself, closed his eyes, and let the dirt fall. He emptied the shovel three more times and then handed it to Eban's brother.

The boy accepted it and filled the pit with what remained of the over-turned soil.

Eban's mother had found her feet by then. "Please," she said softly. "Forgive me. I never imagined . . ."

The man didn't meet her eyes. He squeezed her young son's shoulder one last time, and then limped away.

They watched him disappear between the trees, heading back up into the foothills. Eban wiped his eyes. His mother looked, in that moment, like someone lost.

Then she turned to Eban's brother.

"You should have left him there," she said. "He would have suffered less if he had died with his child."

His brother looked from her to Eban. "Why are you crying, Eban?" he asked. "If I'd left him there, he wouldn't have been able to get out. There was no water or food down there."

Their mother stared at him. She began to answer and then stopped.

No one spoke as they walked together back to the house. Eban's mother returned the rope to the drawer and the shovel to its hook. Then Eban saw her step toward the open door. Outside, his brother could be seen far down the outland road, where he'd begun to run again.

Eban and his mother watched him grow smaller and smaller in the distance, until they couldn't see him anymore.

He realizes Judy is standing beside him, and for a brief moment, she lets her hand rest on his shoulder. As if she knows what he is thinking. Then she lifts the pack onto her back and says, "Let's go."

He's ashamed that she is carrying the weight for them both, but also relieved. Each step he takes tires him further. He wonders, and then worries, how far he will be able to travel without rest, as he trudges on.

As the sun sinks into the valley, a weariness settles into Eban. He knows he is moving too slowly, that Judy is fighting impatience at their meagre progress. But he finds himself helpless to do better. Tomorrow, he tells himself. He will wake rested with his muscles strengthened by a half day's use. He'll do better.

Judy walks slightly ahead of him, stops to wait. He tries to guess at her thoughts. It will bother her that they have no other plan. No alternative if she is wrong, if they are still weeks or more away from Heaven.

When they knew she was pregnant for the first time, Judy belonged more completely to him than ever before or since. "Tell me now," she would whisper at night as they lay in the dark. "What is it doing now?" And he'd describe the way two cells became a human being, the pictures he remembered from his mother's books.

"Will you help me?" she asked once as he sat mending some tool or another. "You know things we'll need to teach him. Her. You had a brother. You know what a child needs."

"I don't know anything like that," he said, and then saw he'd upset her. "I mean, I don't know anything that you don't know. I think it's the kind of thing we'll figure out together."

That pleased her; he could see it did.

And then the day came when he had to tell her it was gone. He woke to find her rocking slightly in the bed beside him.

"What is it," he asked, still drowsy.

"Nothing," she answered, and he heard in her voice that she was afraid.

He found her with her knees drawn to her chest, a blanket wound between her legs to staunch the bleeding.

"It's okay," she said.

"How long?"

It had been all day. All day she'd hidden it from him. She didn't know what it meant except that there was some unhappiness ahead for her or for their child. She hadn't wanted him to know.

"Something's wrong with him, isn't it?" she asked him. "With her?"

He opened his mouth and made no answer.

"Can you fix it?" she asked.

He shook his head.

Judy lowered her face. "But will she be born? Will I hold her? Will I see what she looks like?"

He tried to shake his head again and couldn't. He let one hand fall over her hair, and they sat like that.

"Does it hurt?" he asked after a while.

"No." But he watched her go on rocking herself from side to side until the blood flow slowed, and then she slept while he took the soaked blanket to the dump and burned it there.

Eban reads Judy's shoulders as she walks ahead, the angle of her elbows, the rise and fall of her pack with each step. Judy has a fixed idea of the person she wants to be, and what that person should want or feel, and that vanity guides and confuses everything she does. Now she will want to be someone who doesn't hesitate or delay once her mind is made up. Who is undefeated by hunger or exhaustion. But she will also want to be someone who is compassionate. She'll wait till dark and then propose they stop. She'll urge it, reminding him of his illness. She'll set her mouth and say it will be fine. Then, once he has settled, she'll suggest that she just run ahead and see what's up the path. She'll promise to be only a short time, and then return hours later. He will pretend he wasn't frightened all the time she was gone.

He is thinking this when she turns around, so suddenly he nearly stumbles into her arms. "We've gone far enough," she says. "Let's stop here."

He watches as she lowers her pack and digs into its contents. Maybe, he thinks, he was duped by her bravado. Maybe she, too, fears what they will find.

Without tents or tarps or snow to build a shelter, and without tools to find food or build a fire to cook it, there is nothing to do but sit beside each other on the ground. After a few minutes, Judy leaps to her feet and murmurs that she might be able to forage something, that she should look while there's light.

But less than an hour later, she returns.

He's leaning against a tree, his knees drawn up. "Did you—"

"Nothing," she says.

He holds up the book in his hands. "I borrowed it."

She nods.

He hadn't wanted to read. He wanted to draw. He thought of the charcoals and paper left behind at the camp, as if longing for another human being. And then he dug out his favourite of Judy's books, which he loves for the lavishness of its art. The illustrations are in deep, rich colours. Some are edged in gold.

"Read it out loud," she says.

He hadn't been reading, only tracing the brushstrokes of the illustrations with his finger. "I'll start at the beginning," he says, letting the weight of the pages collapse onto the back cover, and turning over the first page. He begins.

It's a story about how things used to be. In the story, a family lives in a city. The youngest daughter climbs out onto the roof every night, when her family think she's asleep. Another family live in the other side of the house, and their only child, a son, meets her there. From the roof, they can look out over the sea of houses around them, and see lights shining from taller buildings, far in the distance. Eban lingers for a moment on the page that shows what the boy and girl can see from their roof.

"It's beautiful," he whispers.

Judy leans forward. "What did you say?"

He shakes his head, but she puts her hand on his.

"I want our baby to grow up somewhere like that," she says. "With people all around."

"But Judy . . . It isn't like that now. Not like in your books."

His mother never told him much about the world before, only that they hadn't understood the threat to it in time.

"We didn't know what those other ones were at first, not for years. And then there were more and more of them. Fewer and fewer of us. And they didn't look any different from anybody else. But they were monsters." They were sitting in the dirt outside their house. She was cross-legged before the solar cooker, rendering tallow, and the stink of it made him sick. The flies couldn't be shaken or swatted away.

"Can I catch it?" he asked.

She shook her head and said it was a deficiency at birth, something missing from those babies, like an ear, but invisible.

"Then I don't have it?" he asked, electric with relief. She looked at him for so long that the relief turned cold. Then she shook her head and said he'd passed every test she gave him.

He knew from the way she said it that something was wrong. She stood and folded her arms over her chest, looking into the distance.

He followed her gaze and saw his brother in the yard, back from running, his shirt drenched and his chest heaving as he gasped for air. And then Eban understood. The sweaty, fetid odour of animal fat hung over them, suffusing even the memory now.

He finishes reading the story, while Judy kneels before him, her head bowed forward. When he closes the book, she stays like that, unmoving.

"Judy?" he says softly.

She doesn't answer.

"Judy, do you still feel the baby?"

Her hand creeps to her belly, slipping under her coat. "I feel it all the time," she whispers.

"Can I feel it?" he asks.

She undoes her coat and peels her sweater up over her stomach. Her belly looks, to him, as flat as always, but he removes his glove and lays his hand on it. Feels nothing.

They sleep, and he wakes only once. He thinks he hears something creeping near in the wood, and reaches for his rifle, but he has none. He calls out and hears nothing answer. Not even Judy stirs. After falling back asleep, he dreams of a face, watching him from those trees. The dark eyes of a woman his mother's age, lines at the ends of her mouth. Her hair, in the low light of the moon, is a silvery gold. She disappears with the dream.

In the morning, they set out again. He can think of nothing but his hunger. Once when he was young, a starved man came to their door. His mother allowed him in because it was clear he had so little time left. He threw up the food they offered him, and his feet were blackened with filth and bled steadily, his blood too thin to clot. Eban asked him why he had no shoes and the man replied that he had eaten them. Since then he had vomited many times and not relieved himself at all, and there had been no sign of that shoe leather, so it must have remained within his body, even as he died, fighting to digest it.

"Judy," he calls. "Are you hungry?"

She stops abruptly, as if annoyed by the question. But she says only, "Look."

Just ahead, the forest dwindles to a sea of blackened spears. There's no ash or smell of smoke in the air, and at the roots of the trees, moss and low scrub have already sprung out of the scorched soil. Whatever happened, happened some time ago. Maybe years.

"They're all dead," she whispers. "For miles and miles."

"Burned."

"Wildfire?"

He runs his hand over one of the charred trunks and then gazes down the line of trees. "Look how this trunk is burned on both sides, like it was surrounded by fire. But the outer edge of a wildfire, spread by wind, would burn the side the fire started from. This burned so evenly. And look." He points to the tree behind it, its upper branches still green with needles. "Scarcely burned at all. Look how square the border is, between trees burned and not burned."

"You think someone did this on purpose?"

"They contained it somehow. They wanted only these ones burned. This stand of trees."

"But it's endless. I can't see green trees in any direction except the one we came from. How many people, how much water would it take to do this?"

"I would rather know why."

They walk more slowly now, looking about them in silence. Laid bare like this, everything revealed, the forest seems darker and more threatening somehow. No creature could hide or hunt in this burned forest—and yet Eban has never felt more sure they are being watched. Every step feels like a performance for invisible eyes.

They eventually pass out of the burned forest into a blackened plain stippled with the stumps of felled trees.

"This happened more recently," Eban says.

They pass human debris; a cartwheel, bent and black. The melted waxen smudge of something plastic, coiled in rusted wiring. Wrapped around one of the stumps, like a marker, is a red scarf, untouched by fire. Judy unties it and slips it around her neck without a word. They walk on.

The sun is dropping, making long shadows of even the shortest stumps, when they find the bones.

First a rib cage. Judy gasps, pointing. "From the fire," she whispers. He shakes his head. "No."

"Where is the rest of the body? The skeleton, I mean?"

"Yeah. I wonder." He continues walking, but she lingers behind him.

"It's so small," she says.

"Yeah."

"A child."

"Maybe." He knows without looking that she'll have put her hand to her stomach.

They find a femur, several jawbones, a skull. Broken bones he can't identify. In one place, a pile higher than his waist, some animal, most human.

"I'm frightened," she tells him.

"I think we're meant to be." It's as clear as if the bodies had been hanged from a post, marked with an *x*. It is a message from the people who burned or killed or fed here. Or maybe did none of these things, but wished them to believe it.

Judy has gone farther ahead than he realized when she calls out to him. He hurries after the sound of her voice, stumbling in the near dark.

She stands at the edge of a forest of trees untouched by fire. As he watches, she walks into it, disappearing inside. He has to run to catch up.

After the day's travel across a scorched warning of a landscape, the green, needled trees feel secretive. Too deliberate an obfuscation, the wood swallows them totally.

Hunger drives them on. And fear and even, Eban knows, some other instinct, something they shouldn't trust. A perverse curiosity that wants to solve the mystery of this wood. Through the dark, they stagger forward, their hands before them, groping at branches and tree trunks to sure their steps. The moon has risen to the centre of the sky when they see it.

In wonder, Judy whispers, "We're here."

VIII

FOR A LONG TIME, they stand without moving.

If only they'd stopped for the night sooner. He'd feared to rest in the burned wood, so clearly within the territory of another. But now, it is too dark to make sense of the place where they've arrived. And sleep is out of the question.

"It's true," is the first thing he says. "It all was true." Even at his most credulous, he imagined that whatever they would find at the end of their travel would reveal a wild lie at the heart of all the rumours. But here it is before them. A city in the wood.

She doesn't answer. Taking a few steps forward, she touches the wall of the first house with her hand and then looks back at him. Something in him comes undone at the sight of her face then. What she feels now, he knows, is the furthest possible thing from the fear that has seized every nerve in his body.

"I thought someone would meet us," she says. "They must have known we were coming."

She stumbles between the first two houses, following the path deeper till the spill of moonlight through the trees no longer illuminates her, and he gasps at her boldness. She is closer now to them than to him. He has no choice. He follows her.

Eleven houses stand in a circle around a stone well. Like her, he turns around and around, as if it all will vanish or alter if he looks away. Wonderstruck. What place is this?

The houses are built of hewn timbers, straight and solid. Roofs of tin or some other metal. Windows of glass.

"What tools do they have?" he asks softly. "What way did they bring all this here?"

A stone chimney erupts from each gleaming roof. But he sees no smoke.

"Are they hiding?" she asks.

Before he can stop her, she has run to the door of the first house, knocking against it with her fist. "Hello," she calls, and then she knocks at the next door, and the next. "We're hungry and have no food." She stands back and waits for the doors to open. More softly, she says, "We've come a long way to find you."

Eban backs away, turning in circles again as he watches the doors of the houses for any sign of movement. But there is nothing, none. Wind passes through the trees that surround the tiny village, sifting moon-light through their branches. "Come away," he says urgently. "Come away from the doors."

Judy looks up at him, an expression of confusion on her face. Then she steps toward the well and draws her hand across the opening. "Cobwebs," she whispers, shaking them from her hand. She snatches a stone from the ground and drops it inside. A moment later, they hear it rap against the dry bottom of the well. "This hasn't been used. Not for . . ." She stands again and crosses to the fourth house.

"Judy—" But already she has turned the knob and, to his astonishment, the door swings open, as easily as if she were invited inside. He hurries to join her, his heart calamitous in his chest. "Judy, stop."

He stands behind her, trying to make sense of what he sees. Blue light puddles on the floor in the shapes of windowpanes. He can make out the dim forms of tables, chairs, a bed.

"Eban . . ." She is already pulling away from him.

"Don't go any farther." He puts his hand over his face, thinking. "We'll use the matches."

"But they're the only—"

"We can't sleep till we know, and we can't go stumbling into these shadows. It's too dangerous. Give me twenty minutes."

She hesitates.

"Please, Judy."

To his surprise, she follows him out of the house. "I'll get the matches," she says.

He gathers up sheets of birchbark and two green switches from the surrounding trees, and then he tears the hem out of his shirt with his teeth. He makes two small, sticky balls of pine sap and wraps them in layer after layer of bark, binding a cone of birch and sap to each switch with the strip of fabric. When he's finished, he hands the torches to Judy and she lights them. They catch quickly and he warns her that though birch burns slowly and the sap will sustain the flame for a time, the bark is dry and its fire won't last long.

She nods. "I'll start with this house. You take the one next door. If you hear or see anything, call out, and I'll find you." Without waiting for his answer, she disappears inside the house. The door floats closed behind her.

"Be quick," he calls and enters the fifth house.

He pauses, despite his warning to Judy, to stare at the doorknob in his hand. Iron. Rusted, but well-crafted. And some smith has notched a design of radiating lines in the plate against the door. For no purpose. Who are these people?

A bead of sap flares in the fire, sending up a sudden bright flame, and he briefly beholds the entire interior. Then the light gutters, and it takes his eyes a moment to adjust again. Putting his other hand to the wall to guide him around the space, he raises the dim, fluttering fire to each surface, in turn, to examine it.

But the momentary glimpse of the illuminated room remains in his mind, radiant and incomprehensible. They are the grandest living quarters he has ever seen. Better even than those Judy described living in with her fathers. He feels his way along the arm of a chair, the posts of a two-level bed. Everywhere are marks of some extravagant, earlier time. A rug of dozens of colours, woven into a winding, wild design. Curtains of delicate white cotton, gathered along the upper frame of every window. The beds are made, draped in heavy, stuffed blankets.

Everything in the room frightens him.

Where did they go, the people who built this house? What could have made anyone leave such a place?

Then his breath stops.

In the wavering light of the torch, he glimpses a face on the far side of the room.

"Judy!" he cries, but there is no answer.

Where did the person come from, where did he hide, and what does he want? Eban approaches him. He stops before a low cabinet of polished wood. A face looks out from the wall above it. His own.

His hand shakes as he takes the mirror from the wall. The glass is mottled with blue-black streaks, and a rim of dust has collected in the curves of the frame around it. Open-mouthed, he stares into its discoloured surface. It is the first time he has seen his own face in eight years.

He pulls the torch closer till his cheek complains of its heat, but he can neither return the mirror nor lower the flame. He had forgotten that his white face is as freckled as Judy's. Months without sun, and yet its marks are all over him, blurring the contour of his full, colourless lips, clustering into gold shadows along his cheekbones and the bridge of his nose. His red-gold hair falls below his chin, and is so dirty that when he passes his hand through, it stays where he has smoothed it. He had forgotten how pale his grey eyes are. Full of fog and hesitation. Looking into them frightens him somehow. He does not know anything of the person they contain.

"Eban."

Even at the sound of her voice, he doesn't want to stop looking. He doesn't trust what he sees, as if there might yet be something in the mirror he hasn't understood.

"Eban."

At last, he lowers the mirror to his side and answers.

"What do you have there?"

He drops the mirror onto the cabinet so hard it clatters, and he fears he may have broken it. "Nothing. Did you find anything?"

"Nothing. No one. No food. No water. Did you already go through the cupboards here?"

He turns to the counter by the window and looks at the drawers and cupboards it contains. He hadn't even thought of it.

"I don't think they left suddenly. Everything is in its place. And I think," she says, pulling open each empty drawer and cupboard door, "they took whatever food or supplies mattered with them."

"How long ago do you think they left?"

"We can tell better after dawn. But there's dust on everything. Nothing has been touched, not for months. Maybe years."

"The things they have. Had. How did they get them here? Or make them?"

"Why did they leave?" She stands looking at him, and he thinks about the face she sees. How she has looked at it all these years. "I'm so tired, Eban. I can hardly feel my pulse."

"We need water," he murmurs. The light of her torch flags then and extinguishes. She curses, and he finds her hand by the remaining light of his own. "Sleep in here," he tells her. "I'll keep watch."

Nodding, she kneels to the ground and curls up there, silently. In her compliance he sees, all at once, how bad their situation is.

With a tenderness he would keep from his voice if she were well, he says, "Not there. Not there, Judy. Let me help you." With his arm around her, he guides her to the bed, peeling back the heavy blankets.

Now she hesitates.

"There's no greater risk in sleeping in the bed."

She bends over to undo her shoes, and he tries to stop her, but she insists, swatting his hands away. "I don't want . . ."

"What is it?"

"I don't want to ruin that beautiful bed."

He watches her for a moment, her fingers clumsy as they undo her boots and pull them from her filthy socked feet. "Then let's get you undressed." She lifts her arms, and he peels her clothes from her, layer by layer. Then she slides into the clean white sheets of the bed, and lays her cheek on the pillow.

He lingers too long, watching her, as she slips into sleep. And then, suddenly, he is in darkness. He drops his torch to the floor and goes outside to make another.

He makes four more torches and then sits on the steps outside the door, a lit torch plunged into the ground beside him. He watches the moon cross the sky above him and then sink below the trees. And without meaning to, he sleeps.

———

At dawn, he wakes out of some kind of dream. He can't recall anything but the sense of having been elsewhere. Ashamed of his carelessness, he pulls open the door behind him, but to his relief, Judy is still asleep in the bed.

His hands shake and a headache has been scissoring his brain since yesterday. He knows they need to find water today, and he sets out to explore the camp. If there is water anywhere, he will find it.

He searches the other houses but finds them just as the first—beautifully furnished, bare cupboards and empty drawers. Dust and cobwebs sealed over everything like a skin.

Venturing back into the trees, he looks for any sign of a spring, a river, a second well. As the tiny village recedes behind him, he is swallowed up in darkness again, and only by the last flickering light of his torch does he recognize a building, emerging between the trees, so close that, with a few more steps, he might have collided with the wall. It is another house, this one built of stone, its windows painted black.

He calls out, but there is no answer. He wonders if he should have waited for Judy. He feels sure something is inside this building. Something important. He turns the brass doorknob, expecting it will be locked, but the latch clicks and the door swings open.

Inside he stumbles forward like a blind man, reaching into the shadows, groping for whatever walls or furniture might be in his path. At the centre of the room, he finds a wooden desk with two drawers and a stool.

He can't shed the feeling that he has backed himself into a cage. Facing the door, which creaks and flaps in the light wind, he opens the upper drawer of the desk. His hand, holding the torch, shakes, but not from hunger.

Inside the drawer is a stack of papers. He raises the top page into the torchlight. And then the next page and the next. Each is the same, a perfect replica of the first. Far off, he can hear a bird singing to the new day.

He recognizes every picture on the page.

It was years after the first test that his mother called him and his brother to the kitchen. It was a summer morning. He remembers that he'd been eager to go outside, could see the yellow grass of August waving in the wind, knew everything beyond the door was moving and busy and full of games to play and things to do, and here he was inside, silently watching his mother lay a piece of paper before him and another before his brother.

On the paper were simple line drawings of faces. It was not possible to tell if the faces belonged to men or women. If they were young or old. They were minimal, a handful of lines to suggest a smile, a frown, eyes wide with terror. Each face was slightly different, but only slightly. He looked from the drawings to his mother.

"Write there," she said, handing each of them a pencil. "On the lines beside each face. Tell me what they feel."

He looked, confused, at the crude drawings. How could he know what they felt. They were only drawings, not people. He turned to his brother, but he was absorbed in the page, bent over it, his brow stitched together in concentration.

The mouth of the first face was turned up at the corners. A smile. He looked to his mother again for guidance, but she had turned her back to him. *HAPPY*, he wrote hesitantly.

The next face had wide eyes and raised eyebrows. The mouth was open. It was frightened, he thought, all at once understanding the game. *AFRAID*.

The others came more quickly. *ANGRY. CONFUSED.* One gave him trouble—*WORRIED*, he wrote and then crossed it out. *THOUGHTFUL*.

Just as he finished the last word, his mother snatched the page out of his hand and looked at it. Then she took the one from his brother. He made a little cry but said nothing as she pulled it from him. She looked from one to the other, and Eban waited. Then she folded them up, several times over, and slipped them into a pocket in her apron. He looked at her face. Her eyes, not looking at him or his brother, but not at anything else either. The line of her mouth. WORRIED, he thought, but wasn't sure. ANGRY? RELIEVED? He didn't know. He didn't know.

"Go outside," she ordered, and both boys went quickly.

"What did you write?" he asked his brother when the door had closed behind them.

The boy's eyes were wide. "I don't know," he said.

"Did you write something wrong?"

His brother tilted his head to the side, as he often did when he was thinking. "Yeah," he said. "Might have written something wrong."

"You don't remember what words you wrote next to the pictures?"

His brother shrugged. "Your name."

"My name?"

"I thought maybe one of them was a picture of you. His hair stuck up like yours. On top."

Eban remembered, vaguely, that the wide-eyed face he'd marked AFRAID had a few vertical lines of hair. "It didn't look like me. Not even a little."

The boy shrugged again. "I thought maybe it wasn't the right thing. I did numbers on the other ones."

"Numbers?"

"I wrote down the runs I did and all the weights you lifted this week. I did how many times you lifted up the weights and how much weight that was. And how far I went and how many times, and how much faster than the time before."

Eban frowned. "Why?"

"She wanted us to write things down."

"But nothing about the pictures?"

"I didn't really like them."

"But you were supposed to write what they were feeling. The people in the pictures?"

"How can I know that, Eban? How would I know?"

Eban didn't answer. Through the window, he could see his mother's back. She stood unmoved from the spot where they'd left her, her hand still resting in the pocket where the drawings had gone.

In his hand, now, he holds another copy of the same drawings. He flips through the stack of pages. It includes several copies of a second test, and that, too, he recognizes. And one completed copy of the first. He reads the words the test-taker chose. Different from whatever he wrote as a child. *Grateful. Pensive. Disappointed. Hungry.*

He throws the drawings to the ground.

He understands nothing. Not this place. Not what happened to his brother. Not what he and Judy have done, whether there was any point to their stupidity or if they would have been any better, any safer, if they had stayed forever where they were. His head roaring, he seizes the stool and flings it against one of the blacked-out windows. And then he freezes.

Lit by the rising sun through the broken window, the room looks different. Now he can see something he couldn't before. A line in the floorboards. A narrow crack that traces a square on the ground.

A door.

Dropping to his knees, he runs his hand along the crack, searching for a hinge.

Perspiration stings his eyes as he scratches at the floor, until his fingernails slide into a notched edge and he pulls. With an ease that astonishes him, the door lifts.

It opens to a hole and a ladder rising out of the dark. Before he can stop himself, he reaches his hand inside, but hits a grate of some sort. A filthy, rusted grate.

And then a face appears behind it, and he understands.

A cage, he thinks or whispers. A jail beneath the floor.

The second thought arrives, almost simultaneous with the first. She is contained there, captive while he is free. He is safe.

But he is wrong.

IX

"THERE IS SOMEONE HERE."

The words slide into her dream, a dream that she is warm. A child again. Safe. At home.

"Eban?" She opens her eyes and sees nonsense. His face—no nonsense there, only an anxious, tight expression on his anxious, pale face that is more same than strange—surrounded by a nonsense room. Sunlit, beautiful. Herself, enveloped in white, nonsense sheets, and heavy blankets. Her head cradled in a nonsense pillow stuffed with nonsense feathers of nonsense birds.

"You have to get up."

"Did you say—"

"There's someone here. I saw her."

Judy remembers, all at once, and shoves back the beautiful blankets, throws herself out of the bed and dresses as quickly as she can. "Where? Did you talk to her? Is she the only one?"

He has turned away while she pulls on her clothes, like he means to respect her modesty. He has always done this when she dresses and it has always irritated her.

Fastening her coat, she asks again. "Where?"

"There's another house. Set back in the wood." He pulls the blankets over the pillows and smooths out the wrinkles.

"Leave it, Eban. We have to hurry, in case she hides again or runs."

He stares at her. "*We* have to run. We have to go—leave this place."

"Because we found someone? Because after all these days and miles, looking for someone who can answer our questions, finally we found them?"

He shakes his head. "You don't understand. There's something very wrong. She wasn't in the house, she was *under* it."

"Under it?"

"Someone had locked her there. It was a cage."

She hesitates. But it's the reason that they came here. If safe was all that mattered, what they had would have been enough, and it wasn't. She is about to tell him she is going whether he comes along or not, but his expression shifts, watching her.

"Yeah," he says bitterly. "I know."

For a moment, she recalls Eban as she first saw him, crouched in the woods, watching the tent where her father waited for her to return. She caught him there and was proud of herself. She thought she'd caught a man, maybe even someone dangerous. But then he turned and he had a boy's wide eyes. Eyes with the trick of making you think they saw you more completely than anyone else. And he would have walked away and left her and Alphonse there, but she called out to him. In the years since that day, he has repeatedly asked her to stay. But she doesn't think he remembers she was the one who first called him back to her.

She doesn't coax now, or even invite him. She never wanted the responsibility of making decisions for him, but he is always giving it to her. Shoving himself into her hands. She is at the door before she realizes she needs him to show her. "Where—" she begins.

But he is right behind her. "Follow me."

The windows are painted black. A threat, she thinks. Why hide what's inside?

Or what's outside?

The door is unbolted but closed and she needs to open it. She doesn't know if there will be anyone waiting inside or what they'll want or do. She longs to be brave, but isn't. Not just now. She has to put her hand on the doorknob before she can hesitate to turn it. She has to open the door before Eban can see her think about leaving it closed.

Only a single, broken window admits light to the dark, bare room. Unlike the other houses—impossibly abundant, crowded with beauty and things—it's empty but for a single desk and stool.

"There," says Eban, pointing at the floor.

She finds the outline of the door between the floorboards and slips her fingers underneath. Drawing her breath in, she throws back the door and stares into the dark hole it reveals.

"Hello?"

Nothing emerges from the darkness.

"We have to get out of here," Eban whispers from behind her, where he kneels on the ground. "If she got out, someone let her out . . ."

"Hello?" She can make out a grid of rusted steel and what looks like the top rung of a ladder beneath it. How deep into the ground might it lead? Could the girl be hiding there?

"Judy, please!"

"Maybe you scared her," she says, almost to herself. "How old did you say she was? Maybe she is down there, frightened."

"Let's go back," Eban urges. "We can check the other houses. Maybe there are other buildings like this, tucked deeper in the wood."

"I'm coming down!" she calls softly into the hole, as she slips her fingers into the grate and lifts it out.

"Judy!"

"If you're down there, there's nothing to be afraid of. We only want to talk to you." She swings her legs around and drops one foot onto the ladder below.

"Judy, plea—"

Eban suddenly falls quiet as she descends the ladder. She is several rungs down when, despite herself, she wonders at his silence and glances up at him through the hole.

He stares back miserably, his eyes wide, as the woman behind him lowers her rifle and drags him to his feet.

At the bottom of the hole, they find a small room. Feeling with their hands against the dirt floor and walls, they learn its limits. They find a stinking tin bucket in the corner. They find a bed, not big enough for two, with a thin woollen blanket folded over top. The bed creaks when they sit at its edge.

They have no water and no food. She can't count how many days they have been without either.

Her pack, with their few remaining belongings, was left at the fourth house. No longer theirs, then.

The woman who led them down the ladder at the point of her rifle didn't speak a word. They don't know if there are any others. They don't know how long she means to keep them here, or why.

Beside Judy, Eban's head keeps dropping to his chest, and then he startles awake. "How long?" he asks her each time. "How long have we been here?"

"I don't know."

The third time he asks, he crawls to the bucket and retches into it before she can answer. The stench of bile fills the room.

"The French had a word for an underground prison like this," she says, as he retches again. "A little dungeon like this, hidden away beneath. *Oubliette*, that's what they called it." She remembers her father Alphonse telling her. He liked to frighten her when she was small. She liked it as well. She'd ask about the most awful things she could think of. Of prisoners from his stories and their horrible deaths. Buried alive, stretched from limb to limb until their bodies shattered or they confessed. "From the word *oublier*. To forget."

Once he lifts his head so suddenly he startles her, his eyes wide and anxious. "Where is he?" he asks her.

"Who? Who?"

He looks at her like he doesn't completely trust her, his eyes sleep-vague and not his own. He is peering out at her from within his parched dreams.

"Who, Eban?"

"My brother," he murmurs as his head drops again.

It makes her nervous that he sleeps. Already, waiting in the dark like this is unfastening her mind. She thinks of the blind son of a peddler who once visited her house by the allotment. His eyes were clear and he would turn his face towards whoever spoke to him. He moved with grace, and except for the vague misplacement of his gaze—never quite meeting her eyes or anyone's—you might not have known he lived in darkness. But here, in this still, silent dark, it is hard to tell when they sleep and when they wake. And whether this hole is a prison or a grave.

And so she talks.

After a time has passed—impossible to count what number of hours or days might contain it—he stops waking. Instead, his sleep is interrupted by fits of convulsion or of long, rasping gasps for air. He pisses himself, and she removes the soiled clothing and wraps him in the blanket. It is the last drop of fluid his body spares—after that, nothing more is produced when he retches, and his fever-hot skin is dry as a bone. Her brain aches like it is being devoured inside her skull, and she is losing the battle for consciousness. Each time she finds she has nodded off, she shakes him as hard as she can; it's easier than checking his pulse or breathing, which are now scarcely detectable. Once she tried and failed to find his pulse and felt her own heart burst apart, when suddenly he shifted in the bed.

To keep herself awake, she circles the room, over and over, first feeling her way across the walls, with her arms raised above her head to touch the earthen ceiling, and then on her hands and knees. She finds that in one corner of the room the dirt floor is damp—maybe some vein of water passes nearby.

"Eban," she says, peeling the name from her dry throat. She drags him from the bed. Miracle, he stirs. He crawls with her across the floor, and when she tells him to, he puts his mouth to the ground and tongues at whatever moisture he can suck from the dirt. Then she leads him back to bed and lets him sleep again. Puts her own mouth to the mud.

She wakes with her cheek to the cold ground, her mouth and throat thickened with dirt.

She dreamed of her child.

For weeks the child has moved in her. First, a dreamlike flutter, scarcely detectable. Then, the child—a girl, she has long known with certainty, a girl—became her own. A life within Judy but belonging entirely to itself. She felt the girl's autonomy, her insistent exploration of her host, her moods. When she slept and when she woke. Judy wondered if her child returned the love she now felt deepening in her. Maybe to her child Judy was only the walls around her, her containment. An *oubliette*.

But she hasn't felt her child since they entered the hole. Not the flickering movements of earlier in her pregnancy. Not the insolence of more recent weeks, the thrusting feet and elbows—her child's brazen claim of territory.

In the dark, she is consumed by the black, clamorous question of her daughter's stillness.

She doesn't know how far along she is in her pregnancy—she has never been able to tell, because her bleeding has never been regular. It is useless to count weeks or cycles of the moon.

Her menstruation, and everything it augured, made her fathers uncomfortable, and embarrassed of their discomfort. The morning she woke, as a child, to find a deep red stain on the bedsheets, she cried silently until her fathers found her, lying stiffly under the covers, afraid to move. And then they were furious with themselves for not having told her sooner.

But still they didn't explain enough, even then. So that when, the night after her father died, she lay down in Eban's bed and took off her clothes for the first time, only he knew what to do. She let him show her, and she was, at first, miserable with shame for her ignorance. It was not her nature ever to hesitate or yield, but under his weight, limbs threaded with his, she hesitated and she yielded.

Naked and unsure and then certain, they were together, and when they stopped and it was over, she went on feeling like it hadn't been him showing her but something they had found out on their own, here in the middle of nothing, at the farthest edge of nowhere, like they had lit something in the dark.

But it troubled her.

And when, weeks later, Eban asked in the gentle, careful way he always spoke to her if she had bled that month, she felt her skin burn as she told him no and waited to know what it meant. When he told her a baby grew inside her, she was astonished. And then she began to worry.

———

When the door opens, Judy is asleep. Restless between dreams of food, of feasting on lavish meals at beautiful tables, of stuffing her mouth with fistfuls of dirt, she hears the wooden door slam to the ground and then the scrape of metal as the grate is removed.

She crawls to the ladder and stares up, squinting at the dim, square light above. The word *hello?* catches in her throat and she doubles over in a fit of coughing.

When she looks up again, a box is being lowered through the hole on a length of rope. When she has unfastened it, her fingers clumsy on the knots, an invisible agent above snatches the rope back to the surface. A moment later the rope returns, tied to a bucket. Having failed to undo the string around the box, Judy seizes the bucket, but finds it empty. Confused, she unties it and waits for the rope to be drawn back up but it doesn't budge. She looks at the rope and up into the hole in wonder, and then understands.

The bucket in the corner is only half-full, because there is nothing left in their bodies to be expelled. She collects it and ties it to the rope, and watches it rise to the top of the ladder, and then two hands appear to take it away. And then the grate is set in place and the door closed, and she is in darkness again.

"NO," she manages at last to say. "No, no . . ." She listens and waits. "Please," she says. "Come back," she says. She whispers the words that sing in her mind down in this dark, spinning around and around and around her starving brain. "We are dying . . ."

But there is no more sound or glimpse of light or movement above. Fighting a wave of nausea, which she knows will end in unconsciousness if she surrenders to it, she pulls the box across the ground to her lap.

She can smell food.

Is it only her dying mind, playing the same games with her stomach it does in her dreams? Is it real? Is there a box, even, and were those hands above, was there light?

She shakes the thoughts away, and bends her head over the box, gnawing at the string that binds it, pulling at it with her fingers till she feels them bleed. It breaks at last and she pulls open the lid. Inside is a heavy steel jar.

The top of the jar is blocked by a stopper her fingers can make no sense of. "No," she whispers to herself, "no, no, no . . ." as she fumbles till it opens. She lifts it to her mouth.

Water.

"Eban!" she hisses. "Eban!"

She cannot make him stir anymore, but he breathes, faintly. She raises his head and brings the jar to his lips. After a moment, he coughs, water spilling from his parched mouth, and when he has cleared the fluid from his lungs, she feels him straining in her arms to reach for the jar again. She lets him drink only a little, and then makes him wait before she gives him more.

"Slowly," she says.

"Please . . ."

And she gives him more.

When he has drunk his fill, she forces herself to finish what remains as slowly as she can, and to save a little. For later, and however long it will have to sustain them.

Then she returns to the box and lifts out a lidded pot filled with some kind of stew. She nearly weeps.

"Eban . . ."

This time he responds. She hears him shift in the bed, and she finds two spoons in the box, as well as a loaf of hard bread, and she brings it all to him. They eat together. And when they are finished, they sleep.

With her first pregnancy, Judy was scarcely ill at all. Only once, her stomach turned, at the sight of Eban dressing a kill. But for that, there was no outward sign that she carried a child. Only Eban, and his certainty. Eban who knew the right thing to do, always, as he would know the right thing to do with this baby, and would tell her. Eban who knew everything about his body and hers, and who swore the baby lived.

He answered each of her questions, and she listened with a humility that felt unfamiliar but not unwelcome. "My fathers didn't like to speak of these things," she told him stiffly, and he nodded, as if afraid to say anything that might cause further injury to her pride.

He said that in the months to come, she would feel the baby move. That hands and feet would paddle in the deep pink dark within her. And she trusted him. And waited.

In those first weeks, she found she liked to imagine life swimming like a fish in the sea of her interior. She wondered if the child would have Eban's patience or her determination or his grey eyes or her black hair. She thought the child might drive out the loneliness that sometimes came over her. She dreamed of sharing her books with a son or daughter, answering the child's questions as her fathers had answered hers.

But she was frightened too. When she felt most uneasy, she tried to call up in her mind a vision of her healthy, growing child, to foresee the life that would be his or hers. And there her imagination began to fail.

She would imagine reading to the child, and then, all at once, she would imagine reaching the end of her few books. She would think of the books left in the outland, too heavy to carry, and then of all the others her fathers had spoken of or recounted in the dark until she slept, books she would never read and neither would her child.

She would imagine answering the child's questions as her fathers had answered hers, but then she would remember how even her fathers' memories of the time before were already threadbare. And how would she answer questions of a world she herself had never known?

And she saw that Eban was the only thing between her and a world in which she was completely alone, and she saw how insufficient he was.

She saw that when she and Eban died—a thing that might happen at any hour, if they ate the wrong root or came upon an animal in the dark or were found by the marauders that stalked the wood at night—the child would have no one at all.

And then she thought of how very little she had to offer her child. Even less than what she had known in her small house by the allotment. All she could give her child was the shaking trees of the wood, and a few skills to try to survive beneath them. The child would have almost enough to fill its belly and slake its thirst. The tools to keep it sheltered. And an everlasting silence.

She never felt that baby move. One morning, she looked down after relieving herself to see a red pit in the snow. That night, the cramps began.

"Can you fix it?" she asked Eban, and he couldn't. He only asked her if it hurt, a physician's inquiry, because it was all he understood of pain.

And when the other babies came, he didn't tell her again about those tiny paddling hands and feet. She never felt them move. And they died without ever giving any sign they'd lived.

Only now, with this pregnancy, which has stayed with her, which has fluttered and roiled within her, does she remember again that first one. How she waited. How she hoped. How she was afraid.

And she waits to feel her baby move again. And hopes. And is afraid.

The second time the door opens, they are ready, anxiously waiting at the base of the ladder to see what will be sent this time.

"They wouldn't feed us if . . ." Eban murmurs.

But no rope or box or bucket appears. Instead, after a minute—a face, its features in shadow.

Judy cannot even tell if it's a man or a woman, but Eban whispers, "That's her! The girl I saw in the hole. That was her!"

They stare up at her, breath held as they wait to see what will happen next. And then the girl raises one hand and beckons them.

Eban hesitates, but Judy already has her hands on the wooden rungs, hauling herself up towards that shadow face.

"Wait, wait . . ." he pleads behind her, but she knows he'll follow after.

Only when Judy has reached the top of the ladder and laid one hand on the floor above does the girl lock eyes with her and then draw back. The girl, she thinks, is young. Maybe only fifteen, or even younger. She is much heavier than Judy was even before they left their hide to find this place. She is curvy at the hips and breasts, with dust-brown skin and swollen features—all cheek and lip.

The girl steps backward, watching sullenly as Judy stumbles onto the floor of the black house and stands.

Even the watery daylight cast through the single broken window is too bright, too much. Her eyes burn, and she squeezes the heels of her hands into their sockets before trying to look again at the girl.

"I'm sorry," she explains. "We were in the dark so long."

The girl doesn't speak or nod or give any indication she has heard or understood.

Behind her, Judy hears Eban scramble to the top of the ladder and onto the floor.

"It's you," he says to the girl. "I knew it was you."

"Are you . . ." Judy hesitates. "Were you a prisoner like us?"

The girl's black hair blazes around her face, wild curls like Judy's own twisting in every direction. When Eban spoke, she glanced at him, but otherwise, she stares only at Judy. After a moment, her gaze slips from Judy's face to her belly. Her eyes widen and she points.

Judy lets a hand slide to her stomach, and—she can scarcely believe it—at that moment, her daughter kicks, with force. A smile bursts over her face, a radiant relief.

The girl frowns and then smiles back. Only a single tooth is missing, and the others are white as bone. She grins wickedly, gleefully at Judy, but as Eban steps closer, the smile drops from her face like a stone.

"She's pregnant," Eban says quickly. "You can see there? A baby. She's having a baby. She will have." He speaks to her not as if she is a child but as if she were an idiot or mad. Judy can't tell if the assessment is fair.

"She knows," she whispers.

"Tell us who you are," Eban demands, as if to take charge of the room, but there is a shake in his voice. "And the woman. Who is she? What do you want? What will you do with us?"

The girl studies him, pulling at her lip with her thumb and forefinger.

"Please tell us. Please tell us anything. We're frightened. Are we safe here? Will they let us leave?"

The girl's eyes narrow and she takes a step towards Eban. He cringes but stands his ground as she approaches.

"Will they hurt us?" He asks again, "Are we safe? Will we—"

Suddenly the girl seizes his head between her hands. He cries out and stumbles backward, but she holds him fast. And then she opens her mouth so wide, Judy thinks her jaw has come unhinged.

"Oh my god," he says. "Oh my god."

And then the girl turns away from Eban and shows Judy what she showed him. She is shyer this time, pulling down her jaw with one hand so Judy can look within.

"Oh," Judy says. Looking into that empty mouth, she feels understanding arrive. "I see," she says. "I know. It's gone."

The girl closes her mouth, so the root of what was her tongue, now cut like a peddler's, is tucked out of sight behind her lips and teeth.

"They took it from you."

Appearing satisfied to be understood, the girl returns her attention to Judy's belly. She reaches her hands out and then her eyes flash quickly up to Judy's, as if to verify permission. Nodding, Judy lets the girl place both outstretched hands on her belly. They wait together for some sign of movement or life, but this time none comes. The girl, however, doesn't seem disappointed. She runs her hands over Judy's belly in circular motions, with a deft, gentle pressure that is strangely soothing.

Glancing up at Eban, Judy sees his expression of distress. He is staring at the girl, and hasn't yet moved since she dropped her hands from his head. In the tightness at his jaw, in the line between his eyes, she sees that he is feeling her injury as if it were done to him.

When the door opens, they are still standing like that, the girl stroking Judy's belly and Judy receiving it, Eban watching them with a look of pained concern, and her wishing she could erase it from his face.

They see first a lean, dark-skinned woman with a sorrowful mouth and heavy-lidded eyes. Behind her is the older woman who drove them down the ladder, underneath the floor. Neither of them appears to be armed. The women close the door behind them and stare at the girl, who shrinks into a corner of the room, waiting watchfully.

The girl doesn't budge from her corner, even as the older woman advances on Eban, and after protesting weakly, he allows her to back him down the ladder once again. Only when she shuts the door over him does he cry out. "Wait! Judy? Judy? Let her come with me—please! Please let us stay together!"

The woman looks angry at the continuing wails from beneath the floor but makes no effort to answer or silence them. She has pale, pinkish skin like Eban's, which seems ill-fitted to the bones of her face, like a slipped mask. She is the oldest person Judy has ever seen.

They study each other for a moment, and Judy thinks at last the woman will speak. But then, without a word, she turns and leaves the black house, pulling the door closed behind her.

At the sound of the footsteps and the shut door, Eban renews his cries. "Judy, are you there? Judy, where are they taking you? Is anyone there?"

Turning her gaze to the second woman, who stands watching her, impassive, Judy raises her foot and brings it to the floor twice, decisively. *Stamp, stamp.* There is a long pause, as Eban tries and fails to understand what she is telling him.

The woman with the long, sad face points to the desk at the far end of the room. Quickly deciding it is better to be compliant, Judy takes a seat at the desk, and the woman slides open a drawer and takes out a stack of pages. From the bottom of the stack, she withdraws several sheets and spreads them before Judy on the desk. Then she produces a pencil and, frowning, twitches it in the air, as though to imitate the act of writing. Judy understands and nods, accepting the pencil from her. She is unnerved by the silence and wonders if they have all been muted like the girl, but she senses that in any case it is better not to speak yet.

Looking content, the woman steps back and beckons to the girl to follow her outside. The door closes, and Judy is alone in the room, with only the sound of Eban repeating her name beneath the floorboards, until at last, he falls silent.

Then she looks at the pages spread before her, at the simple drawings of faces on the first page, and then the ink-sketched scenes of mother and son, the shadowy images of men and women bent over in laughter, crying out, brandishing injuries. Again and again, she shuffles through the pages, trying to make sense of what she sees, of what these people want from her. Beside each image is a series of empty lines. She is meant to fill them with something, but what? At last she takes the pencil and begins to write.

He always wanted her to look at him, she writes beside the mother and the son. *But she never would.* Beside the man whose face is contorted in pain as he clutches his stomach, she writes six paragraphs, fitting the sentences in the margins around the drawings, a scrawling chaos that stretches up, over and around the edges of the page. *He began his life expecting nothing,* it starts.

A long time later, when she has filled every page with all the words she can think to write, the sad-faced woman enters the room again. She takes the pages from Judy silently, and indicates that she must now return under the floor. Judy is halfway down the ladder when the door is closed above her, and then she lowers herself to the ground and waits.

X

THAT LITTLE BIT OF food and water seems not only to have restored Eban's health but to have charged him with a new, feverish energy she has never seen in him before. The moment she steps from the last rung of the ladder to the ground, he begins to question her. What did they want from her? What was she doing, so quiet for so long? Where have they gone? How many are they? What will happen next?

"I don't know," she says. And again, "I don't know" and "I don't know."

He continues to batter her with questions until at last she shouts at him to leave her be, and then he falls into a reproachful silence. In that dark quiet, she feels relief, and her thoughts begin to assemble themselves, one after another, until she has made sense of things as best she can.

"There were drawings," she says at last. "The woman made me sit at the desk, and then she gave me drawings to look at. I was meant to write something on them."

"She told you to?"

She shakes her head. "They never speak. None of them."

Eban hesitates, and she guesses they are both remembering the open mouth of the girl.

"Do you think they all—"

"I don't know. Maybe. I don't know."

Sitting beside her on the bed, he asks, "Were they the drawings from the desk drawer? One of the tests?"

He surprises her. "I think you're right," she says slowly. "I think it was a test."

"The simple faces or the pictures of people together?"

"Both. What do you know of it, Eban?"

"I saw while you were sleeping. That first morning. When I came here alone. And . . . and I've seen those tests before."

"Before?"

"When we were children. My mother tested us. My brother and me."

When Judy first met Eban and his mother, she and Alphonse still bore Dan invisibly between them. He was everywhere, and he was lost, and it marked them: the missing lover, the other father.

But Eban rarely mentioned his brother or his death, and carried no artifacts of that loss. Eban and his mother were bound together like a single being. Like a sum that yielded an indivisible number.

It intrigued Judy. Between them they had exactly and only what they needed to survive. She found in herself a desire to penetrate and dismantle their bond. To take them apart. To become necessary.

In the first weeks of knowing each other, Eban mentioned his brother to Judy only once, casually, as if he were someone already known to her. When she questioned him, he grew vague and looked unhappy. He didn't mention him again for nearly a year, while his mother never once spoke of the second son she'd borne and raised and lost.

"What do you mean, she tested you? What was she testing for? What was I meant to write?"

Before Eban can answer, the door over the ladder opens again, and when they creep into the puddle of light, they see the sad-faced woman looking down. She beckons to Eban to come up, but when Judy attempts to follow, she shakes her head, and the door closes behind Eban. And there are no more sounds from above.

When Eban returns, it's Judy's turn to torment him with questions, but he seems reticent now.

"Was it the same?" she asks. "They gave you the test?"

"Yes. Both tests."

"And they were the same tests you took as a child?"

"Yes." And then, "I think so."

She thinks she should leave him be, but she wants to know more. What do those women mean by playing with this childish puzzle—those crude drawings and facile faces, which each seemed to say only a single thing, feel only one way, when no one Judy has ever seen has had such a face, a smile or frown like a letter that makes only one sound?

She pushes him until finally he tells her what he remembers.

The last test, his mother called it, when she showed him the second set of drawings. In three days, they would have packed and left the outland house where he was born. But, he says, he didn't know that then.

"And your brother?" Judy asks.

He doesn't answer.

"Was it before he died or after?" When he says nothing, she sighs and accepts his refusal. "Tell me about the test."

What Eban remembers best are the three images of a mother and child that appeared on the second test. In one they seemed to be fighting. In another the mother had gathered the child up in her arms and was looking at him with love. In the last the child was playing alone, and the mother stood in the doorway watching him.

"Yes," says Judy. "That's how it was. On the pages upstairs. It was the same."

He nods.

"Tell me what the mother is thinking," his own mother had said, and Eban remembers that he was stuck on that one. He touched the mother's face, as though he might feel her thoughts with the end of his finger.

"She loves the boy."

"Yes."

"She likes to see him play."

"Yes."

He didn't know why, but he said then, "She is worried about him."

His mother, who'd been standing over him, her hand resting on the back of his chair, took the chair beside him. "Why," she whispered.

He didn't know. He honestly didn't. There was some intensity in his mother that distracted him so that he couldn't straighten out his thoughts. What was difficult, too, was that the thing he saw most clearly in the picture was that the boy had far more toys than he'd ever had, and it was hard for him to look at the mother when the toys were what interested him most in the picture. He struggled to find the right answer. "It's because she loves him."

"Yes?"

"She's worried because she doesn't know what will happen to him."

He looked at his mother quickly to see how she received this answer. Her eyes were very bright. She said, "But he's only playing."

"I guess . . . I guess she's worried about what will happen after."

"After?"

"After. After he's done playing. Whatever happens after that."

"What could happen to him?"

He had no idea. His shirt collar, too tight, was hot around his throat. He wished he could go do his exercises outside. With that thought, he cried out desperately, "He might go out of the house later. Something could happen to him there. He could . . . fall, or get lost, or someone could hurt him, maybe." Suddenly he saw it rise up before his eyes, all the possibilities taking shape. He saw, in fact, that the dangers were enormous. "He could hurt himself. He might trip or, or, eat something bad that made him sick. He could go out on the road, too far from his house. He might be so far that when he called, she couldn't hear him. She wouldn't know where to look for him."

His mother pulled him to her then, tucked his head under her chin, and put her face into his hair, so that her breath made him even hotter, but he didn't fight her. "And so many other things," she said quietly. "And so many other things."

When he finishes telling her, Judy is quiet.

"That's all I remember," he says.

She nods, though she knows the gesture is lost in the dark.

"But after . . . after the test was done, she took a book from the shelf. A text I'd never seen before, on neurochemistry. She must have sent a peddler to find it for her. She made me read a chapter about the orbito-frontal cortex and the amygdala."

"You know I don't know what those words mean."

"They're parts of the brain. If they develop wrong, things don't function the way they're supposed to." He paused. "The book listed a syndrome I hadn't read about before."

"What does it mean, Eban?"

"We'd been reading about neural development," he says, as if he didn't hear her. "For four months we'd been reading and reading again the same chapters . . ."

They had spent a great deal of time on disorders that began in the earliest stages of embryogenesis. Cranial nerve palsies and ophthalmological defects that bloomed into systemic disorders by infancy or even later. He didn't understand why the subject was so important to her, and so when she showed him the new syndrome, whole pages on a complex of indicators he'd never heard of, he asked her, "What does it matter?"

She didn't respond, and so he added, "It's just that I'm not likely to ever see a person suffering from such a rare syndrome."

"It was a stupid thing to say," he tells Judy now. He says he studied injuries and diseases he'd never encounter, and could never help if he did. He'd read about principles of biochemistry that would only be of use in the kind of lab where she once worked, and that he would never see. There was something else she was getting at with all of this, an idea they were completing together, and all of it mattered, and his question was an insult to the endeavour she'd begun with him the summer he turned twelve.

"Eban," Judy says again. "What does it mean?"

When he speaks, his voice seems to come from a long way away. "When we were done reading, she took a silver pin and pushed it into the palm of her hand while I watched. I cried and she made me record my pulse. I would have put a hundred pins in my own body and it would have hurt less. It would have been less terrible."

"Why? Why did she do that?"

"She asked me if I could see it. If I understood. She said there was sweat on my brow, that the freckles on my face looked darker because my skin had turned so pale. She asked me if I noticed that I was breathing more quickly. She said if she could take the temperature of my tympanic membrane then, it would be elevated. She pointed to the number I had written down, and said that that number, my face, they were like books where she could read what I was feeling. She said they weren't just feelings, they were physical, chemical, electrical processes of the human body. She said those processes make us what humans are. If they fail, we become something else. And she said for a person to be altered in that way was a catastrophe."

"Eban, who was she talking about?"

He says, "She told me people like us feel pity even for those who don't know how to feel it. She said people like that, those other ones, think our pity is a weakness. She said we couldn't let them be right."

Then he refuses to say anything else and they fall quiet, and eventually, they sleep.

Food comes again. And water. When the door opens, Judy is waiting at the ladder, prepared to meet their captors once more. But she can't see even the hands that lower the bundle of provisions. This time, only cold bread and an open tin of beans. They devour it, and then the water. They don't save a drop. Without speaking of it, they have both become convinced that soon they will be released or killed. It won't be long now, either way. It occurs to Judy even to wonder about the food itself, but she would rather die with a full belly of poison than starve in this hole.

They return the filled bucket and empty food box, and when the rope appears again it is yoked to a clean bucket and a square package, wrapped in cloth. Judy seizes hold of the package, tearing at the string that binds it.

"What is it?" Eban asks, behind her.

She nearly forgets to remove the bucket, and from the other end of the rope comes an impatient tug. "Get it, Eban. Get the bucket."

He acquiesces and then asks again, "Judy, what is it?"

She stares at it, shaking her head. "I can't . . . I don't understand them."

"Judy?"

She turns to look at him in wonder. "It's a book."

The cover is crudely made, a scrap of heavy leather stitched at the spine to a stack of rough paper, the edges neatly cut. She feels the weight of the book in her hands. She turns its pages. She looks at the narrow black writing that fills them. For no good reason, tears begin to drop from her eyes.

And then the door, which she had not even noticed was still open above, closes, and they're plunged into darkness again. She hears her voice shout. "*No!*"

"There's something else. Judy? There was something else in the bucket. Let me check it."

She can't account for the intensity of the fury she feels. The words that had only just emerged before her, the first glimpse of any meaning or answer, vanished into darkness.

"Look," he says, "here, look." She can see nothing, of course, but he puts them in her hands. "Candles. Matches. And something else, I think it's . . ."

Her hand shakes as she lights the match and stares at the object he holds toward her. "A pencil," she says.

The match burns her fingers and she drops it into the dirt. Darkness again.

"We should conserve," he says, as she twists the three candles into the dirt and lights one after another with a single match. "There might not be any more."

She ignores him and opens the book. After a moment, he asks what it says and she whispers the words.

Written at the top of the first page is this: "*Haven Colony,*" she reads.

And then underneath: "*These free people came to this place on April 11th, 2062, seeking to live among those who share our clement hearts.*"

"When is that, 2062?" Eban asks. "When did that happen?"

"Why does it say 'Haven Colony'? Why not 'Heaven'?" She reads on: "*There were fifty-seven of us. (See list, below.)*"

And then someone has added something, squeezed into the bottom in a different hand, the ink-blue shapes of the letters jagged and wild.

"*We have chosen to live by the rule of silence and to protect and enforce the rule. In this way, we protect ourselves from those who would find frailty in our charity. The rule is binding for all who freely choose to live among us.*"

"I don't understand it. What do they mean by 'silence' . . . they never speak at all? That's why that girl's tongue was cut? She freely chose that?"

Judy is turning the page. "There's more writing in that same blue ink . . . *Someday, if we live, there will be those who wonder how we came and what sort of people we were. With these words, we answer them.* And it goes on for pages, and then again here and there throughout, sometimes for pages, sometimes only a line. The rest, the parts in pencil, is only the list. Fifty-seven names, heights, weights. It says *tested* beside each one, and a date. And other things . . . here, this one says *engineering, carpentry, reading*, and that one says just *cooking, firearms*."

"Do you think there are fifty-seven of them now? How long ago did they come here?"

She counts the names. "I think there *were* fifty-seven. Some have an *x* after the date, and a second date. Maybe when they died?"

"Or left?"

"But there are more names. It goes on. But they aren't the same." She shows him. "All different handwriting. No dates or measurements. This one just says, *After the first snow.* And then the passages get longer, and longer, some of them several pages."

She reads from a page at the middle of the book: "*As two we came, sisters both, no others known to us, and those who knew us dead below, where a house once stood and burned, where there were once five houses and five families and a farm that grew good seed and where we kept animals for meat and fur and fed ourselves and were warm in winter and drew water from the ground in summer, and were not troubled till the fires came and the seed did not grow and the animals sickened and*

we ate the meat left on their bones and the fires came and our houses
burned and there were no others left but we two sisters who knew no
others, and we came into the hills, and walked without knowing where
we walked, the smoke behind us, the hills burning, and no water to be
found, and there in the hills we found this place and yield to what end
we find here, be it sanctuary after long travel or—"

"I don't understand why—"

"And some are only short. This one can scarcely write his letters:
A man alone come from up the barrens where there is nun now and
many dangurs, can find birds in ruff also the rabbit, good with knife."

"Why?" Eban repeats. "Why are they writing this down?"

She finds herself turning back to the entries written in ink, a blue
thread of continuity between the accounts of these strangers whose
fates they can only guess. The blue entries are meticulously dated, but
the handwriting becomes shakier as they go on, the letters losing form,
till they look like they were blown across the page by a wind. *Nearly a*
year we prepared, reads a passage that begins on the back of the first
page, beneath the list of pencilled names. *I wish we'd had ten times as*
much, but it still wouldn't have been enough, considering everything we
had to learn and get done before making the big move. The trip took
only three days, and we had a lot to carry—

"It's a record," she says. She takes the pencil in her hand. "It's their
history."

"But why have they given it to us?"

"Because we're part of it now."

She finds the last marked page, and enters their names beneath the
last person it lists. Beside her own name, she writes, *Winter. Black hair.*
Brown eyes. Book-writing and binding, hunting. She hesitates, unable to
think of anything else she knows about herself. She hands the book
to Eban and then snatches back the pencil to scrawl, *Pregnant.*

He looks unhappy as he writes a few words and closes the book.

"What does it mean?" he asks, and she doesn't answer. "What does it mean?" he asks again. "Judy?"

After the first baby was lost, Judy began to ask for the jobs that would take her farthest from their hide. She had always liked to linger in the wood, enjoying the return to Eban (Eban, soft of voice and touch, the way he held her, always a little too long, and looked at her as if he saw everything) as much as she enjoyed the time alone. But now she took on all the hunting and water-carrying work and walked for hours before even lifting her eyes to look for running water or a kill. When she finally turned back, her steps fell heavier, and she often arrived hours after dark to Eban's anxious face, which she found she no longer liked to look at.

But he seemed to understand. He thought he understood. She felt his patience, daily unspooling, till he had reached the end of what he believed was a fair period of time for her to grieve, and then one night, as they lay together, he whispered, "We can make another."

And she knew what he thought. That she grieved the child or blamed him for its loss or some other thing that could be solved by making another, as easily as a put-out fire could be lit again.

And she looked into his pale, wide eyes and knew they didn't see her at all. The thing that made her—more than sorrowful or even angry— the thing that made her savage with fury wasn't what had happened to their baby, but what would have happened to it had it lived.

Long after the candles have burned down to the dirt, the door opens above, and they tie the book to the rope and return it. The door doesn't close, and after a time, they begin to climb the ladder, haltingly. When they reach the top, the three women stand before them, flanked by two black-haired men who seem to share the same long white face.

"Twins," Judy says softly, and the old woman narrows her eyes and crosses to the desk. She throws open the book, which rests there, and points at a line of handwriting. *The rule is binding for all . . .*

"Yes," Judy begins, and then she nods instead. She understands. But the woman thrusts out her thin hands and clutches Judy's face, drawing her close. One hand closes over her mouth, so she can feel the knotted fingers against her lips and teeth. She stumbles backward, trying to free herself. Eban reaches towards her, helplessly, and then his arms fall to his side, his mouth open and empty of words.

Judy nods and nods again, as hard as she can. She understands the rule. Silence. She understands.

At last the woman releases her, looking unsatisfied still. She points again to the page. *To protect and enforce.* Only when Judy puts her own finger to the line *The rule is binding for all* does the woman nod and seem appeased. She then turns to the second page and touches a name. *Sladja.* Her own name. The eighth one listed in the record. She has been here since it was made.

Sladja then beckons to the others, one by one, and finds their names in the history. The men are called Romeo and Bobby-Rae, and their names appear on the same page as Eban and Judy's. There are no other words by their names, no indication of even the season when they arrived, and Judy wonders how long ago it may have been.

The sad-faced woman is Oona, and she, too, was among the fifty-seven who came here first. And the young woman is Golda. Her name is the last before Eban and Judy's own.

Sladja then closes the book, unlocks the second drawer of the desk, and places it inside. Laying her palms on the desk she watches them, her eyes darting from Eban to Judy, as though waiting for something more that might happen in that moment.

There is, Judy thinks, a kind of animal happiness. Here and there she knew it in her childhood. A physical joy. She remembers it ringing in her body, a tide rising in her veins. She recalls certain sentences she read in certain books that lifted her out of herself. Sinking into the blue cold water of a brook. Nights when the air was as warm as touch, and the sky clear and drowned in stars. A sudden fall of rain. Her father lifting the child Judy from the ground after she fell, and in discovering she was not hurt, the child wept in relief and allowed herself to be soothed, and felt trust as blindly and deeply as it could be felt. The feeling sang out in her and she'd draw in her breath and sustain it as long as she could. She has not felt it for years. And she feels it now. She is in the hands of this tiny, wretched company of people who can tell her nothing. They might not help her—might harm her, even. She doesn't know what will happen next.

But she feels herself lifted from herself, in a heady, weightless, animal joy. At last, she thinks, *at last* something has happened.

Sladja approaches and Judy doesn't shrink from her touch this time. She lets Sladja lay one hand over her belly and then withdraw it, without looking at her.

The woman beckons to Eban, and he looks from her to Judy and then follows. Judy takes a step toward them, but Sladja stops at the door and turns, shaking her head, and Judy understands she is to stay. Their eyes lowered, Romeo, Bobby-Rae and Golda follow after, as if they've been silently summoned away.

Only Oona remains, standing in the corner, one hand at her throat. Judy wonders if she was wrong to think her eyes were sorrowful. They might only be tired. Or, she thinks suddenly, angry.

From a cupboard in the far wall, Oona takes out a roll of blankets and a pillow like the one Judy slept on in the strange, beautiful bed of the fourth house. She spreads them out on the floor and makes a bed, while Judy watches. Then she offers it to her, with a gesture of her hand, and leaves. Judy hears the bolt turn in the lock.

The thin light that leaks in through the window dwindles and soon disappears.

XI

IN THE DAYS THAT FOLLOW, Judy remains in the black house. Twice a day, food and water are delivered to her. Three times, the sheets are stripped from the bed where she sleeps, and taken away, along with her soiled clothing. When they're returned, they smell of soap and are rough to the touch.

At first, because she's exhausted and half-starved, she's grateful to be cared for in this way. She imagines that Eban is being similarly cared for, wherever they've taken him. She feels sure, almost sure, that if they had wished to harm her and Eban, they would have done it by now. Instead, she and Eban have entered their names in the record, just as the others did themselves when they arrived. She and Eban are part of this place now.

The hours recover their meaning again. By counting the meals delivered to her, and watching light swell and fade through the broken window, Judy is able to count the passing days. She sleeps until the light outside is bright and even, and sometimes lies awake, drawn out across her bed, long after dark has fallen. She sleeps with a hand cupped to her belly and wakes sometimes to feel her baby turning inside her.

Not since she was a child has she been cared for like this. Food and water arrive without her fetching it. Her waste is carried away in a white pot each morning, and another set down in the corner to replace it. As she grows strong again, she begins to feel a twitch in the muscles of her limbs, which long to be put to use. She circles the floor of the black house to exercise her arms and legs, but a physical restlessness has taken hold of her that soon spreads to her mind.

She begins speaking to herself, and occasionally to her child. She can't bear the unending silence, and imagines measures she might take to force the people who deliver her meals to talk. But she doesn't know if they even possess the tongues to form words, and fearing for her own tongue, she doesn't dare open her mouth when they appear at the door, and only nods at them in wordless thanks.

I was never alone, she thinks one morning, sitting on the wooden floor of the house with her legs spread out before her. And then she says it to her child: "I've never been alone."

As a girl she was always in the company of her fathers. None of them ever left their home, except to walk or meet a peddler on the road. And it wasn't safe to do either alone. She can recall playing by herself in the dust yard just outside the door, but she always knew that Dan or Alphonse would be watching from a window, and sometimes she'd refuse to raise her eyes from the dirt only so as not to see their eager waving. So she could, for those few minutes, relieve the burden of their steady gaze.

Now, unseen, unheard, she wanders the vast liberty of aloneness, which stretches out around her as widely as the walls contain her tightly. "Your father never let me be," she tells her daughter. "Since we came into his hide, he kept his eyes on me, same as when I was a child bound to that house. When it was my turn to hunt or get water, I'd pretend I got lost or struggled. He thinks, even now, I'm no good as a hunter. But it was lies, so I could steal an hour or two to myself in the wood, where I didn't feel his eyes forever watching me."

She performs the physical listening she has learned to do, feeling for a movement from her baby, some signal of allegiance or argument. But there is nothing. "You think I'm unkind. You're wondering what sort of mother you have. Being watched like that isn't the same as being loved, you know."

Still nothing. "And I never told him. I never said it to him. I only went into the wood and came back when I was ready."

The third time she searches the black house, emptying the contents of the wall cabinets and upper desk drawer, she finds something she had previously overlooked. A stump of pencil like the ones Eban would sometimes sketch with—a stick of charcoal wrapped in waxed string. It's soft and dull, and so little of the string remains that her hand soon turns black when she uses it. But it's a treasure. The most precious thing she has.

She begins to keep records of her own, writing on the backs of the test pages from the desk drawer. She rotates the pencil carefully as she writes, a quarter turn every few letters, so it sharpens with use, and not a mark is wasted. She would write all day if she could, but the three inches of pencil are a measure of all the words she can have, and so she chooses them with caution, the way she would mete out food from winter stock.

5 days. Her heels at my ribs. Kicks all night. Rain.

The parsimony frustrates her. Words run feral in her mind all night. She whispers them aloud. "Why am I thinking so much of Daniel? Of his moods. I didn't understand them when I was a child; I thought they must make sense in some adult way that would become comprehensible one day. They would drift in like systems of weather, and you'd watch the dark spread out across the sky. He'd go for longer and longer walks, and Alphonse would plead with him to come back, trying to make a joke of it, for my sake, I think now, and sometimes he'd lose his temper and shout at him. He'd lead Dan home like a child. And then he'd tell me not to worry, that my father had a wandering heart and it was in his nature to want to travel too far, farther than was safe.

"And then Dan would stop going for walks altogether and be in his study at all hours, and we'd hear his footsteps pacing overhead. 'You'll wear a hole in the floor,' Alphonse would say when he appeared, wan and silent, at meals, and this was also a joke, but I could see he was worried, and I thought it was because of the floor that he looked that way, so I was always fearfully watching overhead, sure one day I'd see my father come tumbling down with the ceiling.

"When it got very bad, he would sit in the chair in his study and not answer me when I called to him from the door. He wouldn't be working or reading or doing anything at all. It was just unhappiness, but I didn't know then what it was; I knew only enough to be frightened by it. Later, Alphonse told me that when Daniel was young it had been all right to walk as far as he wanted. He had loved to walk in forests and rivers, and would go away for days and days with just his knapsack and specimen kit, studying life in the water and fields and trees. All the tiny alive things that no one else saw. And so although he loved us, it was horrible for him to live in our house—to not be able to ever really leave.

"And if he were here in this place instead of me, he would risk everything to escape it. And then I think of you, how I carry you inside me, and I feel you thump at the walls, and I wonder if you are just as desperate."

And then in the morning, she writes, *6 days. Hoar frost. Steady kicks. Daniel, again.*

On the eleventh day in the black house, the door opens at first light to reveal Eban, uncertain, holding the food tray out before him like he mistrusts it.

"You!" she says, pushing herself up from the bed with the extra effort it now takes. In the last week, her belly has begun to press more insistently against her clothes, and she sees him notice it.

He shakes his head sharply, and doesn't come inside like the others do. Instead he bends over the doorstep to set the tray on the ground, moving so slowly she finds herself irritated with him, when seconds earlier she was as glad to see him as anyone she'd ever seen before.

And then two whispered words, so faint she can scarcely hear them or be sure that they have issued from his bent form: "*Take it.*"

"Eban?"

He doesn't answer but remains doubled over, making slight, enigmatic gestures over the tray, pretending, she understands suddenly, to be fixing something there.

Only when she has knelt to the ground before him and accepted the tray does he speak, a hurried murmur in her ear, their eyes never meeting: "We can't say anything. They may be watching. If they send me again tonight. Then. When it's dark. Promise me, Judy. Don't speak."

He rises to his feet and stares for several seconds at her body, the roundness of her belly, with an intensity she doesn't recognize—worry? anger? hunger? Then he looks her in the eye and she hears the words he means her to understand as though he's spoken them again. *Don't speak.*

And then he gently closes the door, and all she has is the hard bread and salt-cured rabbit he left, and the hours till he comes again.

It's some time before she notices that Eban didn't bring a fresh chamber pot, and yesterday's is near full. So she holds her bladder and waits for the evening visit, feeling the pressure swell as though she might burst.

That afternoon, the baby kicks more than ever before, so sharply that Judy holds her breath to keep from crying out. She becomes desperate enough to try to raise the door in the floor, thinking to creep down into the dark below and squat there in the dirt. But the door has been locked with a key, and she pounds her hand against it in frustration.

She would never admit it, but she has begun to fear her daughter's arrival. She knows nothing of childbirth beyond the simplest facts, and that many women die in their labours. In the books she has read, no birth has ever been described—the cleaving of mother and fetus happens between pages, insinuated screams within the silence.

Now, drawing short breaths to bring her mind away from the pain of her bladder, she tries to guess how it will feel to deliver a living thing into the world.

Eban returns at dark, tapping at the door and then, after a moment's hesitation, pushing it open.

This time, he comes inside, setting the tray of food on the desk and gathering up the dirtied dishes, watching her anxiously all the while. She says nothing, sitting on the bed roll with her legs outstretched, determined to hide the soiled cloth beneath her. She won't move until he leaves.

He notices the filled pot as he sets a new one beside it, and looks at her sharply. Glancing quickly to the door, he whispers, "I'm sorry. I forgot it. I didn't know."

"Don't speak."

He looks startled. "Don't . . . ?" Again, he looks to the door.

"*Don't speak*." She waits for him to react and then says, "Isn't that what you told me?"

"I didn't mean to . . . I only wanted to keep you safe. I don't know what they will do to us."

She knows it to be true. She knows he's right to be cautious. And yet, she feels angry. Not at the people who keep them here, but at him. "I'm here, day and night. Who could I speak to?"

"I only meant . . ."

She looks away from his earnest face. "Is it really okay now?"

He shakes his head. "I don't know."

"Are they watching you? Watching us?"

"I don't know."

"Why do you bring the food now?"

He shakes his head again. "She gave it to me. Oona. She makes the food and she just put the dishes in my hands. There's no way to know more. There's no way to ask any questions."

She draws the blanket up more tightly as he steps towards her, and he stops.

"I shouldn't stay long. I suppose . . . I suppose they might be testing me."

She feels a stirring in her stomach that isn't the baby. She thinks she might be sick. It's only now that it occurs to her how long her time here might go on.

"Judy, it's not a bad place. There's a job for everyone. There's food twice a day, and always enough. Better food than we ever had. Oona cooks it for us. But I said that already. I don't know what to tell you. We all sleep under the houses. But we can come and go as we want. They let me work, and they're . . ." He pauses, and then says shyly, "They're pleased with me. I can tell it. Every day I'm allowed to do more. Today I fixed the roof of the house where Romeo and Bobby-Rae sleep. They have tools like you've never seen before. Everything needed to do it right, to make a good job of it. No one speaks, but they're kind to one another. It doesn't feel like there's any danger at all. I know we must be careful. I'm very careful. I follow the rule and do what they show me they want me to do. But I feel welcome here. I can tell that—"

"Eban, are we prisoners?"

He stares at her. Then he turns his back and crosses to the filled chamber pot, carrying it carefully to the door and setting it down outside. He leaves the door open, swinging gently in the evening wind. "I like it here. That's what I'm telling you. That's what I mean. I like living with these people, in these houses. It's a good place."

She waits until he looks her in the eye as she repeats her question. "Are we?"

He hesitates and then answers softly, "Weren't we always?"

She watches without moving as he balances the pot over the dishes in his arms and leaves.

For a moment she thinks he forgot to lock the door behind him, but then, after a time, she hears the drawing of the bolt into its place.

She forgot to ask how many there are.

The idea took hold in her mind the day she found a dumping ground she hadn't seen before. Years earlier they had searched out and buried all the dumping grounds for miles around their hide. But that day she had wandered farther than the usual path and found a place where people, years ago, had gone to cast away what they couldn't use.

She found the usual things in the new dumping ground. Pieces of machinery made for unfathomable purposes. Rotten shreds of clothing. The plastics. And then she saw something else, lying beneath a sheet of rusted steel roofing.

It was, she realized, after dragging the sheet away, a chair. A chair that looked like a machine.

The chair sat on four wheels, two large ones at the back and two small ones at the front. There were metal plates for the feet of the person who sat in it, and two tattered straps that must have bound the feet that rested there. Two plastic-covered shanks projected from the chair back. She rested her hand on one, and her fingers settled into purpose-made grooves. Handles, she thought, but not for the person who sat in the chair.

She looked at it for a long time. She thought of the person who made the chair. Of the person who sat in it. And of the person who held the handles and pushed.

And then she went back to the hide, where Eban sat sewing patches on her winter coat. He raised his face to see her.

"I want to go to the cities," she said.

They argued till it was dark, and then argued until it was light again. *She* argued. Eban only received her argument and shook his head, staring at her helplessly. "But why?" he asked and asked again, until she wanted to take the words in her hands and heave them into the woods. "We are safe here, we have all we need . . ."

She took his hands in hers and said, "There were good people once who made good things, did good things. It can't all be gone. Whatever is there now, there might be good left too. Buried there among the rest."

He refused her. Patiently, gently, kindly, he refused her. And she knew he believed she couldn't leave without him, and she thought she might believe it herself, and despised them both for her cowardice. And the patience and gentleness and kindness she had loved in him became something different. Complacence. Weakness. A trap.

And then she was pregnant a second time. And then a third. And the argument went on.

The next day, Oona brings the food. Judy studies her face as she lowers the tray onto the table with a steadiness she admires. That evening Oona returns, slipping into her house with the same soft step and laying out the new dishes and sweeping up the old with a single motion, surprising in its grace.

Oona delivers the food each day after that, until the first morning of Judy's fourth week in the black house, when the door opens to reveal the white-haired woman. Sladja.

The woman shuts the door behind her and leans against it, seeming to consider something. She presses a finger to her mouth, her eyes fixed on Judy. When she at last steps away from the door, her lips are white, drained of blood by the pressure of her finger.

Hastily setting the food on the floor like she just remembered she carried it, Sladja crosses towards Judy so quickly that she instinctively draws back.

The older woman holds her steady with one hand and pushes the other into Judy's belly, as though feeling for something there.

Judy fights to free herself, but Sladja holds her tightly, one hand pressed against her back as the other digs deeper, palpating the flesh of her belly and then slowly sliding up, coming to rest at last above her navel.

Just when Judy is about to scream for Eban to help her, to protect her from this woman who seems bent on crushing their baby with her probing hands, Sladja suddenly breaks into a smile, the lines of her powder-white skin arching from her eyes to her jaw. She meets Judy's eyes with such a nakedly pleased expression that all at once Judy feels sure her baby is safe. This woman won't hurt her child. What's more, she knows something about it, something Judy doesn't know herself. Some good news of the child, hidden in the invisible interior of her body.

To her surprise, she smiles back at Sladja, nodding and closing her hand over the woman's own and pressing it more firmly to her belly to show she understands. Yes. This baby lives.

The grin fades from Sladja's face and she seems to search Judy's eyes for something before dropping her hands and releasing her. Abruptly, she returns to the door and gathers the dishes she left there, depositing them at the desk. She doesn't set them out for her, assembling the meal, as Oona does. Instead, she stares so intently at the tray that Judy's gaze is drawn to it too. But it isn't the food that has caught the woman's attention.

If she had been closer, Judy would have snatched up the paper before Sladja could take it, but instead she only watches helplessly as the woman lifts it to her face, holding it inches from her eyes and squinting as though she struggles to read what Judy has written there. Silently, Judy admonishes herself. She should have returned it to the drawer with the other pages. She has grown careless.

After a few moments, the woman crumples the page into her fist and wrenches open the upper drawer. Pulling out the other pages, she holds each one up in turn, reading them as she did the first, so that the paper nearly grazes her face. When she's finished, she gathers up the remaining papers from the drawer, even those Judy hasn't so much as marked, and tucks them under her arm, pausing only then to look back at Judy.

In any other circumstance, Judy would expect that she was about to speak, to ask her something urgent. But instead, after a moment, the woman reaches into a pocket in her long skirts and produces a key. Glancing briefly at Judy, as though checking to see whether she understands and agrees about what will happen next, the woman then opens the locked lower drawer.

She withdraws the bound volume that Judy first read down in the hole she now stands over. A second volume is revealed beneath it, thinner than the first, and a stack of papers, and then Sladja shuts the drawer and locks it. Returning her attention to the first volume, Judy watches as the woman opens it over the desk, flipping to the page where Judy's own writing appears. The woman slides a new pencil with a pointed tip between the leaves, marking the page where, Judy understands now, she is to write.

From across the table between them, the two women share a look of understanding. Yes, Judy thinks, as though the other can hear her. She'll write it there. Her story. Of now, and everything that came before. Of her and Eban both. More than the bare, stunted lines they first left on the page. She'll tell Sladja, write it all there on the page as though everything that's happened to them is something she has carried and can now lay down.

Satisfied, Sladja backs away from the table, lifts the filled chamber pot from the floor and, bent over its weight, leaves the black house without looking at Judy again.

When she is gone, Judy takes up the pencil and writes until nothing is left between her blackened fingertips.

XII

This is what she writes:

We were three. I lived with my fathers in a house with glass windows and a yard of dust. The sky was grey nearly every day, and the air thick. But on the clearest days, fields of yellow would appear at the farthest point we could see, a yellow line tracing the sky. The end of what was ours.

Once my father Daniel walked with me as far as the gates of the resource allotment and we stood staring out over those fields. Here and there the soil was bald, and what grain grew looked sun-scorched and sickly, and I knew it was all the food there was. We kept our own garden, because Daniel knew how to make things grow—my other father often said he could have raised roses from a stone. When it was warm he would bow over the pots in our yard, spending hours prodding at the soil, divining, like the snake charmer in one of my other father's books. The year we had two chickens, he would keep the shells of their eggs to rake into the dirt. Sometimes he would haul buckets of our filth into the yard and that, too, he would use. When the chickens died that summer for lack of water, he wouldn't let me bury their poor bones, what was left after we had eaten what we could. Even their tiny bird skeletons went into the pots.

But there were seasons and years when his pots yielded nothing and we had to buy our food from the peddlers, same as anyone, and pay whatever unreasonable price they asked. Alphonse would always pay, because it made Daniel go too quiet, haggling with a stranger in the yard surrounded by his pots of desiccated seed, a garden aborted in the dirt.

So though he hated it, he knew and I did without him saying that without those yellow fields we would have starved. He warned me not to touch the gate, but he let me stand close enough that I could see how the machines that ran the irrigation system had gone red with rust and must have been made long ago.

"They won't last forever," he told me.

"They'll make more," I said, but he didn't really hear.

They send Eban again that night. She feels there is a purpose in sending him, but can't guess what it is.

Again he hesitates at the door and she does nothing to invite him inside, waiting instead until he makes up his mind.

He comes to the table where she is writing and when she doesn't look up, he whispers, "I have your dinner."

"Either they are listening to us or they aren't," she says, still without raising her head. "Whispering doesn't help."

He lays the dishes down one by one and then says, in a slightly louder voice, "You're angry. You're angry with me."

She knows it's true but doesn't understand why, so she only shrugs. At first she was unable to tell, but now, each hour, it becomes more clear—her hatred of this place, it creeps in over the windowsills, smuggles through the keyhole in the floor. She is furious to be caught like an insect in this house. She is furious to be learning nothing more of anything . . . of an existence beyond this one, or the lives of people below these hills. She feels farther from it all than she has ever been before, drawn instead into another mystery altogether, one that is no use to her.

And still there is nothing in any of this that she can blame him for. But for her, they would have grown old in their hide, bent and white-haired, his voice the only voice she heard, his face the only face she saw. She would have blamed him for stealing her chance to know who she'd have been without him. She would have hated him as a way to hating herself.

It has now been years since she felt what she had taken for love become a kind of gravity, a force she couldn't resist or remove. Eyes closed, she could recognize every part of him with her hands. He pressed into the space that should have been hers alone. He occupied her. And if it began in love, now it feels like something much bigger and darker and less. It feels like a robbery.

They argued for a year before she said she would leave without him. It took that long. And then she had to keep repeating it to believe it herself. She'd never been without him or her fathers. It is true, what she now whispers to her daughter. As alone as she felt, she'd never truly been alone.

And so they left that place. She took him from it. She brought him here. And now she despises every stone of the house that contains her, and the ghosts of whoever they used to be, those people who built this place, and the ghost of him, disappearing before her, in this room, wanting to be like them, to die among these empty houses, to sleep beneath their floors, mouthing their silences.

"Tell me why you like it here," she says. "Tell me what it is. What it is that. . ."

"That . . . ?"

That lets you live among these tongueless people and see no horror here. "That changed your mind. That makes you trust them."

"I don't think they mean to hurt us."

"But you are whispering."

She takes satisfaction in his frown, in the long pause before he attempts a reply. When he finally opens his mouth, she interrupts him.

"How many of them are there?"

"The others? You know. Only them. The ones we met here."

"Only those five? Are you sure?"

He shrugs. "I haven't seen anyone else."

"But there are almost a dozen houses . . . I counted them . . ."

"You know from the book. There were more. But not anymore. Maybe not for years."

"Why?"

"There could be any reason. I see these people every day. They live like a family. Each with a house of their own, except for the two brothers who share their house together."

"The girl. The girl they locked beneath the floor. Is she family too?"

"They all sleep under the floor."

"All bolted from above?"

He lifts his hands and drops them. "You always thought I was too careful. Now you tell me not to trust them? These people we've hunted for, walked miles to find?"

"Why do they keep me here, when you're allowed to live among them?"

He looks troubled now. "That I don't understand."

"You trust them that much? You leave the mother of your child under their key?"

He winces slightly at the mention of her child, as he always does, and eyes her belly as if that's what he doesn't trust. "I wonder if it's because of your . . . pregnancy. It seems to matter. It seems to be important to them. They believe you'll bear a child."

She understands his meaning. They believe and he does not. She means to let him feel the keenness of her anger, its sharp edge. But her voice when she speaks is pleading. "She still lives, Eban. I still feel her. Alive in me."

He nods and averts his eyes. "I thought . . . when they first came in here and she—Sladja—examined you. I thought I could see what she did. The shape of you seemed different. Like the baby might . . . it might still . . ."

She is flooded with a sudden impulse to put her arms around him, but when she stands he steps backward, and she sees that he fears her. As softly as she can, she says, "Goodnight, Eban."

He seems sad as he turns to leave. At the door, he tells her, "They make me useful. Sladja comes to me and makes me show her what to do with herbs to heal burns, and had me sew three stitches into Golda's leg when she fell on the rocks gathering water. I have value here. That's why. That's why I feel safe."

She sinks onto the stool again and smiles briefly and almost tenderly, hands already restless, reaching for the pencil, while he shuts the door.

I was fourteen years old the day we saw the deer.

It was Daniel who spotted it first, and who noticed that it limped.

"There," he said, when he had called Alphonse and me out to stare across the dust to the shape scuttling past the gate to the allotment. "And look how it favours its right hoof."

"A deer?" Alphonse said in disbelief. "Out here?"

"Out here and not for long." Daniel set down his field glasses then to look with his naked eyes at the dark shape. "The cameras will pick that up."

"Will they kill it?" I asked.

"If they do, it won't be to eat. Maybe to study it. Or they might shoot before they have the chance to do even that—I don't know if there are people behind the guns they train on anybody fiddling with the gate there."

And then it was Alphonse who set out down the road carrying a lidded bowl of vegetables retrieved from the cellar. Daniel and I passed the field glasses back and forth, and saw the animal's reluctance, the nervous way it sprang away from him, but not fast or far enough.

"Sick maybe, as well as injured," Daniel said. "Or starved."

The deer never came close enough to the yard for me to see it well. It followed the trail of shrivelled carrot that Alphonse laid down for it, but only at a distance.

"Please," I begged, but Daniel shook his head.

"If we spook it, it may bolt for the allotment, the only place with shade for miles, and it will mean the end of it. I know you want to see it, but you might do it harm with your good intentions."

"Young, isn't it," said Alphonse when he returned.

Daniel agreed. "Maybe a yearling."

Alphonse stared at the animal, which stood at the end of the carrot trail, head and ears upright and high, watching us in wonderment. "Did you have any idea there were still deer in the world?"

Daniel made an expression of ambivalence. "I wouldn't dare try to guess what is or isn't out there."

The silence then seemed anxious to me, but I couldn't tell why. And then Daniel said, "No."

"Stupid of us, though. We'd eat without a worry till spring."

"No," Daniel said, just as gently.

"No," Alphonse agreed. "Not even if we starve."

"No way of knowing what's out there, but like all of us, that's one half of the future. Only half a chance there'll be another, and who knows how many such half-chances live out there in those hills yet. It would be a crime to rob the wilderness of one with so few left."

Alphonse was quiet for several minutes. "I didn't even think of that," he said at last.

"What do you mean?"

"I just thought even now we aren't desperate enough to kill something so lovely."

Daniel looked away from the deer for the first time, his expression disapproving as he regarded Alphonse. "You really think it deserves to live

more than the other creatures we've eaten? More than the hundred speci-
mens pinned or bottled on my shelves upstairs?"

Alphonse shrugged and said a special law ruled over the beautiful.
Particularly beautiful living things.

Daniel smiled briefly and noted that they would outlaw him for think-
ing that way in the cities.

"Fairness occupies their thoughts more than mine. I always favoured
mercy over justice."

The deer had eaten the last of the carrots and given up searching for
more. We held our breath for one long moment as it looked back in the
direction from which it had come, and then all at once it bolted, its lame leg
no longer seeming to hinder it, heading, as best we could guess or hope,
towards the hills.

"Well, your way isn't merciful to those insects up there," Daniel said.

"No. No, it's not."

The three of us watched the deer until it vanished from sight somewhere
in the distance. Then we went inside and ate a supper of turnip stew.

For several nights in a row, she dreams of tiny beings of all kinds—
human, animal, insect, once even a slender sapling on a steep, bald hill.
There is no connection between the dreams except the vulnerability of
these creatures. A newborn mouse, pink and blind, trapped in a jar. An
ant attempting to carry a load much too big, which it drops and picks
back up, again and again. It's when she dreams of the human infant,
lying on its side with its back to her, succumbed and motionless, that
she understands these are all dreams of her baby.

Eban once told her that fetal cells can migrate from an unborn child
into its mother's brain, annexing her anatomy to serve its needs. She
thinks maybe this baby is shaping her for mercy, creating in her a dangerous tenderness, which she will host like it is a parasite when the baby
arrives. The parasite will ensure that to deny the baby will be an act of

unbearable self-harm. If need be, Judy will starve to feed her child, and not because of duty or even compassion. Because when the baby is unfed, they will hunger together.

She has never seen a baby. The youngest person she has ever known is the girl whose name was Elinor, who came to their first hide in the hills, whose illness infected Eban's mother and her father and killed them both. Daniel had a photograph of himself and his sister as children in a garden in white clothes, and she used to stare at it, as a girl, and attempt to understand how her father had once been this smiling, neckless boy with fat hands and perfect teeth.

In books she has found pictures of them, babies as angels and as fairies, babies in the arms of their mothers, babies stolen or sobbing or watchful. She knows that they aren't just tinier people but differently put-together ones, with wider eyes and larger heads, round bellies and short, thick limbs. She knows they are born preposterously weak, more helpless than new-hatched birds. But there are so many things she doesn't know. How quickly do they grow? How long do they need to be spoon-fed and carried? When and how do they learn to speak?

When the other babies went, their passage made sense to her in a way she could never have explained to Eban. The inexplicable exits belonged to the mysteriousness of babies—these creatures that were incontestably human but clearly also something else. Something other and more. They grew in darkness. And died there. And whatever they were, invisibly, or could have been and weren't, is their secret, which they keep.

Daniel was a collector, but he didn't call it collecting. He called it keeping things. It was his work, but only coincidentally. You could tell that he would do it anyway, no matter what. He had jars filled with rock and sediment, samples of bark, shelved in lines across the wall over his desk. He kept insects pinned to paper after he'd finished examining them. Alphonse

called it macabre and once threw out a box filled with their desiccated
remains, thinking Daniel wouldn't notice, but he was furious and didn't
speak to Alphonse for three days. At breakfast on the third day, I chided
him, and said he shouldn't disturb Daniel's work, which I believed to be
very important. (I was so proud when the riders would come to collect his
papers.) But Alphonse said the work was done, and that wasn't the reason
Daniel was angry. "He misses them," he said.

The first thing I kept was a watch escapement made of brass.

Alphonse had once owned a fine watch that ran on a battery from
before, and he wore it bound around his wrist with a strap of leather. Long
after they stopped making such batteries, he would show his watch to every
peddler that passed through, and offer enough in payment that sometimes
they would return months or even years later with acid-corroded batteries
they had salvaged from old houses or pried out of spent machines at the
dump, or wherever peddlers find such things. Sometimes the salvaged batteries even worked. But eventually there were no more to be had, and then
his watch stopped for good, and the last peddler he brought it to in des-
peration frowned so deeply that my father understood it was hopeless. But
that same peddler returned in summer with a watch on a chain that kept
time all by itself, by only winding a spring. I was standing at the door when
the peddler pulled it from his coat, with that gift all peddlers have for
drama, producing it like a star plucked from the sky. And I watched as my
father threw his arms around the man and wept.

Alphonse told me the watch on the chain, hooked over the button of the
jacket he wore summer and winter alike, would never stop. He was as proud
of it as if he'd crafted it himself, and in fact I often saw him put his hand to
it and study it as though he would have liked to take it apart and make it
again. He wound it at the table every night after we ate, and for several years
took great pleasure in declaring the hour, though no one had asked.

And then one evening as he wound it, he looked out the window at the
pinking sky and then back at the watch in his hand, and an expression of

worry passed over his face. "No matter," he mumbled and put the watch back into the pocket where it was kept. But the next evening and the next, he took to standing at the window staring out at the sky, holding the watch out before him like a specimen of study. "What is it?" I asked him, but he didn't answer, and Daniel shook his head at me, so I knew not to ask again. After a week had passed, and he had begun taking his dinner standing beside the window, searching the clouded sky for the sun, one night he suddenly hurled the watch to the floor and Daniel and I both cried out as it clattered over the tiles and slid to a stop at the wall.

"We dine at six," he said. "That has always been our way."

Daniel remained seated, pity in his eyes. "Dining is a grand word for the way we eat these days, my love," he said lightly. "And I don't know that I've paid much attention to the timing of it."

"Always at six," Alphonse repeated, like he hadn't heard.

"I am certain you're right."

He turned towards us, as I crept across the floor, trying not to be noticed. "Have you ever known the sun to set at six in summer?"

"No," Daniel said, "I haven't." And he stood and took my father in his arms, and they rocked from side to side in that embrace, ever so gently, like dancers. And as they rocked, I held the broken watch face in my hand and saw that the springs and wheels that had rolled over the tiles would be difficult to ever bring together again. And in the nights that followed, Alphonse tried to do it, squinting through a special glass that made small things look large, but the parts never even turned again, and there was no one who could be found who knew how to make an old and broken watch keep time. One day when I was given a sack of garbage to drag to the dumping ground, I found inside the shining pieces of my father's watch and I kept the largest one.

Eban doesn't return the next morning. Instead, it's one of the twins who slides the door open and heaves his load across the room. Watching him lumber back and forth like a bead sliding along a string, setting down one thing and picking up another, Judy's impatience slowly eases. This isn't Eban's hesitation, but something else—a languorous caution that is somehow interesting to her.

Backing away from her, he looks up for the first time, and she nods at him. Almost smiles. His eyes are wide, faintly mystified. She imagines him asking what she's doing here, and why he has brought her these things. She puts the word *why?* in his mouth and shakes her head in answer to the imagined question. She is overwhelmed by the desire to speak. To be understood by this lean, silent man with his worn face and watchful eyes.

She tries to think of a gesture to communicate to him something, anything. Awkwardly, she lifts her hand and then, unsure what to do with it, simply opens it in the air, as if to signal her attention to him, or call for his. His eyes drift to her hand and then he lowers his face again. He leaves so slowly that she imagines he is at the edge of some change of mind, and watches each step, expecting him to suddenly turn back to her. Instead he slowly opens the door, slowly walks through, and slowly is gone.

After that, it is the twin who comes every day. Whether it is the same man or his brother, she doesn't know. Each time the bolt is drawn, she imagines Eban at the door, and sometimes there is an instant when she seems to see his face, before the imagined features resolve, submitting to the face of the other man.

Three seasons passed without any riders appearing on the road. All my life, they'd come quarterly, a veil of dust gathering at the horizon to forecast their arrival. They rode their horses fast, hurried hooves beating at the dirt, so their arrival was easily distinguished from the plodding approach of a peddler and his cart. Whoever first saw the dust rising from the road in the distance would call to the others and then stand watch. It might be hours till the rider reached our door.

Always, Alphonse would offer a meal, a night's rest, but the riders refused even water for their horses. They wouldn't ask for Daniel or his papers, which Alphonse and I would have copied and stitched together over the preceding weeks. They just waited, reins in hand, until he came to them.

Alphonse sometimes was offended or made a joke of their self-seriousness. "Like zealots," he'd mutter. "For all the world like zealots. Missionaries here to retrieve the holy word." "They've come," he'd announce to Daniel. "First Knights of the Equine Order of Entomological Data."

But he respected Daniel and the work he did, however he mocked the men and women who arrived to collect it. He spoke of it with a reverence of his own when he told me not to bother Daniel in his office, or touch a selection of specimens lined in jars at the table. "Like measuring the world in teaspoons," he whispered once as we watched my father at his microscope. "Taking its pulse with butterflies." Because Daniel didn't like to talk to me of his work ("It worries him," Alphonse once admitted. "He reads upsetting things there, the way you and I read words on the page. I don't think he wants you to see into that book"), it was Alphonse who explained phenology to me. Though I never properly understood how it worked, because he didn't, I saw its importance, and was pleased my father possessed this other literacy, the world's own language, and could receive its communications. From looking at things invisible to most, he saw what had happened to us—and what would.

And somewhere there were those who didn't want invisible things known. Or at least, that was my understanding and the reason for the reticence of the riders, the secrecy around my father's reports. "Like teaching Latin to the commoners, so they don't need the Church to hear the word of God," Alphonse said once, cryptically.

And so as early as the first season when no veil of dust lofted over our road and no rider arrived to our yard, Daniel was worried, and we were worried for him.

———

Almost three weeks pass before Eban comes again. It has been long enough that she imagined, as her mind unreeled over the long and silent days, that he might not ever return.

He steps inside without his usual hesitation. There's a changed energy about him. An intention. Still, he raises his eyes to her in the customary way that has long exasperated her, like he is both searching for something in her face and afraid of what he might find.

"I thought I'd seen the last of you," she says, her tone uncertain. She's not sure whether she means to accuse him. She doesn't know what's happened in the weeks since she has seen him, and somehow she is reluctant to ask.

He doesn't answer, and she says, more gently, "Every time the door opened, I was hoping it was you." The words surprise her own ears. She supposes she means them as an apology, because she was unkind for no clear reason when she saw him last. But he starts like she has hurt him with the remark.

"Eban?"

She feels alarm swelling in her chest as he tightens his mouth and sets to work, laying out the tray of food and drink, and exchanging one waste pot for another.

"*Eban*," she says sharply.

Now he ignores her, not even slowing in his work as he stacks the dirtied dishes onto the old tray and hangs the dirtied pot over his arm by the handle. Like her, he has eaten better and more regularly than ever before in these last weeks. His face is softened, and there is a bright, warm colour in his cheeks. He always argued that they were fortunate in their life in the hills, that they were secure and well-fed, without fear for their survival. And it was true—they never starved, but she had been accustomed to a tightness in the belly, a want that was only ever briefly satisfied. All these steady, plentiful meals show on him, and she guesses they show on her too.

The thought reminds her. "Look," she says, lifting up her layers of sweaters to reveal the unfastened buttons of her pants. She has used a bit of string to draw the pants together under the round belly now rising over her broad hips. She enjoys her spreading body and new sense of weight and strength.

His mouth falls open as he looks. He turns his chin back to the door as if trying to tug his gaze away, but he is held by what he sees. Watching now from the corners of his eyes, as if he is being told a lie, he takes in a long, deep breath and then another. She frowns, trying to make sense of his silence, when it is broken by the sound of all the dishes in his hands clattering to the floor.

She gasps as if Eban himself had fallen to the ground. He is still staring at her, hardly noticing the broken plate, the spilled white pot.

"It's okay," she whispers, hurrying to him. She picks up the clay plate, which has come apart in three clean pieces, and peels off a sweater, using it to wipe at the filth seeping from the white pot over the wood floor. "It's okay." She is frightened of him, this dogged, steady man who now stands before her like a stranger. "I can clean it up."

She cuts a finger on one of the segments of clay and puts it to her mouth, instinctively. Only then does he seem to awaken to himself, dropping to his knees and reaching for her hand. She produces it, shyly, for his inspection. He looks at it for so long, she thinks at first that something must be wrong, that he's worried about the wound or how to dress it. Instinctively, she attempts to snatch it back, but he holds on too tightly, clutching it beneath his bowed head and hidden face.

"*Eban?* Eban, please say something to me. Why won't you—"

And then she understands.

He lives by their rule now. He won't speak again, not even to her. The realization fills her with horror, and a wild, lonely sorrow. Now, she understands, now there can be no question. She is imprisoned here. And she can't tell if he is, too, or if he is one of those imprisoning her.

"Oh Eban," she says finally, surprised to find herself near tears, as if he's someone gone from her, someone to be grieved.

He lifts his face and his expression is so anguished that she can't be angry with him or even show her worry. "It will be okay," she tells him. "Take the tray back, and the pot, and I'll clean up the rest. You don't have to come here again."

She's thinking to herself, as they stand, that she'll have to leave without him. A chance will come, and she'll get free of this place. But he won't.

"Goodbye, Eban," she says, turning away.

And then from behind her back, she hears him whisper, so quietly she might have imagined it, "What did I do wrong?"

She thinks, I don't know what you're asking. She thinks, I don't know how to answer. But she does, and she says nothing. And he's gone.

After the riders didn't come anymore, my father became quieter. He spent more hours alone in his study, though he produced no more documents for Alphonse and me to copy, and he began taking his meals alone, upstairs.

Alphonse, too, spoke less to me, even as he did everything he could to reassure me Daniel was fine and we would be too. But I saw the troubled way he watched the door and stood in the yard, staring to the end of the empty road.

I heard them whispering when they didn't know I listened.

"Who stopped them?" I heard Daniel ask again and again, wildly. "Who stopped them coming?"

Alphonse's answers were always too quiet to make out, and I understood only from the gentleness of his voice that he was attempting to soothe Daniel.

But Daniel disagreed with whatever words Alphonse spoke. "You don't understand. You don't see the risk I'm taking, that we've all been taking. If they've stopped the riders, they will want me stopped too. And it won't be hard for them to learn—"

Finally one night, after he was locked inside Daniel's study for nearly an hour, trying to calm him, I heard Alphonse shout, "Because you aren't important enough! Why should you matter to them? We know nothing even of who they are or what they want, but what possible trouble could you bring them, an aging scientist in the outland, counting bugs and keeping diaries of their every twitch? How can you be stupid enough to think that anyone cares what you write?"

And then there was silence. And then Alphonse appeared at the door, pale-faced, closing it behind him. And then there were no more butterflies and beetles, no more notes and no more charts. My fathers seemed to less often remember me, and cared for me only absently, and they scarcely spoke to each other at all. Once, I pushed open Daniel's study door, expecting him to scold me for interrupting his work. But there was no work. All the papers on the wall, the drawings, the stacks of books, the jars and slides and maps, were gone. He sat at an empty table, in an empty room, staring at his own hands with tears in his eyes.

I was the first to see my father dead. We had just returned from a walk, and in the distance, I saw his body poured over the ground outside the open front door. "They killed him," I said as Alphonse lifted him from the steps where he had fallen. "They killed him." I sobbed, "He did matter. He did. The things he wrote were that important. And they killed him for them."

And my father, holding the body of the man he loved like a baby, said nothing.

A day later, we travelled up into the hills. And I knew there were things that I'd been told that were wrong. I knew that it was not for love that my mother had given me to these two men. And I knew we weren't safe anymore.

Waiting is a strange practice. By the time sixty-seven days have passed, Judy has begun to feel like an insect trapped in a lantern, flapping at the glass. Some days she paces the rectangular course of the room until dark. Some days she sits in taut, uneasy stillness, squatting at the centre of the floor, listening for the approach of whoever brings her food today. She scarcely sleeps, but forces herself to remain in her bedding until sunlight pricks through the broken glass. With no way to count or measure the dark hours, the nights stretch to impossible length. When the black begins to lift and blue in the first minutes of day, she is ready to sob with relief. There is nothing but waiting. She waits and she waits and she waits. Her mind has gone crooked. Occasionally she'll hear what sounds like a step land outside her door, and in the moment that lasts until the hand can be heard pulling back the bolt, turning the knob, she suddenly knows that she could not have waited a second more. The wait for the last sequence of sounds before the door will open is all but infinite.

And then sometimes she has made a mistake; she hears no bolt drawn, no hand pushing open the door. It may be minutes or hours until someone comes, or longer than that, a sum of time she can't even imagine, and she will wait it. The wait is impossible, and happens anyway.

Early on the sixty-seventh night, she hears a heavy step outside the door, which flies open before she can even feel the usual lift of heart and vanishing of patience. Sladja leaves the door open and walks directly to the table where Judy sits with her pile of pencil-scrawled pages. She smiles at Judy, and it is the first time anyone has smiled at her since the last time she came. Judy can only stare back in shock.

Sladja extends her open hand and Judy is slow to understand what she wants, but follows her gaze to the papers before her on the table and reluctantly turns them over.

Sladja's eyes narrow and she holds the pages up close to her face. She turns the pages roughly, and Judy winces as they crumple in her tight grasp—she herself has treated them almost tenderly since they were given to her.

Her brow still lowered, her eyes slitted, Sladja nods and nods again as she reads. She shuffles the pages with increasing speed and then, finally, lets the hand that holds them fall to her side.

She looks down at Judy with clear, shrewd eyes and smiles once more. Hesitantly, Judy lifts her hand to retrieve the pages, but Sladja tucks them into her jacket and produces a key from her pocket. Stepping to the other side of the desk, she unlocks the second drawer and withdraws the stitched volume Judy once glimpsed beneath the stack of tests. Sladja opens the history to the first page and shows it to Judy, who nods slowly. *Ourselves*, she begins to read, and then the older woman snatches up the edge of the page and tears it from its binding.

Judy is as astonished as if the woman had peeled away a limb.

With an expression of intense concentration, Sladja opens her jacket to reveal two objects slipped inside a deep pocket, laying them on the table before Judy, side by side. One is a sheaf of empty pages, and the other is a wooden box. Opening the box, after Sladja's nod of encouragement, Judy finds a steel-nibbed pen and a pot of deep blue ink.

Then Sladja sweeps up the pen, the ink and the history, turns her back and settles onto the floor, bent over the torn page so that Judy can't see what she is doing with it. Judy hides her frustration by flipping through the stack of pages Sladja has given her. The paper is thinner and smoother than any she's seen before, and she wishes she could ask how it was made.

After some time, Sladja pulls herself from the floor, her age making the simple act of standing a feat of strength and will, and Judy has to resist the urge to help her to her feet.

The page Sladja lays before her now has been altered and amended in the wild and wavering blue hand Judy recognizes from the history. Whole sentences have been struck out with a single jagged line, and new words scrawled above. She stares from the page to Sladja's hands, which shake even clutched in fists as they are now. She understands that there is something wrong with those hands, and maybe with Sladja herself. And then she understands everything.

I'm to write it, she thinks. Sladja can no longer do it herself. She wants the history written again, and I'm to write it.

Judy looks into the older woman's eyes. As if Judy has spoken aloud and as if she has heard, Sladja nods.

Then she lays the page on the table, smoothing it with both hands like something cherished, and locks the volume from which it was torn inside the drawer.

When she is gone, Judy doesn't hesitate. She opens up the ink and begins the work of copying both old and altered words onto the clean and empty page.

The last words Judy writes of her own are these:

Alphonse loved to tell me stories of the baby I once was. He was more sentimental than Daniel and would have to wipe his eyes as he spoke of just how small I had been, of a foot that fit perfectly in his hand, of a season of nights spent at watch over my cradle, which he'd sawn apart a chair to build.

"You were a being of time," he said once, eyes closed and the tip of his nose a little reddened as he recalled my smallness, when I had been unable to move or eat but for the loving care of my fathers. "You would pin us to a single moment, as we waited and watched you breathe or sleep or drink. The long hours of the night would pass in slow seconds as we looked at your tiny face and thought that we would be content to watch it for the rest of our lives, to do only that, only look down over this small being and forever know, Just now she is safe. Time had become something else altogether, something remote and measureless, a kind of grace.

"But then, all at once, over a single night sometimes, we would see how time had travelled through the room while we weren't looking. Your face would be bigger, your body longer than the day before. A gown no longer fit. A hand could clasp what yesterday it couldn't. And we understood that time had never altered or shown any compassion for us. You grew and grew and grew, and would not have stopped even if we'd wished it."

"*Did you wish it?*" I asked him.

"*No and yes and no. You taught us how long hours are, and days, and how quickly they pass. That's what babies do. They are an education in time. Its constant alterations their perpetual becoming.*"

"*Would you have wished me not to become—to stop?*"

"*But for the fact that I know what stopping is. A single certainty, instead of all that possibility. You can't want that, and it's the only other choice.*"

But Alphonse stopped. We came into the hills together and Eban found us on the ninth night we slept in our tattered tent, frozen and grieving and afraid. Eban was carrying a rifle when I caught him watching us. He turned and it was I who was caught, in his pale eyes that were kinder than any I'd seen before, and he glowered for a moment, as he does when he's unsure, but I knew from his eyes not to fear him. I still can see him as he was, standing there in the near dark, a figure of mercy with a weapon in his hands.

And it wasn't long after that that a girl so wild she scarcely knew a word to speak brought some sickness to us, and Alphonse became a single certainty, in a pile of dingy bedding, in the middle of the wood I understood I'd never leave. And the girl stopped, and Eban's mother stopped, and after that, he and I continued, moved high up into the hills with all our possibility, which somehow felt like only one. And the babies we made together grew and ceased, unborn, becoming other certainties.

I would have liked to love Eban. This is the cold, unthinkable thought that I have now. I read it on the page and am not certain I believe it. But I find I don't have the imagination or the memory to convey me across the great distance between this time and one when I was sure of him and believed we'd find happiness together in the hills.

And what belongs to us now, which he mistakes for love, is something so much less it makes me want to flee these hills or let you leave me locked in this room forever. Because I knew what love was. I lived in its house.

And what I saw in my fathers' faces, heard in their voices, felt part of just for standing near them, is not here or anywhere nearby.

XIII

THE YOUNG SLADJA, who put her pen to the first page of this book when it was new, wrote in a hand that bears roughly the same resemblance to the newly scrawled addenda that a young, straight back might bear to an old and crooked one. The earlier writing is confident, each letter shaped with care, the passages long and breathless. The corrections she made moments ago, bent over the page on the floor, are scarcely legible, the wildness of the shivering blue lines contradicted by the words themselves, which are stilted and overwrought.

Judy reads both sides of the page four times before she lifts the pen from the table. The first passage has been considerably expanded, extra words crowding even the title, and she can't guess the significance of the changes.

The Second History of Haven Colony

Like in heart and like in mind, we choose this life. Those named here joined together in this choice, freely made, guided by our shared conscience, hidden from a world that has fallen under shadow. Drained of the human graces, it belongs to others now. Where we hear, they are deaf. Where we see truly, they are blind. Where we are plied by mercy, they are iron.

These free people came into the hills on April 11th, 2062, and in this waste made a place of refuge for all under our care. We number fifty-three, named in these pages. We have chosen to live under the rule of silence. By its enforcement, we protect our own from those who would turn our hearts against us, pervert our pity and bend us to their will. The rule is binding for all who freely choose to live among us or who enter into our watch.

To those who wonder of these two worlds, the one fled and the other built by careful hands, with these words we tell you who we were.

Judy notices that from the list below of fifty-seven names, four have been removed. She wonders why.

The last passage, entered in blue beneath the pencilled names, is marred by so many excisions and additions that it is hardly readable. Sladja's changes fill the margins and seep past the page edge, continuing on the other side.

Nearly a year we prepared. We might have prepared for a decade and not been ready. But the travel took only three days, even with heavy loads of food and seed and each of us carrying our own belongings, stripped to fewer possessions than we'd ever imagined possible. "Leave it all," Ren had commanded on the night of our last assembly, meeting the eyes of each of our number, honourable and proud, worthy of the faith they have awarded him. "All but what will enable your survival." He paused and studied us, as though he guessed where weakness might exist, a reluctance to renounce the lives that now belonged to that before, an extinct time and place. "Our survival," he said.

And so we left the village and left the world that was. We climbed into the hills, bent under our packs, and fast learned what had been forgotten and what should have been. The houses were ready and sufficient to our needs. For the year of readying, twenty men and women in our number had camped in the hills for months at a time, cutting wood, hauling stone, digging, sawing, nailing, and preparing this new place. The last place, for us, the last people.

Judy slides her finger down the list of names, but sees no *Ren* among them. At the edge of one of the blots of ink that have expunged four names from the list, she thinks she glimpses the contours of an *R*, but isn't sure.

Alive in a way she hasn't felt since she was bottled up in this black house, she fills the pen with ink and begins the work of copying the history. She writes until it is dark and the words impossible to read.

Sladja arrives at the end of the next day, when long beams of blushing sunlight are retreating across the floor, slipping out the broken window. She takes the new page and the old from Judy and reads, signalling neither approval nor disappointment. Then she tucks both pages in her jacket pocket and tears out two more. This time she sits down on the stool, which Judy yields, and makes her changes on the desk while Judy stands aside, trying not to watch.

From that day on, Sladja appears every evening to accept Judy's work and mark new pages for her. Sometimes she brings a candle and stays on into the night, turning over so many pages that it takes Judy most of the day to copy them.

After that first night, Sladja leaves the job of bringing Judy's meals to Romeo-or-Bobby-Rae, who sometimes lingers so long that she feels sure he is near to addressing her, but he only raises his eyes to her at the door before he closes it. Eban does not come again.

———

And as the weeks pass, Judy learns the story of the people who first came into the hills, and what drove them there.

The first dozen pages of Sladja's account follow the process of the colony settling into their new lives in the wilderness. In great detail, she explains the back-breaking labour of hand-ploughing and planting the four-acre garden, the endless problems with the solar-powered pump that was to irrigate the orchard, and the disappointing yields of their first efforts at hunting, and foraging. An entire passage describes an outbreak of trichinellosis after a bear was felled in a rain of lead by a panicked novice hunter and the elaborate sequence of baths in brine and smoke failed to kill the parasite.

The account is at first instructive and objective, a report on lessons learned or brought from the other civilization. But as the colony adjusts to the new conditions of their existence, they grow bored, and conflicts begin to emerge. At one meeting, a couple with two young children speak of leaving the hills. Then, three pages are blotted out and there is no more mention of the family.

Ren figures frequently and importantly in the account, resisting the erasure Sladja seems to have attempted when she struck his name from the register, as Judy is now convinced she did. In each appearance he is portrayed with such respect—his proud little speeches recounted in full, his features described more completely than those of any other—that she guesses he was a leader of sorts to the colony.

None of our number has taken to the forage with such success as Ren, who returns from the forest with his sack filled of amaranth, chicory root or fireweed, and knows always with certainty which roots and leaves are safe to eat and which must be left untouched. Even in this drought, he has found beds of mushroom nestled deep in the cleft of a tree or huddled in its shade. "All that we need can be provided to us in these wilds," he answers modestly when we wonder at his knowledge. "We must learn to know the trees we

live among, which we can and cannot trust, as we once knew our neigh-
bours and whether they should be avoided or sought."

Often as we eat, we whisper among ourselves that we might have
starved waiting for our scorched gardens to grow, but for the fruits of his
daily trips into the forest. The hunters bring back kills only intermittently,
and whether fewer animals yet live in this forest than we supposed or their
skills are less than they claimed is anyone's guess. In the world before this
one, Ren ate no meat and disdained even the cow's milk and hen's eggs that
could then be bought at any store. But he understands that in this new
world, even principle must sometimes yield, and he surrenders it as easily as
he surrendered the possessions that were no longer fitted to the lives we lead
here. Yet to eat of the hunters' kills gives him little pleasure, and he swal-
lows only what meat is needed to survive.

As she reads further, the grandiloquent prose becomes faintly less stiff,
and Sladja's neutral pronouns falter, her *I* springing up among the endless, affectless *we*. And in this change, Judy notices a sort of alliance
between her and Ren. Many pages later, she comes across a passage that
seems to indicate they were something even more than that to each other.

On our ninetieth night in these hills, we were brought from our bed by a
knocking at the door, and when Ren opened it he saw Gretchen, who kept
watch that night. In hushed and hurried words, she told us—

With a sharp intake of breath, Judy rereads the passage. *Our* bed. She
reads on.

In hushed and hurried words, she told us that a man and a woman had come
out of the forest, awaking several houses with their flashlights and loud
voices. She said that their English was poor and she could scarcely under-
stand them. They were looking, she said, for a place they called Heaven.

"Heaven?" I repeated.

"I think it's a misreading of the sign," Gretchen answered. "I think they mean Haven."

When we first came to this place, Ren asked an eleven-year-old boy to post the name of Haven colony at the path, honouring the future we had founded by choosing the youngest among us for the job. But the boy's parents hadn't disclosed that he had never gone to school, and the sign he produced read HAEVEN. The error troubled Ren. "We will need to be careful with words," he had said during our final climb into the hills. "We are shaping a paradigm for future generations with our lives. Every choice we make, every gesture, every detail is a symbol. And so everything we do must be deliberate and precise." But he had hesitated to remove or replace the sign, wishing to spare the boy's feelings.

"We'll take the sign down," I said.

Gretchen shook her head. "No need. It blew down in the winds last week. These people didn't stumble upon us. They already knew we were here. They came looking for us."

We had long expected and planned for this development. The last people, we are also the first, pioneers in these hills, and we knew that in the months and years to come, many more would flee as we had fled. And by accident or intent, they would find their way to us.

"And when they do, will we turn them away?" Ren asked when we had first spoken of it. "Will we deny them what was hard-earned, because they lacked our foresight or our courage?"

I knew for him the answer was clear, as all truths were to him. And yet a shadow dwelt in my heart.

Sladja didn't explain the shadow or its meaning . . . was it the same shadow alluded to on the first page, or some other, private worry? But as if it had poisoned the events that followed, the next many pages recounted only unhappiness. The couple adjusted poorly to the conditions at the camp, and proved to be of little use to anyone. The man, Alexander, was bad-tempered and stole fruit from the orchard. Sladja found him creeping through the colony after dark for no apparent reason. And his wife, Josefine, seemed untroubled by his behaviour and uninterested in the routine of the colony and its inhabitants . . . only Ren seemed to hold her attention.

And I ask him what is meant by the long hours Josefine keeps at his side, and he tells me only that she is frightened and has endured more than we did, having lingered longer in the troubles of the old life.

"What fears does she have?" I asked him. "What troubles has she endured?" For she shows no weakness that my eye can perceive and seems to lack the gentleness of character that might allow her to suffer.

"When we earn her trust, she will tell us," he promises me. But if she tells anything, it's to him alone. She is as close-lipped as her husband among all others. She follows Ren to meals, darns his clothes, and spends her only hours apart from him gathering herbs in the wood that she boils and claims will ease his asthma. But his fits of wheezing have only grown more frequent in the months that he has been without the medication he once took (though he doesn't know I hear him when he wakes at night, gasping, and leaves our bed for the outdoors, thinking he keeps his secret). And twice I have had to drive her from our own house.

He asks for my forbearance. He asks that I await her trust. But has she proven worthy of ours?

Sladja's apparent jealousy balloons over the succeeding pages, as seemingly meaningless incidents between Ren and the woman, or conversations between Sladja and Ren, are recounted with forensic detail. But then abruptly, the couple disappears from the account, eclipsed by an incipient crisis, as the drought that took hold weeks after the colony arrived shows no sign of abating, and the rainless crops fail one by one, costing them not only the intended food supply for a year but also the source of future seed. When eight months later the well runs dry, fourteen men and women decamp for the foothills, and in passing, Sladja notes Alexander among them. She doesn't mention what became of Josefine.

As the remaining colony struggles to make it to their second spring, Sladja focuses on reporting the details of crop-tending and water rations. There's no further sign of the brief turmoil caused by the arrival of the couple, though Judy notices that over the following year, Sladja dedicates herself to the study of medicinal herbs, and her accounts of Ren are no longer limned in wonderment. But in one short passage, fitted between records of seed storage, she writes cryptically of refugees, and Judy guesses who she means.

He tells me not to worry. My ljubavi, *my own happiness, he whispered in the dark that night, laying his cheek to mine and putting his hand over my bitten fingers. We are safe. We are safe. We are safe.*

But there will be more refugees. They will always find us. And we would crack in half to harbour them all. And we would never know whom we'd let enter, what snake we had brought into our house. At night, I think of it, and how we might know the wrong ones to turn them from our door.

By the colony's third year, only half its original number remain, but they have found a viable way of living that seems to bring them peace. Of their cherished orchard, only a single peach tree persists, which Sladja notes will run the clock of its short life in another decade. What is left of the four-acre farm, once maintained by a dozen dedicated workers, is now overseen by Oona alone, who also prepares the nightly meal. And Judy notes that it is now Sladja, rather than Ren, who addresses the colony when extra hands are needed to harvest the garden or help must be called to repair one of the houses. She encourages the others with words that appear sincere, and there is no sign that her zeal is flagging after the obstacles they have faced. But Ren, when he is mentioned, seems to be forever away in the hills, alone, foraging whatever he can in the dying wood.

The day Judy sees Eban again, a cold-looking rain drills the roof for hours, puddling on the floor before the broken window. She is staring out the window at the sodden snow still clinging to the ground, wondering whether this unending season is winter or spring, when she sees him.

In this dark weather, he is little more than a shadow darting between the grey trees. But before he steps close enough for her to glimpse his face, she recognizes his shape and stance with certainty.

She tells herself there's no point in calling his name. And so she just watches him, trying to guess why he has appeared there.

"What are you doing," she murmurs as he creeps from the shelter of one tree to the next. And then she hears a snapping noise, as if something has given way, and as she watches, he lifts a trap from the ground and studies his catch. She shakes her head. He has driven some poor rabbit from its den in the rain and chased it to his trap. She wonders if he even realizes how close she is.

Even though she knows what comes next, she watches him.

With nothing showing on his face at all, Eban seizes the rabbit by its ears and raises it from the cage. The rabbit beats its feet frantically and struggles to lay its teeth on Eban. As Judy watches, Eban grips the rabbit's feet in one hand, lowers a thick branch over its neck, and then, so quickly neither she nor the rabbit can quite believe it has happened, he snatches the rabbit's body back and steps onto the branch, disarticulating its neck. When Judy uncovers her eyes, the rabbit is limp in his hands. Though she never cries, she cries then. And she blames the baby, weakening her, cell by cell. Wiping at the tears with her hands, she feels a terrible pity.

It must be for this reason that she calls to him then. "Eban?"

He doesn't answer or stop. He is tying the rabbit to the branch to carry, but there is something intent and resolute about the way he moves now and she knows he hears her.

"Eban . . . I wish you'd look at me."

With hands that appear steady, he knots the string and lifts the branch over his shoulder.

"I've been reading about them," she calls to his back. "About the people who first came here and made this place. Sladja gave me their book to read. Their history. She wants me to copy it out again. She is changing it and I don't know why. But I'm learning what happened here."

He hesitates, adjusting the burden over his shoulder, or pretending to.

She searches for the right thing to say to him now.

In the first months and years that they knew each other, she envied Eban his talent with his pencils. She could never understand if the talent was in his hand or his eye, but he could look at a thing before him and then make its shape on the page with exactness. Or something even better—a trace of life itself. In his still images was a taut, ready vitality, so that looking at one you very nearly believed whatever he had drawn there was only temporarily still. Its next move and the onward lean of time were invisible but somehow present, strung among the pencil lines, already in wait.

She thought he could teach her to draw as he did, but the distorted shapes she put on the page had the precise opposite quality. They were as far from life as the machines her father used to tell her about. Unnatural, somehow. An aberration.

But Eban was patient with her. As often as she was willing to try, he would sit by her side as she drew, gently noting details she hadn't drawn or even seen. She thought it was strange that you could not see the thing you were looking at—that is, you could see it, but not know what it was you saw.

"It's not about seeing," he told her again and again. "We both see it. When I tell you, you know just what I mean. It's not as if you disagree with me or see something different."

"But why don't I see it till you tell me?"

"I think we must be used to looking at things as if they're only one thing. You know what a leaf looks like when it's held up straight before your eyes, but if it's turned on its side it might be some other shape—it might be just a line. Your eyes can see that line is a leaf, but when you draw, your hand doesn't know how to make that leaf into a line. Your hand wants to make it look like what you already know. It wants it to look like a leaf."

One day when it was so hot they couldn't bear to do anything else—nothing useful or routine—Eban had shown her a rabbit he'd caught in one of their traps. The creature was huddled against the farthest wall of the cage with its back to them, shivering. It was trying not to exist. It had done the best job it was able to do of disappearing.

"We'll both draw it, and then we'll switch and see what we saw that was different," Eban told Judy, handing her a book of paper and a piece of charcoal. She liked working with just the charcoal, even though it blacked her hands. Eban used pencils the peddlers brought him specially to make his tidy lines.

Of course what she drew was nothing like a rabbit and when it was time for them to make their trade, she gave it over so roughly it tore at the corner.

Eban smoothed the page with his hands till they were black like hers, and studied what she'd made.

"It's awful, I know."

"It isn't."

She looked miserably at his drawing in her lap. He'd drawn the rabbit at the very centre of the page, so small it seemed to be hovering help-lessly there. Unmoored. So vulnerable you almost wanted to look away.

"Why didn't you draw the trap?" she asked.

He frowned. "I don't know. I guess . . . I just wanted it to not be in there."

She looked more closely. Tiny as it was, the drawing contained everything about the rabbit. The dim, narrow lines of its form seemed tense with the same energy of the still, trapped rabbit before her. It was protesting, she understood. As the other rabbit protested the cage, this rabbit made only of pencil lines was protesting the page that bound it.

"Can I do something to yours?" Eban asked. "Would you mind?"

She peered over his shoulder at the dark, angry-looking smudges she had made. Drawing the bars of the cage had bored her, so she'd made them roughly, too thick and unvaried—with no qualifications of light or shade. The rabbit itself was out of proportion with the squares she'd drawn around it—too big, erupting from containment. She wondered if she should have drawn the cage first. But how would she have fitted the form of the rabbit between the bars?

She was prepared for him to redraw what she had done and wondered how he would erase such dark, clumsy marks on the page. But he made only three changes.

She had missed the way the very edge of the rabbit's eye could be seen, even though it tried to bury its face. And that eye, she realized, looking more closely after seeing what Eban drew, was watching them.

She had missed, too, that though both ears were turned back so far they were buried in its fur, one turned ever so slightly up at the end. She thought at first that the rabbit had cocked its ear to listen to them as well as watch, but the effect on the drawing, when Eban's work was complete, was altogether different. With that slight change, the altered angle of the farther ear, the rabbit seemed to be not listening but *resisting*.

The last adjustment Eban made was to the hunch of her rabbit's spine. He traced above the hasty line she had made, reshaping the curve, and revealing the last thing she had failed to see: the rabbit's head was much smaller than she had made it. She had drawn the head to be a size that seemed proportionate to its body. But the real rabbit's head was strangely small. And all the urgent, outraged energy of the rabbit, coiled in its corner, ended there.

"You can see it now," she murmured as he returned her drawing to her.

"See what?"

"How that rabbit wants us to believe it has disappeared."

He smiled slowly, his pleasure in her words as plain as his confusion. "I hardly did anything, Judy. You were most of the way there."

"You caught it," she said, shaking her head. "I wish I understood how."

"Do you remember that other rabbit?" she asks him now. "The one we drew?"

Eban is far enough away, shuffling through the rain with his chin tucked to his chest, that she thinks maybe he really can't hear her anymore.

"You took my drawing from me. Remember? You drew right on the page."

Now he's gone, out of her sight.

"You made it beautiful," she says.

Whenever Judy had asked what happened to the world, her fathers had been too vague and Eban too specific. "Human society has its own currents and tides," Daniel would begin. "The orbitofrontal cortex," would answer Eban.

Only now, reading Sladja's history, which circles back to the past with increasing frequency, does Judy understand.

I can't tell when it began. Did he always talk so, or is it only these last days or weeks? He is so long in the woods—all day and sometimes overnight. He doesn't like me to worry about him, and so I follow him when I can spare the time, and otherwise I trust, because I must, that he'll return.

But when he does, in those few hours that he sits by me after the evening meal, or lies with me in our bed after we put out the lanterns, he talks only of the way we lived. Before.

"I used to take you dancing," he said last night, waking me from sleep as though we had been in conversation all along. "I knew it was wrong but I was proud to dance with you. I mean it was wrong to take pride in your beauty, to want to show you to strangers, like a prize. But there it is. I loved it anyway."

"We stopped that long before we came here. We hadn't danced in years."

"We should have, though. I should have taken you out so much more. Every Saturday, we should have been dancing."

"I don't see how it would change a thing about where we are now."

"I didn't say that. Did I say that? I only said we should always have gone dancing. When we could. You danced like a ballerina. It wasn't really the right way to dance—even if we were only waltzing, you would point your toes and lift your elbows high like you were a little girl in dance school and your teacher was watching. You were always performing, never following like you were supposed to do. But that was okay. I followed you."

And then, three days ago, in the morning after he kissed me goodbye, he said, "We should have had children." And I was unable to think how to answer him before he went off into the wood.

Because it wasn't my choice not to. Or not only my choice. We agreed together, and we never questioned what we had decided. If he has had doubts, he has never shared them until now. And then to say it so casually, as though it was something we'd only forgotten to do.

We'd decided after his sister's child was tested. Though we'd long known, as everyone did, that anyone could have a child test positive—it wasn't a measure of weakness in you. That would have been less frightening. That, at least, you could predict, if not control.

We worried we wouldn't have the strength to relinquish such a child. We knew ourselves. We knew, like his sister, we might be tempted to keep such a child, whatever the risks.

As a girl, I went to school among them, of course. We all did. We didn't know better.

In those early days, we were supposed to be sympathetic. We were supposed to help them understand us. Though their sickness shared a similar neurological profile to antisocial personality disorder, they had, we were told, no will to harm. They want to understand, we were told. Tell them what they need to know.

For several years, researchers mistook the sickness for a variant of autism, because of the similar impact on emotion recognition and ability to read meaning in faces. We were taught not to attempt to show them pleasure with our smiles or grief with our frowns. We were taught to tell them, "You have pleased me." "You have made me unhappy." Then, we were told, they'd understand, and respond as any of us would.

But continued testing revealed that they lacked the deep empathic capacity of those with autism, who might struggle to process emotional expression but were highly sensitive to emotion itself. For unknown reasons, the brains of the sick ones were devoid of the faculty for affective empathy. No explanation of another person's pain could cause them to feel it themselves.

And meanwhile they kept being born. The school-administered battery of affect recognition and autonomic response tests was soon replaced by a simple brain scan that could be performed in infancy. By the time I was twenty-one years old, the year of the first tsunami, two of three babies left the delivery room with a confirmed diagnosis.

But for a long time we didn't truly understand how the sickness altered those born to it. The difference between us and the sick was far greater than we first believed. It was vast and unbridgeable. In the architecture of their brains there was no chamber laid ready to receive the experience of another. They could injure without suffering or knowing the suffering they caused. They lived among us like a human sham, remaking the world to their preference, bereft of the quality that had formerly defined even the worst of our species, the innate physiological response that registered guilt, shame, pity, and was the root of all human aspiration towards goodness. Civilization relied upon refraction of emotional experience—if a victim's pain produced no echo in the hearts of those who caused or witnessed it, there could be no remorse, no conscience, no moral foundation to human action or the laws that governed it.

When, at last, we saw what our blindness had hidden—when we saw that imposters had made a perversion of our humanity. That all which had been ours belonged to them. That there were enough of them to run our government, and enough to vote them to power. When we understood the computers we used did their affectless work, and we were now led by their science and by their laws. By a good they defined, which bore no compassion for the liberties and lives of men and women.

When they witnessed our suffering and spoke only of data projections and rations. "You have made us unhappy," we said to them. And they were no more moved to action by our words than they were moved to pity by our faces.

When, after their arrival, the world fell dark. When drought came. And famine. And they told us water and crops would no longer ship outside the cities. When they told us resources must be centralized, and energy conserved, and didn't regret the businesses they shuttered, the homes they left in ruin. When they rationed and then withdrew the fuel, and ceased to maintain the roads, so we could go nowhere but where they took us. When they cut off the power that we used to light our homes and cook and keep our food. When the consolidation orders were issued, and we watched communities empty like turned-out pockets, and we stood our ground and made our protest but knew we would fail because we were so few and they were so many.

Then, finally, we came to understand that they were not the pitiable victims of chromosomal deviation, but something dire and enduring—an "evolution," as they called it. A new and terrible world.

And into that world, he wonders now if we should have brought a child.

When he woke this morning, I was dressed and ready. "Do you want to go back?" I asked him. I meant it viciously, but he answered like it was an honest question.

"No."

"How can I believe you? After your talk of dancing and children, and the food we ate and the people we knew, of our house and our things and our families . . ."

"No," he said again, so surely that I listened. "Even if there was nothing in those cities. Nothing to fear. Even if we could go back to everything as it was, I would stay in these woods. We should have come years ago. There is such a clarity here. I think that's why I'm able to see now, at last, what I never could when we lived down below."

"What on earth would that be?"

"How happy we were."

The next night, it's already dark when Sladja arrives to collect the pages. She enters the house carrying a lantern like the ones Judy remembers from her fathers' house. Made in the old style, with an ornamental glass chamber, it casts a splintered yellow light around the room.

On other nights, Sladja has taken the finished pages from Judy without so much as looking at them, and then immediately unlocked the drawer and begun work marking up the new pages. But this time, for some reason of her own, she sits down at the desk and begins to read what Judy has copied, word by word.

Judy watches her, trying to guess from her face what she is looking for or confirming as she reads. She seems to linger over certain lines, her gaze arrested, her thoughts a mystery as she stares into the page. Once she turns a page over to read again what she has already read.

At last, she lays the papers on the table and sits for a moment looking over her shoulder into the shadows that dart and shudder along the wall.

Standing at the window, her hands at rest on her rounded belly, Judy feels strangely moved by the older woman. She imagines for her there is something stinging in the past, some sharp hook of regret that has caught her thoughts.

But the mood, whatever the source of it, drops away abruptly and completely. With an air of impatience, Sladja jams the key into the locked drawer and tosses the history onto the table. She seems to cross out more lines than ever before, with only a few brief, scribbled words to replace them. When she has finished, the pages she pushes across the table to Judy are scarcely legible.

As Judy bends to take up the pages, she feels a sudden, violent tightening in her womb. With a gasp, she drops the papers, which waft and drift across the floor. And the pain comes again.

She finds herself on her hands and knees and doesn't know how she reached the position. Whatever is happening to her won't stop happening. All that had held together—one thought to another, one moment to the next—cleaves. Between pains she looks up to Sladja, who stands at the table, white-faced. She looks much tinier and older than she did when she came into the room. Judy can see every thought in her head. She is afraid.

For a moment, the two women regard each other from either end of this event. As Sladja's lips part and Judy imagines she might speak, Judy slides a hand into her pants. When she pulls her hand out, it is red.

There's a crash as Sladja shoves aside the stool, which falls to the floor. She stumbles across the room and throws open the door. Catching hold of a rope Judy has never noticed before, she strikes a bell that must be hidden in the eaves. The bell clangs and clangs, but does nothing else. Summons no one.

Sladja drops the bell pull and turns back to Judy, who thinks now she'll come to help her. But instead she opens her mouth and howls.

The sound seems to repeat in Judy's head, ring in her bones. The long wail repeats, repeats, and ends.

When it does, a third person is in the room. She slips inside the door and stands with her fists at her sides, looking from Sladja to Judy. As Golda slowly edges towards Judy, Sladja pushes past and vanishes out the door. The lantern winks out just as Judy realizes that the pains have stopped.

In the dark, she hears Golda crouch to the ground beside her. And then the girl's arms wrap around her. Her embrace is too tight to be comforting or comfortable. But Judy finds herself clinging to the arms that have encircled her.

Sladja returns with a pot of hot water and a small sack of herbs, which she mixes into the water and forces Judy to drink. It burns her tongue but she drinks it all. She feels Golda's eyes on her as she lowers the cup to the floor.

Together, as though they share an understanding, Golda and Sladja guide Judy to her bedding. In the light of the candles Sladja brought back with her to the black house, Judy watches the two women. When they think she sleeps, they blow out the candles and leave.

In the dark, Judy shakes with exhaustion. There is no more pain, and no more bleeding. She doesn't know what has happened to her. She waits and waits to know.

In her fist is the key Golda pressed into her hand when she helped her to her bed. And in the table behind her is the drawer it will unlock.

XIV

FOUR, FIVE, SOMETIMES SIX times a day now, Sladja comes to check
on Judy. If she finds Judy out of bed, she guides her back to it with a firm
hand and a frown. Judy learns that if she waits until Sladja is gone, she
can safely take an hour out of bed before she appears again. And so every
time the other woman leaves, she listens for the scrape of the bolt and
then unlocks the drawer, and sits at the table and reads. She notes the line
of sunlight on the floorboards if the day is bright, and makes herself stop
reading when it has shifted by more than the span of her hand. If the day
is dark, she just guesses at the time, but sometimes she becomes lost in
what she's reading, and knows she's in danger of staying out of bed too
long and being caught. She doesn't know what Sladja would do if she
found her at the table with the open drawer and the history in her hands.

Now and again, Judy once more feels the clench of her womb, and
occasionally it is sharp enough to take her breath from her. But in time,
it passes, and there is no more blood. Whatever has happened or almost
happened remains at bay, for now.

When she has locked the history back in the drawer, Judy slides

the key halfway under the table leg. She hopes that when Sladja at last
notices it missing, she'll think she only dropped it.

Each time she pushes the key into the lock she wonders how it came
to be in Golda's hand, and then slipped into her own. She tries to imagine when Golda might have noticed the key, abandoned on the table
where Sladja left it. The two women seemed to have been by her side
until they left. But what is strangest of all is that Golda guessed it might
be useful to Judy.

When she first saw the girl, she was frightened of her. The terrible
violence of whatever had been done to her tongue seemed to cling to her,
an endlessly echoing threat. But Judy sees now that the girl is a victim.
Like Judy, she is trapped here in some inscrutable way. Though she's
permitted a measure of freedom—more, it seems, than Judy—within its
confines, she is captive. She is kept, thinks Judy, and then, *I am kept.*

Judy wonders if Eban knows what happened to her, and then tries and
fails to imagine how it could possibly have been conveyed without
words. In the long quiet hours of rest and worry, she has found herself
missing him. When she lost the other babies, he would make her stay
in bed for days, as Sladja does now. And he would struggle by turn to
entertain or comfort her. To guess which was what she wanted. At the
time she wished only that he would leave her alone, but now she thinks
that she would like him to be here.

She feels as though she is creeping towards an understanding, if she
could only get a little closer. She no longer recalls what she's searching
for, but she retains the conviction that whatever it is, she might find it in
the pages of the history.

Two days into her reading, Judy's eye catches Josefine's name on
the page. The history has recounted six years of life in the colony since
she was last mentioned.

———

We've met four times to discuss what to do about Josefine. But no one has any ideas. None that we can live with, none worthy of the kind of men and women we came to these hills to be. She can't be sent away, not after so many years. But she can't be kept. She shows great interest in the children, but she frightens them. She carries the youngest boy, James, around in her arms like a baby, even though it makes him scream and fight her, and his parents say she takes him with her deep into the woods when they are at work. Things have gone missing that can't be accounted for except by her presence at the time they disappeared. She eats as she pleases, from the fields, from our stocks, and wastes as much as she eats, leaving picked potatoes to rot in the mud where she dropped them, or forgetting to re-tie the sacks of dried fruit she plunders, so that they become infested with grain beetles. At night she doesn't seem to sleep but just wanders from house to house, and several people have reported waking to find her standing just inside or just outside their door. She hardly answers us when asked what she is doing or why. And none of us seem to be able to reason with her.

Last night I told Ren she was unhinged, and I could tell from his expression that he was annoyed. It has been a long time since he gave up speaking to her, but he never pretended to understand why I asked it of him. Or to think well of me for asking. Since then, he has been true to his word. I don't know how he explained it to her, but I haven't seen a look or word pass between them ever again.

And so when I said her name he flinched like I'd slapped him, but didn't answer.

"Something will have to be done," I told him. And still he just studied the staff he was carving—since winter he's had a persistent pain in his left knee, and he thought a cane might make his long climbs in the hills a little easier—and said nothing.

"Everyone has said their piece, but still no one does anything. They're in need of leadership. A decision. A sure hand."

"Maybe," he said.

"I used to think you were that kind of person." I looked at him as I spoke the words so he'd know I meant the sting of them. But he didn't look stung in the least. He looked sorry. And I saw right then how old he'd grown.

"I thought it too," he said only. "I thought it too, Sladjana."

I wished he called me "my ljubavi" as he used to. For the first time, I realized it had been years since he had spoken those words. But the thought didn't make me sad as all of our conversation seemed to be making him sad. It made me angry. "And what has changed?" I demanded. "You're no less needed now. And so what's the change? Where is the man we followed here, the one we listened to, whose every word we hung on? The one I listened to. The one I followed here. Aren't you that man?"

I wanted to make him angry too. I thought my anger would break the strange calm that had settled over him, the look of hardly caring about anything at all.

"I don't think so," he said slowly. "Not that man. Not anymore."

When I grew up, it was unusual to marry young. It was rare and considered unwise to know only one lover. I can't remember why. Was it because you were meant to wait until you had grown old enough to know yourself, as if the person you are was a fixed destination, an address to roll into like a driveway and never leave? When we met, we were nineteen years old, both of us, born just three days apart. Which seemed meaningful to us, in those young years when everything was meaningful, everything important. We won the disapproval of our parents, which was as good as a blessing. We were alike in everything, except in the ways we were different, which were perfect too.

Or was it because you were meant to try out those feelings, before you owned them permanently? Was it so you could learn the ways of other bodies, and then know what was him and what was sex itself, so it wouldn't feel as if you had invented it all, together, something as alive and wondrous as that, belonging all to you. Or was it because if you loved only once, you would love too hard?

"*I was pompous,*" *he said.* "*A blowhard. It makes me sick to think about it. I spend all day forgetting it, and then I come home and I remember. When we came here, I was certain about everything. I thought we were going off to live in an idea. But it's not an idea. It's this shitty cough I can't get rid of and no drugs for it but those expired ones you hock like snake oil in a pillbox. We'll all die of things we could have cured at the counter of a pharmacy. It's the awful food that tastes so good it's depressing, because we're all half-starved. It's all these people, who have come here with us and gone half-crazy with us or maybe always were. It's how hard we work. It's how much we care. It's how the woods smell, every single day. It's how the weather changes everything. It's the way you look now, with your hair grown long and turned white like it has. You are relentlessly beautiful.*"

He didn't say even those last words with tenderness. But I didn't want any. "*Pompous?*" I repeated.

He nodded. "*I used to talk and talk and talk. And I believed everything I said.*"

"You *believed?*" I knocked the staff out of his hand, and the knife too, without meaning to. He watched them clatter to the floor, and kept his head lowered. "*I believed. Was it pompous?*" I asked.

"*We didn't know anything,*" he said, which wasn't an answer.

"*I thought we were going to do something magnificent, something so unlike anything our parents ever did. All those people from before. They watched everything they had known fall apart, and let their lives happen to them. But what we planned? Before we came here, I could see everything, I knew exactly how it would be. We would begin together. No one else got to begin again.*" He had dropped one hand to his side, like it was thinking about picking up the staff or the knife, but hadn't made up its mind. He was still looking at the floor. "*But we didn't, did we? That's what you're telling me now. We just got old in a worse world like everyone else.*"

Years and years ago, when we still lived in the city, which was still the

original city, Ren signed us up for dance lessons. It was a kind of a joke,
but we went every week, faithfully. In an old church that had been remade
for weddings and parties instead of religion. We did the steps better
than anyone there. We were always first to get them right, and I knew it
reflected well on us. I knew the other dancers thought we were a better
couple than they were because of it. It was spring after a long winter, and
at the lesson's end, while the other dancers lingered to practise or make
shy conversation, we would burst through the church doors into the pink
evening. I would hang on his arm, matching my steps to his as we hurried
down the sidewalk, because we were that eager. We were young and
beautiful and other people envied us. I don't know if I knew it then, but
we cared for no one but ourselves. And we were as happy as we would
ever be.

I don't know what made me think of that.

"I've let you down," Ren said at last.

"It's her," I told him. "It hasn't been right since she came."

"Who? What are you talking about?"

I spat her name. "Josefine. She has ruined everything."

He stared at me and I thought of things my mother used to say. I loved
to hear her talk. I loved her strange Serbian idioms. Merak nema cenu.
Your heart's desire has no price. Progledati nekome kroz prste *meant to*
look at someone through your fingers, as I looked at her. I couldn't rightly
see her until she was dead. As a child, I thought she was remarkable.
I thought her life was original and interesting. Later I saw it was all waste.
But I miss her language. I feel tired of talking in English. I want to speak
and know there's no chance he'll understand and no hope he'll even try.

"I didn't know that was what you thought," he said quietly. "You're
wrong, Sladja. It never had anything to do with her. It wasn't her who
did this."

"Then who was it? Tell me that. Who did it?"

He didn't say the words, but I heard them. He didn't say anything. He just picked up his staff from the floor and slid his knife into his pocket. Then he touched my hair and left the room.

We did.

That evening, the full moon casts down enough light for Judy to read on into the early hours of the night. She reads until her eyes ache, huddled by the broken window, squinting in the blue near-dark. She reads of how the colony finally sends Josefine away, of how she walks into the wood, willing and sullen, and Sladja watches till she's gone. And then page follows page of crop reports, weather chronicles, the routines of finding and preparing food, repeated over and over. The pomp of the first years has drained from the recounting of these tasks. They began as pioneers, devoted believers. They left their jobs and talents to toil in the woods as clumsy farmers and terrible hunters, for love of an idea. And now, what was left of that novel society was a joyless and increasingly fractious body of people. A tattered family, who knew each other only by habit, and were bound together by resentment more than care.

Sladja writes more and more frequently of Oona. The two women seem to have drawn closer over the years, and they are often alone together. Oona sometimes hunts with Sladja, while Sladja takes to helping Oona skin and cure the meat. There is no indication of what the two women talk of, or if they talk at all, but they seem to seek out each other's company, and Sladja writes of the other woman with respect, and even warmth.

Judy looks up, startled, and finds the twin at the door. Somehow she didn't hear him pull the lock or even push open the door. She heard nothing until he stepped inside. Now he stands staring at her, a torch in one hand and something else in the other.

Judy's thudding heart sounds in her ears. She's dizzy, her fingers clawing the edge of the page, and her eyes dart to the still-open drawer.

Does he understand what she has? Does he stand there frozen because he is about to run, to bring someone to show what she has done? She has closed her hand around the page edge. She could slide it in the drawer and hope he has never seen the history before, or has forgotten it. Or knows no better than she does why it matters.

The light of the torch scatters over his face, and falls against the walls of the room, which swim into view as he steps closer. No one but Sladja has ever come here after dark. And he carries no food or drink with him, no pail. She can't guess what he means by standing there.

Still watching her with his strangely steady gaze, he reaches out his hand and reveals its contents. With a frown she peers at a soiled cloth wrapped in a ball and then, answering his encouraging nod, she opens the cloth. Inside is a knitted object she can't identify, made of the same greasy grey wool as all of the colony's hats and sweaters. He reaches his hand closer, and she takes the bundle of wool from him, holding it up to the moonlight.

It's a doll. A dingy doll, with a faceless knitted head and body, and braids of wool for its arms and legs.

She is glad there is no possibility of speech between them. She doesn't know what she would say. She doesn't know what even to think. Is it something he made, or saved from his own childhood—which she can see, from standing so near him now, was not so long ago—or some cast-off bit of trash he found somewhere?

He points at her belly and then takes a sudden step backward, as if the gesture was too great an intrusion.

Her eyes sting, unexpectedly, as she smiles. Nodding and shaking her head by turn, she pulls the doll to her belly, to show her understanding. Her gratefulness.

He doesn't return her smile, but neither does he leave. He shuffles slightly from one foot to the other, his eyes settling on her belly. She is suddenly, unexpectedly, reminded of Beau.

An impulse strikes her and she takes up the book from the floor where she laid it. As he watches, she turns pages until she finds the one where his name and his brother's appear. Unsure if he understands or can even read, she points from one name to the other, looking up with the question in her eyes.

Hesitating, he reaches for the book, takes it from her and stares for a long time at the page. And then a smile breaks over his face so abruptly she is startled. He turns the book around and lays one finger under his name. *Romeo.*

She mouths the name, and his smile widens. Then, suddenly he is laughing, and after a pause, she laughs too, not understanding why, not understanding anything.

With one hand, he pulls a lock of black hair away from his forehead and leans toward her. She is confused, and then he draws a finger down a long, pellucid scar that runs down his face in the shape of a scythe. The blade of the scythe curves under his eye, where now, she realizes, she will always be able to glimpse it, if she looks closely enough. And now they know each other.

He drops the hair and she shapes the name again with her lips and tongue. *Romeo.*

This time, he only nods, and then he shuffles out the door and is gone.

After Romeo leaves, the moon is too high to illuminate the window, and she lays the history aside until morning. She pretends to sleep through Sladja's dawn visit, and then when the woman is gone, she retrieves the history from the drawer. Impulsively, she takes the book to bed, where she reads under cover of the blankets.

A long and unexpectedly fruitful summer passes before Josefine appears again. Sladja returns to a formal, impersonal prose that now strikes Judy as unnatural. Many passages are only long lists of crop yields, and she can sense the relish with which they are recounted, the words themselves swelling on the page as if with appetites of their own.

Maybe it's out of this sentiment of abundance and satisfaction that Sladja welcomes Josefine back. The young woman arrives at night, near summer's end, and is found waiting by the fire when Oona rises to prepare the first meal of the day. Judy draws her breath in sharply as she reads, *Her child will come in no more than three months.* How can Josefine have become pregnant, and so far along as that, in the season and a half she'd been away? Or was the father of the baby someone in the camp? The history shows no interest in such questions, but accepts her return as gently as the members of the colony do.

Even Sladja shows her something near affection, producing the last yields of the dying peach tree for her to salt away, and fixing up a house for her to live in all by herself, as no one has ever been allowed to do before.

Josefine is permitted extra rations of food, and dismissed from the chores that occupy other members of the camp. And so she grows round and idle, hunched over the fire, humming to herself as autumn cedes to winter and still the baby hasn't come.

The account of Josefine's labours when they arrive at last is terse. Her pains go on for two nights, through a windstorm. The woman who once delivered the babies of colony members left camp some time before, so Sladja and Oona tend to Josefine.

The baby, a hairless, wailing boy, is born smaller than expected, given her size and long pregnancy. After his birth her pains continue unabated, and they fear she will die of hemorrhage as one member of camp did years earlier.

But to their astonishment, several minutes later, she pushes again and a second boy is born. All at once, Judy understands, even before she reads that the woman names her sons Bobby-Rae and Romeo.

The two boys are raised as much by the camp as by their mother, who is seldom referenced in the pages that follow. Whenever she is named, it is regarding some mishap that befell her sons under her care, or a minor offence meriting sanction. Sladja appears to look on her with continued kindness, showing no relish in describing her transgressions, while Ren is enthralled by the twins. He fashions cloth slings, and daily carries the babies into the hills with him, murmuring ceaselessly to them, as if they understand.

Though Josefine's behaviour is no less strange than before she was sent away, no one seems troubled by it anymore. If she is found creeping through camp in the dark, she's gently returned to the home she now shares with her children and Oona, who is charged with watching over the babies at night. Her thieving of food is indulged; it's no longer a time of scarcity but of abundance, and there is more to spare, and, as Sladja writes, after birthing two hale boys, she needs to regain her strength.

And then one winter morning, Oona wakes to find mother and children gone from the house. The colony searches for hours and at last the boys are found far up in the hills, standing in the creek where the colony fishes in summer. But it is long past summer, and the mountain water is ice-cold.

The boys are breathless with sobbing, their legs, which only learned to stand in recent months, shaking beneath them. From the bank, their mother watches them, turning narrowed, defiant eyes on Sladja and the other members of camp as they approach.

When the boys have been dried and bundled in warm blankets and carried back to camp, Sladja and Oona question Josefine. She tells them the boys needed to be punished. She says they had cried all day and wouldn't listen when she told them to stop, and that night she dreamed they tormented her still, and it was then she understood they were wilful and demanded her correction.

After that, Josefine lives in her house alone again, and Oona and the twins are given a room in another house until a house of their own can be made ready. Josefine is never left alone with her children, though she is given supervised time with them each day.

But still Oona worries, confiding in Sladja that she believes the boys will not be safe as long as their mother stays at camp. When Sladja discusses the matter with Ren, he argues that it would be a greater hardship for the boys to be deprived of their mother. "We'll keep them safe," he tells her. "There are so many of us watching over them."

And then one day Josefine becomes fixated on the boys' hair, which falls over their eyes in dark curls. She is granted permission to cut it, Sladja noting approvingly that she has begun again to show interest in her sons, but the man who was intended to supervise the haircut must have turned his attention away. When Josefine and her sons appear at the fire that night, both are shorn to the scalp, and Romeo's brow has been cut open by the iron blade of the scissors.

We can't keep both mother and children safe. No more argument can be made. And yet all night we argued in our house. Ren begged me, as he had begged the others, not to turn her out. "Our pity is what unites us and what divides us from those we fled," he said. "We can't let our hearts harden against this woman, when she needs our mercy most."

At dawn, exhausted and no longer sure, I agreed to speak to Josefine.

She sat in her house, on her unmade bed, and didn't stand when I entered the door. Her eyes unnerved me as they always do.

I saw no point in evasion, so I told her, "We don't want you near your children anymore. You put them in danger. We sent you once from camp, and you returned to us. We let you return to us. But you're no longer welcome here."

"What will happen to them?" she asked me in her odd, childlike voice.

I told her we would keep them and that she could trust us to raise them well and with love. "They'll be safe here," I promised her. "Whatever happens, they'll be fed and cared for and kept safe."

She looked away then.

"Do you hear me? You don't need to worry about them anymore."

"What will happen to me?" she asked.

I hesitated. "I can't tell you that. You'll be on your own. You'll find your way in the wood, as you did when you went away the first time. You know how to forage. It will be summer soon, and easier to find shelter and water and meat."

She answered me like she was reading from a page. "I know I'm not a good mother. I know I've hurt my children. I don't know how to help them. I don't think they're like us. I see in their eyes something that scares me."

"What do you mean?"

"The other ones. I see the look of the other ones."

I didn't know how to answer her. The twins are too young to be known. They are only needs and impulses. They smile and cry and feed, and cannot so much as speak. But I have never been a mother. Is it possible that she instinctually perceives what it will take years for us to see? I remembered Ren's sister saying, after her child was tested, that she had always known.

But I told her, "You can't know if they're infected. There's no way to know that yet."

Her cold hands fastened on to mine and wouldn't let go. "Will you help me?"

I answered honestly, "I don't know how."

And then she said she wasn't well and never had been. Before coming to the hills, she'd been steadied by doctors and drugs, but they had always been only ties, tethering her against a great wind. The wind never ceased to blow, and then everything changed and all the ties were cut. Still it wasn't her fault, and she couldn't be blamed any more than the ill can be blamed for their disease.

I saw the truth of it, all of it, the unfairness, the helplessness, the harm we risked doing to a woman who already suffered. I heard and felt, as Ren had asked me to hear and feel, and I pitied her.

A special house is built for Josefine. A house far from the others, outside the clearing they circle, set amidst the trees. She is permitted to stay in the house, and meals are brought to her there. But Oona learns that the twins have taken to slipping away whenever their caretaker's back is momentarily turned, to come to stare at the house where their mother is kept, and that she calls to them from the windows when she sees them, and tells them things that frighten them. And so the boys are watched more closely still, and the windows of Josefine's house are painted black.

Judy knows she must put the history back in its drawer, but she is nearing the end of the written pages and so only reads faster and faster, her hand turning over each new page with the sense of plunging down into darkness, hoping to find something there. And snow falls outside the broken window of Josefine's house.

The next page contains only six lines and then a great empty space.

The parents of the youngest boy, James, noticed first. And then all the parents woke and found their children gone and rang the bells. All the bells of the camp rang as we searched for them. We went to Josefine's house like fools, worried for her children, and they were gone, and she was gone. Eight children, with hers. And all of them gone.

Judy traces the words with her fingers, closing her eyes. How long ago did it all happen? How long ago did the woman sleep where she sleeps, wake into the darkness of her black-painted house and do whatever terrible thing she had done to her own boys and all the children of the camp? She reminds herself that the twins live. They were returned. They are here still.

A page is left white and blank, as if to separate the writer of the next page from what came before, to avoid touching even the words. And on the new page, the handwriting has changed from Sladja's cramped, uneven script to a steady, slanting hand. Judy has read half a page before she understands.

My ljubavi. *You don't speak to me or anyone. You don't answer me. You hear, but you don't answer. If you did, my love, I would know what I can only guess. You grieve as we all grieve, but there is more, you have taken shame upon yourself. You think it happened because you let it. You think if you had been sterner, harder, if you had driven her from camp after the haircuts, or sooner, or never let her come at all, driven her and that man, whose name I do not even remember, back into the wood the night they came to us seeking help, you think then we all would be safe. The children, all asleep in their beds, the parents with unbroken hearts. You and I as we once were, beloved to each other.*

And I don't know how to bring you comfort, because I know so very little. I don't know what words she said to lead them away, or even how she left her locked house. I don't know why she wanted to flee camp or why she wanted those little boys and girls by her side. I don't know why the mood left her, why she tied the children there in the wood—did she think to punish them or us or to leave them where we could find them? The oldest three, the ones we haven't found, may live still. You must remember that and hunt yet, not lose courage to search. They may still be with her.

I don't know even if you are right to blame yourself. Or if you blame me, and are right in that too.

I wish I had been the one to find them. I wish it had been me and not you. I wish I'd taken up their little bodies and warmed them in my arms, wrapped them in blankets before you or their parents saw, so you wouldn't carry in your head the way they looked discarded on the ground, the two who escaped, face down in the snow like little dolls. I wish you hadn't seen the way James still huddled beside the still-breathing twins where they were bound, his thumb in his mouth, so you thought he too lived until you touched his cold tiny hand.

But we will never have not seen these things or not know what we know or not have done what we did. And everything we have done in these hills is defiled by it. The poison of it runs through the houses we built, the gardens we dug, the lives we made.

We lived a dream for a time, a world we'd made ourselves. I fooled myself that it was a real place. Now it seems a fancy so threadbare I can see through it to all the things we never spoke about. What we pretended not to know. We didn't make a world; we retreated from one. And we brought with us all the same capacity for calamity and irreparable mistakes.

Oona says we were wrong to pity the woman, that we should instead have pitied her children, but who can make such a choice? I know you think now she was one of the infected, and perhaps she was. Or perhaps the boys are, as she feared. I look for certainty, which once was the contour of everything. But I find it all shifts when I look at it; nothing will hold still for me or surrender to my grasp. It took courage to make our lives here, as we always used to say, but more than that it took certainty, and there is none of that anymore.

It's for this reason I leave with the others. And it's not you I leave. If you would come, I would travel with you. I would go back to the world by your side.

Would I stay if I loved you better? I don't know even that. It seems to me like a very great fight to love another person, even you. And there is no more fight in me.

———

When she finishes reading, Judy lays the pages on the ground beside her, meaning to tuck them away later, but she falls asleep. She dreams of men and women she never saw, all the members of the colony, streaming down the mountains like an avalanche. In her dream, there are thousands of them.

XV

JUDY WAKES IN A dark room, and doesn't know if anyone came and
went while she was asleep. With her outstretched hand, she feels the
pages, resting where she left them. And then the door opens and Sladja
enters the black house.

She sets her lantern on the desk and takes something from her coat.
Though she can see only a pool of light on paper, Judy guesses it's the
second history, what she has copied out for Sladja so far. The older
woman, who hasn't yet looked at Judy, spreads the pages over the desk,
sorting till she finds what she's looking for. She beckons to Judy, her
mouth at a slant—almost a smile.

Judy doesn't dare move the papers on the floor or slide the cover
overtop—to turn her attention to them in any way might summon
Sladja's gaze. Instead, she rises from the bed and lets the other woman
show her the page on the desk. With a gesture, Sladja urges Judy to sit
on the stool behind the desk, and then she lays her finger on a revision
she has made on the clean first page of the second history. She touches
it the way a person might touch the hand of someone they love.

Judy recognizes the list of names that began the history, the list she copied for Sladja with four names excised. The erasure of the people who belonged to those names is complete—Judy has no idea what significance their existence had, or how profound its omission might be—save one. And it's that name that has been restored to the list, fitted under Sladja's own.

Ren Takami, Judy reads and looks up, searching for an explanation in the face of the woman standing over her. Sladja points again and then draws her hand away, letting it rest at the edge of the desk, touching Judy's own. Their eyes meet and it seems to Judy that Sladja believes an understanding has passed between them. But Judy understands nothing.

Hastily, Sladja pushes the pen into Judy's hand and then reaches for the drawer. In an instant, seeing Sladja's other hand fly to her pocket, Judy understands that she's looking for a new sheet of paper, on which the words will be recopied, with the missing name restored. But before her other hand can discover the empty pocket, with just the slight pressure of her fingers closing on the knob, the unlocked drawer skids open, toppling to the ground and releasing a flock of fluttering sheets of paper.

Sladja stares at the drawer and then at the hand that found nothing in the pocket where the key should be. She takes in the room, the desk, the four dark walls, the coil of blankets where Judy sleeps, and the pages she left on the floor.

Very slowly Sladja bends and picks up the key from where Judy slipped it under the desk.

Only in that instant does Judy understand the magnitude of what she has done in Sladja's eyes. She has peered into what Sladja sought her help in forever erasing. She has seen what was to be hidden—and even now doesn't entirely understand what that is. A recalibration of a grand agenda . . . or maybe a deeply private shame. Shame of weakness, or of unwillingness to yield, or only of an error in her doctrine—for losing the man she loved or failing to protect the children in her care or for the dwindling end of the world fifty-seven men and women tried to build when they were young . . . Or was it something else altogether, something that has eluded Judy, an answer Sladja will never give to a question Judy will never be able to ask?

Without words, there is no way for Judy to defend what she has done.

So she only looks on as Sladja picks up the papers from the floor and reads the last page Judy read, the one written in the hand of the man who came with her into these hills and then left them alone.

When she has finished reading, Sladja drops the last pages of the first history on the desk. Judy stands, determined to face with strength whatever is coming. But Sladja steps past her, lowering herself onto the empty stool and using Judy's pen to strike out page after page in the first history and then in the second. She makes no effort to hide her work, and Judy stands beside her, watching until it's complete. The pen performs the work of an axe, cutting a man from where he stood, removing Ren from the only place where he remained.

She waits to see what will happen next, if the histories will be taken away from the black house, or if she will. When Sladja makes no move toward the key that still lies on the floor, Judy picks it up and offers it to her in her open palm. But Sladja shows no interest in the key or the woman who holds it.

Instead she crosses to the broken window and stands at it for a long time. From behind her, Judy sees what she sees—a white spray of stars over a black sky. But she cannot guess at what she feels.

After a time, Sladja turns away from the window. She doesn't take the key or the old pages or the new. She doesn't show her face to Judy, waiting anxious at the middle of the small, dark room. She leaves the house without a backward glance, leaving the lantern still burning and the pages spread over the table in careless disarray.

———

Judy waits all night and day, but no one comes to the black house. Enough water remains in the jug to mete out over a week if need be, and a day without food is nothing to someone who has lived so long in these hills.

At first she leaves the pages untouched, expecting Sladja to return for them. But when she doesn't, Judy gathers and orders them, setting them at the centre of the table in a tidy pile. And then, when dark falls again and the lantern burns on, she pulls the stool to the table and reads the last pages of the history.

Fewer than a dozen of the original colony members now remained, and none of child-bearing age. After the leaving of the bereaved parents and of those demoralized by grief, which spread like a contagion through the camp, Sladja wrote her account with a tone of stoic disinterest. She recognized with a flick of her pencil, a sharp word or two, that nothing, after all, would be built to last in these hills. The people would die one by one, as Ren had written, and then the houses they had lived in would crumble. No new generation would lift up the burden of their imagined future.

And so instead, Sladja found a new purpose, amending her cause and that of the colony itself. She wrote of the need to keep safe those in her trust. The threats were manifold; she would have to prevent them from the folly of leaving camp, like those before them, to face incomprehensible dangers. And she would have to keep others from entering camp and imperilling this last place of refuge. But in enforcing these directives, she needed to also ensure they didn't cripple the very faculty they had sought to protect. They would have to turn away all threats without becoming ruthless.

Without discussion, Sladja invented and imposed the rule of silence. She presented it to the camp with a prepared speech that she recounted in the history. "We came into these hills to hide from them. But even here we aren't safe. They find us, or enter from within. They know the weapon that weakens us, makes us lay down our defences willingly before those we might have easily defeated. They make us hear and feel, and they steal our pity. And they do it with words.

"Lies," she said, "are told by words. It is the only way lies travel. But truth speaks in our eyes and faces, where it can't be silenced or forged." She reminded them of the peddlers; no one knew if they were born mute or if their tongues were cut to ensure they wouldn't report to the cities, but their silence preserved their own safety and that of the people who lived in the hills.

If, she wrote, after making this speech, *I hadn't listened to Josefine. Or even to* ___ (here, three letters are scratched out by a slash of ink, but Judy knows the name they spelled). *If I had driven her out instead of letting her manipulate me with a sad story. I can't let myself think of how it might be different now. They fool us that way, those other ones. Move us, as she moved me. Persuade us, as she persuaded all of us to let her stay. But they can't read our faces or lie with theirs. Those like us can share what we feel and need without ever speaking again, and then we'll have denied them their last tool to harm or deceive. We should have been so much more careful with our words.*

A week later, the rule came into enforcement, and by then, all but six members of the camp had left in protest. Only Sladja, Oona, the twins and one senescent couple remained.

In her speech, Sladja had also announced that all newcomers to Haven would be subjected to the same tests they had faced in their youth, before coming into the hills. She cleared out Josefine's house while Oona and the couple dug a pit beneath its foundation, like those they had dug beneath their own houses, where they themselves would now sleep, in hopes that those who found Haven would think it long abandoned.

It took eleven days to build and contain the fires that burned the surrounding circle of forest, so they could more easily spot and track approaching strangers. Those strangers would be brought to Josefine's house and cast into the pit until they could be tested. There is no indication in the record of what would happen to those who failed the test.

The entries become terse and infrequent. A dozen years tumble past in a couple of pages. Sladja's handwriting is increasingly difficult to read. In passing, she complains of a tremor in her hands. *What a joke,* she wrote. *The same palsy that wrested away the mind and body of my mother now doubles back for me. All the way up here it came, slunk into these hills to find me. Not even that have I escaped. A great, devouring joke. And there is no one to laugh.*

The summer after the couple died, five days apart, Sladja recounted a conversation with a man she had first mistaken for a peddler.

I found his footprints in the ground of the burned wood. I could make no sense of them at first, till I tracked him to his tent. I saw then that he used a pair of purpose-made canes to walk, to minimize the weight borne by his arthritic knees. Strange to see a runner, which is what he claimed to be when I woke him, walk with a limp. In the tent beside him was a young girl, whose age I couldn't guess. She was wild-eyed and silent.

The pages that follow make clear that runners were not, as Judy first thought, agents of the resistance like the riders who had collected Daniel's work. The man was one of a company of people who travelled through the hills and other, farther places, charged with finding those who had escaped the cities and their records. She reads how runners like the man, whose name was Lincoln, were given photographs of the missing, and sent to search out where they hid. Some were rumoured to do their work for the other ones, and were feared. But Oona had hired Lincoln long ago to find her sister and her child. The sister, whom he had located at last in the outland, had been ill and had not survived the journey to Haven. But the child, Golda, knew her aunt on sight from Oona's resemblance to her own mother, and Sladja wrote that the two held each other as though they would never let go.

Lincoln wasn't well, and Sladja allowed him to stay in the camp for three days, watching him closely. He slept in Josefine's house, but not in the pit beneath the floor. He agreed readily to the rule, and didn't say a word again. By the third day, his colour and cough had improved and Sladja visited him with a rolled sheet of paper in her hands. On the page, she had written out the terms of an arrangement. If Lincoln gave up his work as a runner, and agreed to make camp in the burned wood and keep watch over its surroundings, she would offer him whatever fuel and food he needed to keep himself.

Sladja wrote that Lincoln had considered the matter for several hours after she left him, but he was old and tired of limping the forest paths, and when she visited him again, he had signed his name beneath her own.

There was, it seems, little to report in the months and years that followed Golda's arrival at Haven colony. They were now so few that they found it easy to provide for their needs, stockpiling surpluses of furs, grain and cured meat to trade, and they wanted for nothing in the way of food or basic supplies. But as Golda grew older, a discontent took hold in her, and she was often overtaken by sour, restless moods, abandoning whatever task she was assigned to wander without purpose in the wood. Her aunt worried for her, and Sladja worried too.

Golda's ventures away from the camp became longer and more frequent, taking her farther each time, until one night she couldn't be found. Bobby-Rae located her four days later, halfway to the foothills, cold, starved and defiant. She fought him all the way back. After that, Sladja assigned one of them to monitor her every day, sticking close by her side to ensure she didn't escape, but three more times she managed to elude them. After her third escape, she was gone for nearly a month, and of that time, Sladja wrote nothing at all in the history. But when she returned, Sladja took up her pen again.

———

26 days she was away from us. 26 days she walked in these woods, wearing the clothes she slept in on her last night with us. Without proper boots or coat, without weapon of any kind, she walked and walked. I don't know where she went. And I don't know what she found there. Oona asks. I can't stop her from asking. I must punish her for that and I can't. She asks but Golda cannot answer. She has shown us what they did to her. When we washed the dirt from her—dirt everywhere, in places that shouldn't ever have been touched—and removed the rags of her clothes, she turned her head toward her aunt and opened her mouth and we saw that they had taken her tongue.

It wasn't enough to keep watch. It wasn't enough for Oona to sleep with her in her house. Now we'll lock the door at night and open it for her at dawn, so she can't go away from us again. But I still see in her eyes that senseless, desperate desire to leave. I wish I could take it out the way they took her tongue. I swear I'd take her eyes themselves if it would do it.

And again and again, in the dim late hours, this thought returns to me: We will be the ones to leave. We'll leave all three of them. When Oona and I are gone, they'll have only each other, and houses and gardens that would take a dozen to maintain, and these words.

I've made so many mistakes. I want to lift them out of these pages now. If it were possible I would scrub them from our history like a stain, till all that remained was who we were when we came here, and what we meant to do.

It grows harder and harder to steady this pen. This diary will end when my hand finally fails. And if I go the way of my mother, it won't be long after that till I struggle to eat, to walk. Hardest for her was the loss of speech—she would look at me with the words teeming behind her eyes, coarse sounds dropping from her stumbling tongue, her wet empty mouth. Those unsaid words blotted up her life, choked the air from her lungs. I thought it was horrible, to be unable to leave your own head, to be bottled up there. To break the joint of speech that connects one person to another. But now I will not even know the day when it breaks in me.

I'm going to stitch this diary into our log. If I could I'd write it all again. I'd speak for all of us, not just my feeble story. I'd hide what no one needs to know—my failings, Ren's weakness, and what we lost up in these hills. We tried to be new and better people. And if it was stupid to think we could remake the world, or just save what was left of it, even just a handful of people—even just the ones we loved—then we should be forgiven for failing. If I wrote our story again, I would write it so that whoever read it might forgive us.

And I would choose better words. Strong, solemn words. When we first began to talk of going away into the wild, Ren told me that words would matter. He said we should choose each one with caution, speaking and writing with the enduring grammar of laws or scripture. "Or poetry," he said. "So that our words become something more, something that will last. An edifice. A bond."

I see now that I chose all the wrong words.

Judy is already angry by the time she reaches the last page, two years but only a few paragraphs later. The words are written in a wilder, more disordered hand than the quaking one of the preceding entries. The twists and knots of letters seem a kind of defiance, unyielding against the force that would dismantle them.

It has been two years since any stranger entered the burned wood or knocked upon our doors. I began to think the hills all emptied out, as our camp was. But today Lincoln came with news for us. He sketched a man and woman for me, wandering in the wood. He wrote only a few words—he went to school only a short time, and can spell little more than his name—but he made me understand. The man is one of his. Someone hunted for. He was paid for the man by someone in the cities, and would claim a good fee if he returned him there. But I emptied out every fur in our keep, half a winter of meat. And I gave him to understand that there would be more if he let this man and woman come to us and showed me where they camped. Together, we will take from them everything they carry, leaving only enough to ensure they survive the trip to us, and that when they arrive they will be in need. Because the woman, he showed me, will have a child.

And so, beyond all hope or possibility, comes a survivor.

And maybe, with that child, the world will begin again.

When Romeo appears, Judy has just dropped the history to the table and turned her back. Anger crowds out the questions—*Who is it that wanted Eban found? And why?*—as she understands at last that she walked into her trap like a fish diving into a net. That it was Sladja who robbed them and let them enter this place starved and weak and that she will never let them leave. She is thinking of toppling the lantern with a swipe of her hand, feeding the history to the last burning drops of oil. And then, staring out the broken window into the black trees, limned in moonlight, she sees his face appear out of the darkness before her.

She gasps and steps back, but he beckons her to the window again and reaches both hands through, pushing their contents into her own hands. She unwraps a scrap of linen and finds a hard, small loaf of bread and a handful of crushed red berries bleeding through the soiled cloth. His hands slide to circle her wrists and she fears what he wants from her. The ground outside is lower than the floor she stands on, so he reaches slightly up to her, supplicant, his face shadowy, the moon describing his silhouette in white.

He's young, she thinks. A boy, really. She thinks of the fatherless babies she read of, the motherless boys in the woods. An older man would have brought her water.

But she is grateful enough to put aside her anger for a time, and let him see her eat the berries with desperate appetite, sucking the juice from the cloth.

His hands have dropped now to the windowsill, but seem to linger there, waiting for something from her. She sets the bread aside, wrapped in the cloth, for later, and stares at him, uncertain. His eyes flick to her waist, and then all at once his hands are on her, and she is about to strike him, shove him as hard as she can to the ground, when she realizes what he wants.

His hands stretched over his head, through the window, hold the roundness of her belly between them. She resents the sudden, unasked-for intimacy, but she's moved by his face and the gentleness of his touch. He rests his cheek on the sill, seeming not to notice the jagged edge of the broken pane. She hesitates and then decides to allow what is happening to happen a little longer, and she moves toward him. His face inches from her belly, he hums just loudly enough that she can hear, a sweet and dim refrain, a baby song.

The door opens as she stands at the window, her belly in a strange man's hands.

Sladja, holding a small vessel of water but no food or pot, stops at the sight of Judy, her gaze dropping at once to the hands at her belly, which Judy impulsively seizes in her own. But Romeo, who seems to see in Judy's face what has happened, steps back from the window and becomes a dark figure among the trees, lingering, listening there.

A hot, bright star of anger flares within Judy, and she seizes the history as Sladja waits, seeming to thin and dwindle in the corner of the room. Briefly, Judy thinks that the pages are lighter than she would have guessed, and then she heaves them at the woman in the corner, the fragile binding cracking to release a flapping, fluttering swarm of paper. Sladja drops the jar of water as she grabs at the pages and it shatters on the floor.

The lantern blinks out as Judy watches the woman fall to her hands and knees, snatching at the scattered history. In the dark, she hears the scratching of her fingernails against the floorboards, and then the opening and closing of the door.

When Sladja is gone, Judy looks out the window for Romeo and sees nothing but the black and reaching trees. Neither ever comes again.

Two more days pass and the bread is gone and Judy thirsts the way a fire burns. And then on the third evening, as rain drums against the roof, the door opens on the last person she guessed would walk through it.

"Eban," she says, and his name, the first word she's spoken in weeks, scours her parched throat.

She sees he has been sent to her. He carries the normal food and water ration and clean white pot. He avoids her eyes as he does the work of laying it out, and she means to wait until he is gone to devour it all, but her legs seem to carry her to the water of their own accord, and she lets it run out the sides of her mouth and down her clothes as she drinks and drinks and drinks.

When she has finished, she turns away to wipe her face dry. Her weakness embarrasses her.

Knowing he won't answer, she says his name again. And then: "Eban, I can't have this child here."

He looks at the floor, arms at his side, doing nothing.

"Are you going to stay here, when I'm gone?" He doesn't answer. "Why? Eban, why?"

His face is round and soft now. The daily plenty of the colony has filled out his thin figure, making him look both older and younger. He raises his head and looks at her, like he wants to show he isn't afraid of what he sees.

"I shouldn't have said I would leave you," she says softly. "That I would leave without you."

As they always have, his eyes undo her. "Little spider," Daniel used to sing when she was small and full of talk and couldn't sleep, "never still.

Spins and spins and spins until . . ." She used to stamp her feet going up the stairs as a child; catch a mood like a cold and run endless circles around the house; lie on her back, staring at the sun, and yell till she was emptied of breath. She always had more strength than she could exhaust, more want than she could slake. Only Eban slowed what spun. When he looked her way, she saw a quiet at the centre of him that found her.

Standing in the middle of the room now, looking ready and afraid for anything she might do, he moves her.

Once, months and months ago, at the end of summer when the leaves were gone to red and the grass was dying, he met her coming back from the brook. They usually fetched water as a pair, or carried only two jugs at a time to fill. But for some reason she had brought all the jugs with her, without saying anything to him. She'd carried one in each hand, another in the crook of her two bent arms and the last in a small pack on her back. Her wrists ached with the weight of the two in her hands, and because of the one in her arms, she'd stumbled many times, unable to steady herself over the uneven ground with her outstretched arms. The one in the pack had come uncorked a mile from camp and soaked through every layer of clothing she wore. Still, it was a good afternoon's work and would spare them the trip for another week.

She was surprised to see him on the path, and he hurried to take the jugs from her, but she shook her head. It was foolish, she knew. He could help her easily, and there was nothing to be gained from carrying them the remaining way except the pride of having done something difficult and unnecessary. She waited for him to protest, but he stepped back from her and looked into her face, a radiant quiet in his pale eyes.

"I see you," he said softly. And then he walked by her side, just a little behind, all the way back to camp without speaking again.

It was the day after she lost the third one.

Now she looks at him and thinks it isn't his fault that he became, for her, the world. In him, she saw the limits of her life. In him, she was confined. He is everything she hasn't done, everyone she hasn't known. He is all her choices. Too much and not nearly enough.

Maybe, she thinks now, she couldn't love Eban because he was the only one to love.

The thing that is unsaid between them is too terrible to speak of. The want, the failure, the dire disappointment of it all.

And so she says instead, "It's about control. That's all they built here. Not a sanctuary, not some new society. They are children who made a toy kingdom to rule. And all of it, the houses, this cell, the silence, it's all tyranny. Whatever comforts you in this, Eban, is a lie or worse."

He is shaking his head and that much gives her hope. She goes on, goading him to answer her. "Out there, there are things to know, choices to make. They can't face it. I've read their history. Do you understand? They're cowardly brutes. They want to crush the world to a size they can grasp. To wield sovereignty over the tiniest possible territory."

She searches for some other thing to say, some way to reach him. "What do you think your mother wanted for you and your brother? Was it this?"

His eyes narrow (*I see you*, she remembers) and he lifts his chin, turning his gaze from her to the door and then back again. She hears the challenge as clearly as if he'd spoken and it startles her. Why doesn't she run? Why has she stayed in this black house, imprisoned by a dying old woman, for more days than she has managed to keep count of? When there was a chance, time and again, for her to push past whoever delivered her provisions? And maybe he'd even expected it to happen every time he came to see her, had prepared to let it happen. . . .

She feels the hot rush of tears, and squeezes her eyes closed against them. She can't now imagine why she stayed here, keeping a diary of her childhood for a stranger, reading that stranger's own account like she was assessing evidence, turning every page like it contained the possibility of truth.

It occurs to Judy then, for the first time, that Golda gave her the key not so she could read the history but because Golda thought it would open the door and free her. And she recognizes a debt unpaid.

"There was a man," she says. "Eban, there was a man who was hired to look for you. It's his job, or was. He hunts for people who've gone missing. People pay him to find people they've lost up in these hills. He had a file on you. Someone wanted to find you, Eban."

She steps nearer and lowers her voice. "Eban, who was looking for you?"

Watching him, standing stricken in the same spot where he has stood without moving all this time, she thinks that there is a whole story Eban hasn't told her. And she thinks of what she wrote in those pages for Sladja, and of what Sladja wrote. She thinks that even Josefine must have had a story none of them ever learned. And does it matter if she did? Does it make better anything any of them has done?

As he shakes his head again, bringing his hand to his face, she hisses, "Leave the door unbolted, Eban. I can't stay here any longer. Unbolt the door for me."

He turns away, walking stiffly, like one who has been struck, and leaves without answering her.

XVI

THERE IS A HEAVY iron bell mounted on a spindle beside the fire where food is prepared and served. Every day in Heaven begins with its sour clang, calling them all from the basements of their houses. Eban's house is the one nearest the fire, and when Oona turns the bell crank, the sound finds him in his bed under the ground like it has hunted him there.

Since arriving at the colony, he has dreamed darkly and richly, his night dreams spilling out of bounds, entering the day, altering the world he wakes to. Every night of dreaming ends with the sounding of the bell. Judy believes he's comforted by what he knows will happen again and again without fail, but what he feels is something greater and deeper than that. He feels love. He loves the bell the way he loves the day's meals, the blue of sky, the changeless gravity of the earth.

When the bell rings the next morning, he lies for a long time, staring sightless into the dark of his narrow chamber under the ground. He leaves the lantern on the floor beside his cot unlit. The floor of his chamber is tiled with white, polished stone, and wooden planks line the walls. He sleeps on a sheet suspended by metal springs, raised inches off the ground, warmer and drier than he has slept since he came into the hills.

When he stood before Judy last night he had to look away from the round pressure of her belly against her clothes. He doesn't know if she noticed how her hands went to it, landing there after every gesture like a bird lighting on the ground, returning to earth. For a moment, her changed shape, the physical fact of it, made him nearly believe what he never had, insisted what he had denied: their child, its possibility.

He can't be sure—they are both rounder, better fed than ever before. What made hope briefly flare in his mind, like a match, could be only a few pounds of extra weight and her own will, which he believes to be a force as powerful as meiosis, as life itself. But he saw then that his doubt was unforgivable.

So now he thinks of Judy, who stood before him last night and for a moment wanted something he could give.

And he wonders if their child, like Judy, would look at him as if he could be seen perfectly, every crack and fissure revealed—as if, with a single breath, he could be blown apart, dissolved to dust.

And then there's the name he thinks and doesn't think. He empties the name from his head, squeezes it out of every thought.

At last he rises, unhooks the door latch and climbs up through the floor above.

The name he doesn't think. The thought he doesn't name. The nameless, thoughtless thing he cannot.

He's the last to take his seat at the fire. He is usually the first. Beside him, Bobby-Rae rolls a twist of paper between his thumbs and forefingers, his plate already empty on the ground. He likes to have a cigarette after every meal, tamping threads of dried tobacco from the garden into papers he gets from peddlers. Eban had never seen anyone smoke before except from a pipe, and he enjoys the smell and look of it, the delicate way Bobby-Rae pinches the cigarettes between his long fingers, unspool-ing smoke with a wave of his hand.

When Eban first arrived, he didn't know how to distinguish Bobby-Rae from his brother, and thought of them almost as a single being. But now he can't imagine mistaking one for the other. He and Bobby-Rae are usually paired for work, maintaining the houses of the colony. Eban would have preferred to be assigned to work better-suited to his skills. He doesn't understand the construction of these elaborate houses or the complicated tools they are given to repair them. He has tried to intimate that he would be more useful as a hunter, but only Sladja leaves the colony to hunt, occasionally taking Bobby-Rae or Oona along if they are needed to help haul or field-dress a larger animal.

But Bobby-Rae is an able worker and corrects Eban's mistakes with impatience but not unkindness. There is a sharpness to Bobby-Rae—from his wry, jagged grin to the lithe way he moves. He laughs a great deal, but silently, with a sense of irony that bewilders Eban, unnerving him even when he understands the joke. Bobby-Rae watches the others and relishes any peculiarities in their behaviour; he often turns to smile at Eban at such moments, as if to share the humour of it. Unlike his grim-faced brother, he seems to enjoy himself, his work and his routine at the colony.

Eban fills his bowl with the usual morning meal, a fibrous grain he can't identify boiled to a paste, and takes his seat. As he does, Bobby-Rae nods to an empty chair Eban hadn't noticed, blocked by Romeo, who is on his knees, tending the fire. Golda's chair. Eban wasn't the last to take his seat after all.

Now that he has noticed the empty chair, he sees he's not the only one. Oona stands at the fire, stirring her iron pot, but keeps casting her eyes over to the chair with an unhappy expression. Sladja, too, sits in stillness, her bowl in her hands, untouched, looking from Oona to the chair. She has been moody and strange for the past many days, but today she looks more anxious still. Eban has seen Sladja pass the fire on her way to Golda's house each morning, where he knows she must unbolt the door to release her from her chamber. They never return to the fire together, but the girl always comes slinking after the older woman, never far behind.

Now, Sladja gently touches Romeo's shoulder, nodding at the chair, and he sets down his bowl and rises, leaving the fire to collect the missing girl. A troubling thought begins to form in Eban's mind as he watches the man go, and then he feels the light touch of Sladja's hand on his shoulder. She has stood to offer him the familiar tray of food and water, the clean white chamber pot. He stares at them for a moment, his head full of fearful, unspeakable questions, and then he accepts them and the task of their delivery.

The sun has topped the hills as he reaches the black house, slanted yellow light guttering between the trees. Even now, at this early hour, its warmth reaches him, softening the air.

He opens the door of the black house. Stepping inside, he stands and stares and wonders what he should do.

The first time he guessed Judy was pregnant, he thought of the night he'd woken, three years old, to his mother's screams, and then another, unfamiliar howl. How he'd crept to the bed where she slept to find the sheets soaked and red, and his mother with a stranger in her arms. How he'd begged to hold the baby she said was his brother and how she told him he couldn't be trusted with something so weak.

And so he was afraid for Judy's child, and afraid of himself, who couldn't keep it safe.

And after she miscarried, he knows he could have made her speak, called out to her across the grief she believed was hers alone, unwound the distance between them with the right word or touch. But instead he startled himself with the limits of his will, the cold they both discovered at his heart. He was afraid to believe in that invisible speck, coiling towards existence, silently beginning and then completing, leaving no mark. He was afraid to want something so fragile. Once he dreamed of the tiny baby who had been his brother, in Judy's arms, telling him it had died because he never spoke its name.

But the physician in him knows he can't be blamed for the loss of these babies—it wasn't a failure of faith or imagination or anything else that stopped them in the womb. Some scrap of the genetic fabric in Judy or in him must be disordered. That might be it. Only that. Or maybe something in their diets. Something wrong with how they live.

Now he stands in what he had come to think of as Judy's house. He looks at the shattered glass, winking light up from the ground. At the sheets of paper that flap and quiver in the breeze through the broken window, a white tide across the floor.

For no reason, he opens the door to the *oubliette* and peers into its darkness. He can scarcely remember the dizzy, starved days they spent down in that dark. He is surprised to feel briefly wistful, thinking of it. Of the two of them, together between those narrow walls.

Maybe if his mother had let him hold the child. Maybe if he'd held his brother in his own child hands. Maybe then he'd have known how to want something so dangerous, something that would never be safe.

He closes the door and then, for lack of knowing what else to do, he sets the tray of food on the table and puts the pot in the same corner where he left it when Judy was still there.

And then he leaves the house he freed her from.

When he returns to the fire, he knows immediately that something is wrong. The flames have been allowed to go out so only a few dim embers remain of the fire that is never cold. Even through the night, it burns.

Now all the chairs are empty except Bobby-Rae's. He is refilling his bowl from the pot, scraping up the last of the meal, and as he drops the pot to the ground, he glances at Eban and twists a smile. Then he turns his focus to his bowl, eating with a calm composure that Eban finds unsettling.

And then Eban knows where the others are.

Golda's house is the farthest from the fire, the first Eban and Judy encountered the night they came to this place. He can hear noise inside as he approaches, and he opens the door unsure what he will find.

Inside, he sees first the ruined room, and then the people.

Sladja is slamming doors and raking her hands across the bottom of every shelf and drawer. Her fury is wild and methodical as she searches for something that must be terribly important. Every stick of furniture has been overturned.

Romeo stands in the corner of the room, ignoring Sladja. His eyes are on Oona, who kneels beside the open door in the floor. She is old and stiff, but she kneels there like a child.

Watching Oona, Eban understands that Sladja isn't looking for anything. He sees that the cupboards are mostly empty anyway. The things she throws to the ground are things that have been there for long years, left by whoever first built and lived in this house. Things that have no use. Things he can't even name.

Oona is so terribly still. When Romeo crosses the room and lays a hand on her shoulder, Eban expects her to strike him like a snake. Instead she looks back at him for a moment and nods, and Romeo leaves Golda's house. They all know he has gone to look for her.

He tries to remember when he left Judy. Had the moon yet risen? How many hours have passed since he shut the door, touched the bolt, hesitating, and then drew back his hand and hurried away? How long did she wait before she tried the door—and what did she expect when she put her weight against it? Did she know he'd do as he has always done, whatever she asks?

He wonders if she came right away to Golda's house, and how she knew which one was hers. He imagines Judy floating through the camp as they slept, wandering between the houses, her face against the windows, her hand at the latch. Did she try each door in turn, searching for the girl? Did she peer down at them in their beds? At him? Did she look at him?

At least a dozen hours have passed, he guesses. Enough time to have travelled a long way. Golda knows these woods, and Judy knows the route back to the foothills. If they're still together, by now they're beyond anyone's reach.

Sladja has stopped at last. The tremor he has long observed in her seems more severe than usual, and she lays both hands against the corner table as though to steady herself. Oona hasn't moved.

Eban looks away from both women, and the thoughts he hasn't wanted begin to come.

What he remembers best about his brother now are the things his mother said. How he was always away, in mind and body, his thoughts elsewhere, his feet hurrying out the door. How nothing seemed to trouble him, except things that made no sense. The wrong things he laughed at. How hard he was to understand.

But if he searches his mind, he catches glimpses there of his brother with his hand out, reaching for Eban's attention. His brother's lanky, fragile body. His brother's crooked, tooth-filled grin, which he showed most often when they were alone. For a time, his brother had enjoyed labelling things. He carried a small notebook in his pocket and a stub of pencil, and he would write things like *Eat here. Sleep here. Sit here* and lay the notes on the table or bed or chair. Then, for a while, the notes grew more complex and bore no apparent relationship to the surfaces where they were pinned: *No more crying Mother* and *Eban be nice*. And one day, there were no more notes. It was always like that with him. Habits flared and ceased. You wouldn't notice the day they finished but suddenly they were only something you remembered. Why did they start or stop?

Once, after a rain, he gave his brother a hard push into a puddle in the yard. His brother had been pestering him all morning, till their mother in frustration forced them both outside. He'd expected the younger boy to catch himself, but he fell to his hands and knees in the mud. Stricken with shame, Eban tried to help him up, but his brother sat cross-legged in the puddle with his head back, laughing and laughing. *Good trick, Eban*, he said, mud streaked across his thin face. *Good trick!*

He remembers his brother returning from a run one evening and entering the room where Eban stood at the window lifting weights. Eban was tired and ready to finish but he didn't want to stop while his brother watched. So he went on lifting till his arms ached, for an hour, longer, and his brother sat without moving, perched silently on a stool that made him look even leaner and lankier than he was. When Eban at last dropped the barbell to the ground, every muscle burning, he was furious to have lost this silent war of will, but his brother only said, *Would you show me how you do that?*

When Eban began to learn medicine, his mother made up a test for him every week. He only ever failed one of her tests, a long one on gross anatomy, and she made him sit at the table and study until he could list every part of every organ system. He read till his vision blurred, fell asleep on his books, and woke with the candle burned to nothing and his brother asleep at the table beside him.

He can scarcely remember talking with his brother or whether he ever showed him kindness. He doesn't know if he's forgotten or if it never happened. For the first time, he thinks: we were only boys. His brother was younger than Golda when he saw him for the last time. Whatever his brother was, he never had a chance to become it, not while Eban knew him.

Oona is still on the ground, her elbows bent over her knees, at rest and in wait all at once. Her head is bowed and her shoulders heave, but she makes no sound.

And then Sladja makes such a sudden move towards Oona that Eban thinks she's going to slap her, to punish her for wasting time, for not watching the girl more closely, for every second that she ever turned her eyes away. But instead she falls to the ground.

Oona receives the other woman like she was waiting for her, her long arms wrapping around and around her, and the women close together like two hands on the floor of the girl's house. They cry together, and the sound shocks the silence. Eban feels frightened and alone and unsure. He stands beside the two women wishing he were anywhere else.

And Judy is wrong. Judy is dangerously wrong. He sees all at once everything these people did, and none of it done for the reasons she told him. They didn't seek out power or control. They were afraid, like everyone else. They are terribly, terribly afraid, and this fear, he sees, is love.

He always imagined that he would stay when Judy left. He knew that one day she would go. He had done to her something like what these two women had done to Golda, trying to capture what he couldn't keep, and when he couldn't even do that, he tried just to stall her, unspooling Judy from him as slowly as he knew how. That was all he'd been able to do. One day, he'd understood, when she wasn't frightened anymore, she would be gone.

He thinks now of the morning bell without Judy. The night's dreams without Judy.

And then someone whispers in his ear, so faintly it could be his own head talking to him. "Come with me," the whisper says, as Oona closes her hand around his wrist and draws him out the door.

She stands just beyond the threshold, looking out at the dawn-lit houses of Heaven. Still he doubts the words he heard, can't believe she spoke at all, and so he waits for some sign of what she wants from him, but none comes. At last he offers her his arm, which she refuses. Her eyes are dry and fierce, and she is straight and tall and steady.

She begins walking, and after a moment, he follows, and despite her age, he struggles to keep up. He sees no sign of Bobby-Rae, not at the fire and not in any of the houses, and he guesses that he joined his brother in hunting for the girl.

Oona reaches the black house some time before him, and when he arrives, she is standing in the doorway, staring past him into the trees. He tries with his eyes to explain what he cannot say, but she won't even look at him as she makes her way back to the colony.

He follows her from house to house while she fills a pack with dried food and supplies. Whether she wants him or not, he'll accompany her when she hunts for the two women. He makes up his mind that he will do that. But to his surprise, once her pack is filled, she shoves it into his hands, accepting help he hasn't offered.

"Take it," she says.

Is it a trick? He hesitates now to even lift the pack onto his back.

"I said take it. And go find her if that's what you want to do. Maybe it isn't. I don't pretend to know."

He draws in a breath, lets his mouth open slightly, maybe testing whether words will come rushing forth with the permission she is granting him now with her own words.

"I did it," he says and winces. She doesn't even seem to hear his confession. "I let her out."

"You let Golda out?" Oona raises her chin, her black eyes narrowing. "You did that?"

He shakes his head. "Judy. I unlocked the door for her . . . She must have been the one to let out Golda. She would—it's something she would do."

Oona turns back in the direction of the houses and steps past him, but he touches her shoulder. "Wait. Please. Wait."

"Wait for what?"

"I don't . . ." He tries to think of what to say or ask. "You spoke. You're speaking to me. You broke the rule."

She smiles with just one side of her mouth. "I never really understood why Sladja thought it helped us, but I know it makes her feel better to think it does. And I'm old enough to have said most of what I needed to say. But Golda couldn't take the silence. My sister's girl. She had it hard enough here. It was the least I could do to talk to her when we were alone. I'd tell her little stories about her mother. Try to reason with her. Try to soothe her. Just little things like that. She'd never have told Sladja, even before those monsters took her tongue."

"Those monsters . . ." He remembers Golda showing them her gaping, empty mouth, the day he and Judy first climbed out of the hole in the floor of the black house. "Was it one of them then? One of the other ones who did that to her?"

Oona makes another half-smile, her face otherwise empty of amusement. "No. No, it wasn't." She takes him in with her level, sharp-eyed gaze. "You're afraid of the wrong thing," she says.

"I . . ."

"All of you fear the wrong things. You always have. Sladja too. All of us that came here, all of us that stayed. Everyone up in these hills and I have no idea about the people down below them. No, we have plenty of monsters right here, creeping through these hills, and one of them got hold of her. It took me a while to figure this out, but most people that choose to live in hiding are monsters of one sort or another, or we turn into one after long enough.

"I followed somebody I loved here, and never thought I'd stay this long. You know, I used to live in the city, back when I was a girl. I can tell you there's nothing much different about those other ones. But the drought went on so long and there just wasn't enough anymore. If it hadn't been them, there would have been someone else to blame."

She tells Eban that Sladja had a runner named Lincoln who used to report to her. She says he went back to the cities every year, though he never told Sladja.

"Lincoln said we got it wrong up here. He said it was because of those other ones that the famine came to an end. He said it made a difference, moving everybody closer. Shutting down the roads and the grid. Setting limits, stopping waste. He says it was because they were different that they were able to do it. He said it made them see farther, see past how people felt about it all and see all the way to what needed to be done. And then, even though it hurt some people, they did it anyway.

"And it makes me think. It makes me remember how one time when we were children, my sister was in the news because she broke her ankle right before she was supposed to compete in some big ice-skating competition. The whole city felt sorry for her. They felt so sorry they started sending cards and flowers. Some of them sent ice skates. It didn't make any sense. I was a kid and even I could tell that. She *had* skates. All she needed was a good left ankle, but people couldn't send that and she had her picture in the paper looking sad, so they sent skates. Maybe a dozen pairs. And meantime there were people right on our street putting water in the milk they gave their kids to make it last till their next payday came.

"People like you and me, people up in these hills, like to think it's the most important thing about us. The way other people's stories make us cry like they were our own stories, like we're feeling their feelings for them. But maybe that's not very important. Maybe it's not even good.

"I'm telling you. You're afraid of the wrong things. You've wasted your whole life locked up in these hills and never thought to leave them. *That* ought to make you terrified."

Oona presses the heels of her hands to her eyes. "I used to think about going back, when I was younger. Seeing the new cities with my own eyes. Finding out what it was we left all those years ago. But I'm an old woman now, and I know I'll die here, and that doesn't matter to me. I like it here. The people used to say we were building a new world here, but it isn't that. It's the oldest world there is. Dirt and trees and sleeping on the ground and never being sure you'll eat tomorrow. That's what I like about it."

She hesitates, leaning toward him, laying a hand on his chest. "I don't know where you're going but if you find her, my Golda, would you tell her how she has broken our hearts?" She shakes her head then. "Maybe you shouldn't, though. Maybe just tell her you'll go with her. Maybe you could make it all the way back to the cities. It could be that it really is better there now. Maybe everything that old man said is true.

"But then again," she adds, turning her back, "who knows what to believe up here?"

He watches Oona disappear back into Golda's house and then, with nothing in his head, no plan or intention, he goes into the wood.

He knows only that he wants to move, to put distance between him and the two old women and Golda's empty house. As he enters the burned wood, he thinks that if he finds a good kill or two, Sladja will forgive him for being away for a couple of hours or days.

The air is warm and the ground soft—each step sinks a little, and he looks back to see the history of his travel in the black, wet dirt. He tells himself not to search for Judy's footprints.

The night he sat beside his mother as she died, after he had apologized for letting the sick girl into their camp and she pulled her hand from him, she was quiet for a long time. He imagined she was past speech. And then she said, "You didn't stop me."

They had never spoken of the day they left the outland. He had rarely let himself remember it even in the dark of his own thoughts. It was three days after the last test. He could still see the faint mark on her hand where she had inserted a pin. He watched it as she spoke to him that morning.

"Eban," she said, handing him a large pack he had never seen before, "take this and fill it with whatever things you'll need when we leave this house."

He didn't understand. "Leave?"

"We're going away."

"Going away where? For how long?"

"I don't know."

"Why?"

"You know why."

He searched his mind but couldn't guess what she meant. "When do we leave?" he asked at last, because he could tell from her face she wouldn't answer the same question asked again.

"Within the hour."

He looked at the door his brother had left only a few minutes earlier. "But he won't be back from his run in time."

She crossed the room in two steps only, taking his face in her hands. "You remember what I told you. What you read with your own eyes. What's wrong with your brother can't be fixed."

"There's nothing wrong with him!"

"Think. Remember what you read, what I told you. You know it's true."

"It isn't," he said, ashamed to feel tears well in his eyes. He hated her face so close to his, hated her seeing him cry. "It isn't. He's like us. He's no different from us."

But as soon as he had said the word *different* he heard the lie, because it was what his brother had always been. They had never been the same. And as he thought this, his mother went on holding his head, pressing her own forehead to his, and she hissed the words she must have been preparing for days to tell him. She had known from her younger son's first weeks in the world that he was not right, too still in his crib, too unhappy in her arms. She'd known it but convinced herself she was wrong.

"It was his father did it to him. He looks just like him, you know. Same queer smile, same way of staring far too long at a person. I never told you what your father was, but you must have guessed."

He shook his head free from her hands. She had spoken so rarely of his father, and he always thought it pained her to name him, as it pained Eban too. He knew the man had left them, all three of them, before his brother was even born. He had spent his entire life stopping himself from wondering why. But now, though he tried to close his ears, his mother told him.

"He was a sneaky one, your father. You might know him all your life and not see what was wrong with him. He could charm you like that. He was better than most at the pretending of it. You'd have thought he felt and cared like any other person."

"How did you find out," Eban whispered.

"I didn't." She lifted her eyes from Eban's at last, looking around the room as if she hadn't seen it before, or as if she might still be able to find the missing man somewhere inside it. "He hated it in the outland. He was always wanting to go back to the cities. He said he wanted me to go with him, to raise you there, but he knew I was never going to leave the outland again. The first time he left, when you were small, I blamed myself. They do that. Confuse you like that. How I hated him for making me look at myself for the flaw, when it was all in him. And then he came back again and I was that glad to see him, I took him into our house and did everything I could to keep him there. I went after his love like I was trying to keep water in my hands. It was like that, just always falling through, gone as soon as you had it. I wanted a father for you, but it wasn't why. I wanted him for myself."

She steadied her voice and faced Eban again. "He went back to the cities fifteen days before your brother was born," she said softly. "Think of that. Think of the kind of person who would do that. And then there wasn't any question what he was, because how could a person do a thing like that if there weren't something broken in their head? It reached and wrecked every cell of the man he was. And it contaminated his seed. The son he never knew has kept him here in my house all these years."

Eban had never seen his mother as she was in that moment. He looked at the door again, searching for words. "He'll be back soon," he said slowly, and only as the words fell from his mouth did he understand what they consented to.

His mother understood it too. "Go get your things," she said. And an hour later, they left.

So the night she lay dying in her soiled sheets, he knew without question what her accusation meant. *You didn't stop me.*

He sat quietly for a long time, touching a damp rag to her white lips like it took all his attention to do so. "No," he said, when her eyes closed and he thought she was gone, dead or asleep, at any rate beyond hearing anything he said. "I didn't stop you."

A sign of annoyance passed over her face, though her eyes didn't open. The expression was as familiar to him as the sound of her voice. "We left him the house," she said, so softly he had to lean closer to hear. "He was perfectly safe there. We left him the house." He felt a slight slackening in her body as she spoke and hated her for it, for the relief she found in those words, which were her last. She drew three more breaths and died, a hint of exasperation showing in the slight pinch of her face.

He walks for hours in the ugly company of his thoughts. He lets the sun set without slowing his stride or taking as much as a drop of water from his pack. A warm, warning wind has begun to slither over and between the branches of the trees overhead. From the hum he can hear if he listens for it, issuing from deep in the hills, he knows what is beginning, one of the wild gales that descend with the arrival of spring. But he no longer trusts the weather of this strange, endless season.

Driven by the wind, the clouds go racing past the moon. Its tilted white smile appears and disappears, trumpeting light and then vanishing. He stares up at this fast and fickle sky, which slips like oil running over paint. It is near to dreaming, looking at something so grand and distant, everything between erased by darkness, drawing the sky so close, the same wind that moves those clouds lashing his face. Back in his and Judy's hide, the mountain winds scarcely troubled them. Their shelter was built in the shadow of the hills, and at the turn of the season they'd hear the winds howl overhead and afterward, in the open plains, they'd see the ruined wake of their passage, but between the trees they were hidden as well from the wind as from everything else. He walks through the night, bowed forward, thinking of that other time. Of Judy.

And then, a few hours after dawn, when the winds have weakened and the sun is high and bright, he finds her.

In the shade of a sagging hemlock, Judy sits cross-legged, her belly cradled in her lap. She has her back to him, so that he doesn't notice her until he has almost passed her, but she must have seen him coming for some time.

As he stares at her, motionless and mute, a smile slices her face. "I knew you'd look for me," she says.

But he wasn't looking for her. He's almost sure he wasn't.

There's an unfamiliar effort in her rise to her feet, an extra step involved in pitching her weight forward over her belly, with a hard push from her right hand. He could help but doesn't.

As she approaches him, she keeps one hand under her belly, which he can't lift his eyes from. He wants to doubt and doesn't. Her head is cocked to the side, looking too closely, too carefully at him.

"You let me go," she whispers when she is close enough that he could touch her.

He drops his head for a moment, thinking, and then slowly, he nods.

"Thank you." She looks ahead down the path. "Golda is long gone by now. I gave her everything she needed to make the trip. She didn't want to wait. She wanted to go alone." She looks to see if he understands. "I think she wants to go back into the valley. To the cities. It doesn't frighten her."

There's something awake in her, something lit and alive that he thought was extinguished years before. He can feel its current humming in her, its charge dangerous and close.

"Eban, it's time to go. You know it. We've waited too long."

If, he thinks. If there it was, right before him, something true and invisible, all at the same time. If her belly hides something already begun and not yet even properly alive, if something so impossible could transpire, what else might? What might she come one day to say to him, or him to her, or to feel?

He squeezes his eyes shut behind his hand, admitting, for an instant, the thought of it. Judy's baby. His. A thing made of them and entirely its own, more new and alive and unknowable and certain than anything else had ever been. Its tiny step on the world would shake the planet.

Judy with a baby in her arms, turning to look at him over her shoulder. Judy knowing what to do if it cried. Or turning to him, a question in her eyes. Him with an answer.

He doesn't know if she has in her the gentleness to care for something small. He thinks everything about her, every gesture of her hands, every expression that crosses her face is clumsy and broad. But small things need to be handled only by fine, careful hands.

"Eban, when we left to come here, we said we were looking for answers. But those people have none. It's more of the same, more of all we've ever had. Other people's words. Borrowed terrors. I went through the houses last night to pack the things I needed. I saw how empty they were." She reaches into the pocket of the coat she wears, which he notices is too thin even for this turning weather. She withdraws something and holds it out for him to take. "I don't want to be safe. I want to know what we're hiding from. Maybe there are other reasons for everything we've been told. Maybe there is more to know. We know so little, Eban."

He takes the slip of paper from her hand. The shining surface of the paper briefly catches a ray of light through the needles of the tree above, singing out with its gold for an instant. A photograph.

We have eyes, he thinks, that slowly cease to see the things before us.

He feels her watching him, the weight of her gaze. "I found it in Sladja's things," she says. "With a note from a man named Lincoln. A runner, she called him."

The boy in the photograph is fifteen years old. His face is unreadable, faintly blurred as he turns his head to look at something over his shoulder, something happening in the distance.

He remembers the peddler who visited that day. They'd never seen him before. His cart was smaller than most, and though he offered them some unfamiliar wares (a device for peeling apples, pear saplings wrapped in burlap, a flashlight that ran on enormous batteries), none of these items were the real thing he was selling. Out of his cart, he lifted a small black case, which he opened delicately, gesturing to Eban and his mother to peer inside.

Eban had no idea what they were looking at, but his mother recognized it instantly. "A camera?"

"And so it is," said the peddler, and both Eban and his mother flinched at the sound. He was the only peddler with the capacity to speak—or the first one willing to admit it—that they had ever encountered. Eban waited for his mother to lead him back inside and lock the door, as she did when anyone dangerous passed through.

But instead she took the camera from the peddler and turned it over in her hands as he explained that it would produce a print immediately, and then named a price. Eban was shocked, but his mother went into the house and returned with an armload of furs, a winter's worth.

"These," she said, her face set. "And there are two laying hens that I can spare."

While the man, with a satisfied expression, loaded the furs into his cart and installed the hens in a cage already packed near-full with other fowl, Eban's mother turned to him. "Hurry now," she said. "Go and fetch your brother."

Eban ran into the house and called for his brother, but there was no answer. He stood at the window, looking out across the barren outland, but saw nothing. Then he noticed his brother's shoes missing by the door.

Outside, his mother and the peddler were waiting. "He's gone," he said.

"Gone?" the peddler repeated, amused.

His mother looked grim. "Running."

"Should I go and try to find him?" Eban asked.

His mother bit her lip and then shook her head. "Come stand here," she said. "So the sun will be on you."

"Ma?"

"Do as I say."

The man grinned a mouthful of black teeth at them. "It's very popular, this camera. Nothing sells like these pictures do. Can't hit a place more than once, so I had to widen my route, but worth every penny I paid for it."

"What's it for?" Eban asked his mother, but the man answered.

"See this slot here? A picture of you, just like you are, will come out there. Like looking in a mirror. Better than any artist could paint."

Eban stood under the glare of the sun, squinting up at his mother, who retreated to the elm in the yard.

"Don't you want to be in it too?" the peddler asked. "Nice picture of you both? Or one of each?"

"We don't have enough," she said. "I just want a picture of my boy."

"Smile," said the man, just as Eban's mother took a sudden step forward.

"Wait!" she said. "He's coming! I see him there."

Eban spun to look where his mother pointed, just as she landed a hand on the peddler's shoulder to stop him.

There was a snapping sound as Eban perceived the long, thin shape of his brother, emerging from the horizon, far in the distance.

He turned back to the peddler just as the man drew a slip of paper out of the camera. "Come see this, boy," he hissed. "You won't believe it."

"Wait," said Eban's mother. "I wanted both boys. My other son is coming now. Wait for him."

"You'll like this one," insisted the peddler. "Wait and see. Just takes a minute or two." As they watched, a shape took form on the paper, like oil surfacing on water. And then Eban's own face was there. Squinted against the sun, slightly blurred by the turning of his head as he looked away from the camera and off to his side, as if someone were creeping up behind him. And the shadow of his mother, at the peddler's side, was flung over him. He could pick out the long, exaggerated lines of her legs cast over the grass and then hinged over his own body, where her shape was imprinted on him.

"Too bad, that," commented the peddler.

"Take another one," cried Eban's mother. "He's not even looking, and it's got a shadow on it."

The peddler shook his head. "You'll have to pay again. Price I told you's just for one picture."

Eban had never seen his mother look so upset. He thought she would give the peddler a piece of her mind, but instead tears welled in her eyes. "I wanted a picture of both my children."

"One picture. Pay again, and you'll get two. I can even offer you a deal."

"I don't have anything else to sell."

"Well." The peddler retreated to his cart. "It's a nice picture of the boy. You'll treasure it later. Maybe it's better like this. Not too posed. More natural. Thing is, he'll grow up faster than you guess. I've got kids of my own. Listen to me. *I* know. He won't look like that ever again, and you'll be glad you can remember it now."

They watched him leave. By the time Eban's brother reached the yard, breathless and all limbs and sweat-shining skin, the peddler was out of sight, and the picture was complete, all the colours and angles of Eban's face as he knew it from his reflection resolved. He held it in his hand as his brother asked, "What?" and his mother, without a word, went into the house.

The picture went up on the shelf over the fireplace, beside the one of their grandparents. Two days later, Eban and his mother left the house, and when he last looked inside from the stoop, just before he closed the door, he noticed that it was the only photograph she had taken. Or he assumed she had. But when she died, he searched her possessions and never found it.

"Eban," Judy says, "how did Sladja get that photograph? How did Lincoln? It's you, isn't it? You recognize it, don't you?" She takes the photograph back from him and holds it up to her face, studying the boy caught in light on paper. She hesitates a moment before speaking. "Eban, you never told me how your brother died."

He wonders if his mother already knew that they would leave when the photograph was taken. He wonders if she had first meant to take it with her or if it was always intended to be a gift for the son—the child—she would flee. *We left him the house.* An empty house and a photograph of the brother who once shared it. He fingers the paper, which is worn by touch and time. Did his brother treasure or resent it? How long did he keep it before he charged a stranger with finding the brother who had left him without a question, just because their mother asked? And could he have in him such goodness that he would call that person brother still?

———

He looks at Judy for a long time. Even now, he loves her, helplessly.

When she lost the pregnancies, he would search for a way to tunnel into her pain, to make a little room for himself, but it was only big enough for her. Now she stares at him with something gentle in her eyes, something that makes room for him.

"His name was Michael," he begins.

"Come with me," she says when he has finished. She is already lifting her pack from the ground where she left it, one hand supporting her belly, as she turns her attention to the path.

"I didn't understand," he says slowly, "until just now, when I saw those two women grieving. I didn't understand that loving someone like that means being afraid all the time."

"No, Eban," she tells him, shaking her head. "Love isn't fear." She adjusts the straps over her shoulders. "It's faith."

This day, its rising light and heat, the world emerging around them from buds and branches, from dirt. Meltwater everywhere, running through everything, the sound all around them of water creeping down the hills back to the valley they've never seen. The colours, the sun in his eyes, and everything suddenly too bright. All of it swallows him. He understands none of it, and is lost within it, made into its mystery.

Before they begin the long walk ahead of them, through the hills and down into the valley, Judy turns and looks back at him.

She looks back for him, one final time, and it's enough.

ACKNOWLEDGMENTS

I gratefully acknowledge the support of Arts Nova Scotia and the Canada Council for the Arts in writing this book.

Thank you to my brilliant agent, Ellen Levine, for the gift of your guidance, editorial insight and support from the earliest draft. I admire and am deeply grateful for your devotion to your authors and fierce commitment to the world of books.

Thank you to Martha Kanya Forstner, magnificent editor and first-rate human being. At every stage of editing this book with you, I've felt lucky to work with you and learn from you. I am moved by your vision, inspired by your integrity, honoured by your faith. It has been a joy to travel through this book with you.

Thank you to my copyeditor, Melanie Little, for your thoughtful insight and and eagle-eyed, don't-miss-a-thing precision.

Thank you to my cover designer, Emma Dolan; my proofreader, Gemma Wain; and my publicist, Danielle LeSage. Thank you to Megan Kwan and the Doubleday production team.

Thank you to my first reader and dear friend, Johanna Skibsrud, for encouragement and direction when I needed it most, and thank you to the writers and friends who lent their ears and wisdom throughout the long process of writing this book: Oisín Curran, Sarah Faber, Stef Lenk, Susan Paddon.

Much of this book was written at the Frick Art Reference Library in New York, at the Dancing Goat Café & Bakery in North East Margaree, and at L'abri café in Cheticamp: thank you to the staff of all three for your tabletops and your patience . . .

Lastly, thank you to my family. Thank you to my parents and to my sisters, Sarah and Lisa. Thank you to my husband, Conrad. And thank you to our son and daughter, who were born as I wrote this book, and who are part of it.

A NOTE ABOUT THE TYPE

The Second History has been set in Sabon, an "old style" serif originally
designed by Jan Tschichold in the 1960s.

The roman is based on types by Claude Garamond (c.1480–1561), pri-
marily from a specimen printed by the German printer Konrad Berner.
(Berner had married the widow of fellow printer Jacques Sabon, hence the
face's name.)